DRAGON QUEEN

THE HIDDEN KING TRILOGY

JEN L. GREY

CHAPTER ONE

My heart stopped while I frantically flapped my wings to get to her. I roared in my dragon form with both fear and rage as I watched my mother tumble to her death.

Thick, fresh blood soaked her dark hair, and it clung to her face even with the long drop to the ground. Her brown eyes, the same shade as mine, were wide with terror.

I couldn't lose her.

Not now.

Not like this.

"Egan, save me," Mindy pleaded as she dangled from another harpy's taloned feet. Mindy's vanilla-blonde hair looked dirty blonde, and her bottom lip trembled in a horrible attempt to look fearful. The tell was that her honey eyes were calm, and the harpy holding her hadn't dug its talons into her like the other one had with Mom.

If I hadn't been worried about my mother, I'd have been pissed at yet another stupid, manipulative stunt the dragon shifter was trying to pull, but her pathetic need for my mate's attention didn't mean shit to me right then. Not when the people I loved were in danger.

The harpy that had dropped Mom smirked at the show. Each time Mom screamed, the harpy's coal-black eyes twinkled with amusement. But I hadn't expected to find humanity in these creatures since they were from Fae and working with Vera and the fae dragon king. It was a no-brainer that they wouldn't care about us.

The harpy's chest shook, jiggling her naked breasts. The harpies' top halves resembled that of a voluptuous old woman while their bottom halves were reptilian. Long, sturdy wings sprouted from their backs. Oddest of all, they all looked identical from what I could see.

Vera's cackle pierced my brain. It was like she was somehow talking into my head like Egan could when she yelled, "She might actually catch her. Shoot the dragon now." Some humor had vacated her voice, and hope blossomed in my chest.

Egan used our fated mate link to talk to me as he growled in his dragon form, *Jade, the two harpies are loading their bows. Be careful. I'll try to distract them.*

Under normal circumstances, his request that I should be careful would've made me chuckle, but too much was at stake for me to find anything amusing.

My eyes locked on my mother, blocking everything else out. She was only two hundred yards away from slamming into the ground.

Her body flipped and spun wildly as she screamed. With the way she was panicking, she would faint before she hit the bottom. Maybe that was a good thing.

I pushed my wings harder, refusing to admit defeat. If Vera was siccing the harpies on me, I had to be moving faster than I realized.

God, I hoped so. I felt like I was crawling—or whatever the equivalent was for a flying creature.

Loud roars ripped from behind me as Egan, his parents, and Draco attacked the harpies. Hopefully, they'd catch the harpies and Vera by surprise since they were all enjoying the action between Mom and me.

Renewed determination filled me as I felt somewhat safer with the dragons' diversion. Even the threat of the poisoned bone arrows couldn't deter me from saving Mom.

Inches from her, I reached out, preparing to wrap her in my arms. Since the harpy had torn up the top of her shoulders, I didn't want to risk digging my talons into her skin. I could deepen the wounds, not to mention the amount of pain she had to be in already, and dangling from my talons, she'd be like a flying target for the archers. Having my arms available to fight would be ideal, but in dragon form, they were way less important.

I zipped toward the ground, abandoning my natural urge to slow. Apparently, in beast form, my survival instinct was stronger. Pushing it aside, I connected with my dragon. If I let her take too much control and she let Mom die, I might not be able to live with myself. Some things were more important than my own life.

The world blurred as my dragon stopped fighting and flew faster. I braced myself, knowing Mom and I were likely going to die. The mixture of gravel and grass was getting closer by the second.

Mere feet from impact, I desperately stretched my arms out. This wouldn't work, but dammit, I had to try. I'd expected only to snag air, but my large, scaly hand wrapped around her arm. I carefully adjusted my grip so my talons didn't graze her skin.

Tears burned my eyes, magnifying all of the new colors

of the rainbow in this form. I hadn't thought I could get to her in time, but somehow, I'd caught her. Not wasting another second, my dragon jerked her toward me and wrapped my arms around her. When her head hit my chest, I shifted my weight upward, and my wings changed directions, pushing us back into the sky.

"No!" Mom yelled as she jerked against me. "Let me go! I'd rather die than be eaten or abused by disgusting creatures like you."

Her words stung, but I couldn't blame her. If this had been my first introduction to the supernatural world, I'd have felt the same way.

Despite my beast's strength, her resistance caught me off guard. She broke free and dropped once again.

My heart pounded.

No, I'd just had her.

I forced my wings to stop, and I dove beside her. My dragon roared in my mind, unhappy with my dangerous plan.

Since I had five hundred pounds on her, I reached her in a second, this time anchoring her in my arms.

I wouldn't make the same mistake twice.

Jade, fly upward now! Egan exclaimed, and my already panicked heart raced harder.

I wouldn't be surprised if I had a stroke. I blinked, realizing that impact was imminent.

Egan's fear melded with mine so much that I couldn't tell where his began and mine ended. The flapping of wings grew closer, and I hoped to God it was him and not a harpy. I wasn't sure how I could fight with Mom in my arms. I needed to find a safe place to set her down.

She squirmed, but I was prepared for it, and my wings sprang back to work, lifting us higher. As my body adjusted to the change of direction, my legs swung forward, and my feet brushed the ground.

Thank God my scales protected me, or my feet would have been in immense pain. Another benefit of being in beast form.

That had been way too close for comfort.

Duck! Egan screamed at the same time that a whistling noise caught my attention.

Dammit, that was an arrow. I rolled to the side despite Mom's distracting screams. I couldn't blame her; she had no clue the dragon was her daughter. The last time she'd seen me had been before I'd run away to college and met Egan when I'd been completely human.

The whistling grew louder, even though I'd altered my course. I spun around to see three arrows spiraling at me. Each one followed a different path like the harpies had predicted each option I had. I wasn't getting out of this without injury.

Draco flew at a harpy as she drew another arrow. He moved so fast his navy scales distorted, his focus on getting to the horrible creature before she shot at me again.

My only option to avoid getting shot was to curl into a ball. I pulled my huge-ass bottom half inward, trying to make myself as small as possible without injuring Mom. I still wasn't used to my dragon form. Before I could get adjusted, an arrow sank into my leg, close to the same place I'd been injured not even an hour before.

Excruciating pain pulsed inside me, stealing my breath. I directed every ounce of concentration I had on keeping Mom in my arms and my wings moving. All I wanted to do was wallow in pain, but I gritted my teeth, resolved to take Vera down.

Egan raced toward me. *I'm almost there. Just hold on.*

He was only ten yards away, but the overwhelming throbbing grew sharper, weakening my entire body. I wasn't sure how much longer I could stay strong. *You need to get Mom.* As long as she and Egan made it out of this alive, that was all that mattered. They both deserved to live. Mom deserved to find happiness before dying.

Cries and growls raged on behind us, but I didn't have the energy to turn around and see what was going on. At least, it sounded like a battle and not a slaughter. I'd have been more worried if all I'd heard was the harpies' war call.

Agony intensified inside me, and my wings slowed. We descended even faster. My body started to shut down, and I channeled all of my strength toward protecting my mother. If we tumbled to the ground, I could shield her with my body.

A low groan emanated from Egan as his golden eyes glowed brighter. *I'm here,* he said moments before reaching me.

I held Mom out to him, but instead of taking her, he wrapped his arms around us both. His dragon was much larger than mine, but I hadn't expected him to be able to take the brunt of my weight.

Hold on as long as you can. Worry laced each word, and they came off like a command.

Normally, I'd be annoyed, but I understood how he felt, and his concern fueled me, overriding some of the pain.

Egan lowered us to the ground, and I looked over his shoulder at the fight. Ladon fought one of the archers, while Draco took on the other. Every time they used their dragon flames, the harpies would fly out of the way seconds before it could reach them.

Dammit, those harpies had to be some of the smarter

ones. It made sense that Vera would want them around her for extra protection.

Each time the guys missed the harpies, Vera threw her head back in laughter. Her once sable eyes appeared completely soulless, and her caramel hair was disheveled more than usual. She watched the fight with a sick, satisfied smirk that was at odds with the white, animated Star Wars shirt she wore.

Egan's mother narrowly dodged a harpy's punch. Kayda's scales were a lighter army-green shade than her fated mate's, and she was slightly smaller like me but still strong in her own right. She straightened, and her dragon flames engulfed the harpy. The harpy let out an ear-piercing screech, but it was cut short as her body disintegrated into ash.

I took that back. Maybe they weren't all smarter, just the two Ladon and Draco fought.

My reprieve vanished as the pain rolled back into my body tenfold. I groaned as my wings slowed to almost a stop.

We're here, Egan comforted me. *You can stop.*

That was all I needed—the reassurance to quit. My feet touched the gravel and grass, and I crumpled to my side, feeling the ground shaking under my weight. I somehow kept from rolling onto Mom.

Looking skyward, I realized how close to the top of the cave we were. We'd landed on the very top of the hill—the very hill we'd used to hide from all of the harpies at the village. We were heading toward a hidden exit that only the dragon king knew about in case something of this magnitude ever occurred.

Mom struggled to get out of my embrace, and I gladly opened my arms. She was scared, and I wasn't in the right mind to fight her, not that I would've anyway. I would tell her everything if we made it out of here alive.

I needed to pull the arrow out from my leg before more poison entered my system, but the pain had immobilized me.

My chest shook as I took in a breath, and my gaze went to the entrance to the hidden village inside the cave.

No more of the winged fae creatures were pouring inside, which calmed some of my fear. I had no clue how many harpies Vera had brought. If these were all of them, most of us should make it out alive as long as we killed the witch before she could do anything else.

"Kayda, please help me." Mindy's voice cracked as she struggled weakly against the harpy's hold.

Her act was wearing on my nerves. I couldn't wait to call her out on her shit since Mindy didn't know that Vera had outed her. Not only had Mindy told the witch who Egan's family was, but Vera and Mindy had also bonded over my future death. Apparently, Mindy was thrilled at the prospect and wanted to kill me like Vera had killed her ex-lover's fated mate, Egan's great, great grandfather. The question bubbled in my mind about how Mindy knew Egan's family was of royal lineage. But that was a question for another time.

Babe. Egan leaned over me, his eyes filled with concern and love. *I'm going to yank this out now.*

I nodded but wished he hadn't told me. Now, I anticipated the moment, knowing it would hurt like hell before feeling better. The longer it stayed lodged in me, the worse the injury would be. *Just do it.*

He grabbed the bottom of the arrow, holding it firmly where it jutted from my leg. *On the count of three.* He sucked in a breath while his dragon hands held the bone arrow just as if he were in human form. *One,* he said and yanked.

Pure shock filled me before the pain. I groaned and sagged against his side as the sharp agony hit then finally receded.

A warning tingled at the base of my neck.

Someone was about to attack.

I spun around, but I couldn't find anything, which only meant one thing. *Egan, Vera's invisible.*

CHAPTER TWO

I searched for something—anything—that would alert me to Vera's whereabouts. Scanning my surroundings, I hunted for the ghost-like apparition that appeared when she astral projected. I was learning that all magic came at a cost or with a penance. For instance, dragons were strong but couldn't connect to their entire thunder. On the flip side, wolves weren't as strong, but their pack link gave them an edge.

However, I didn't see anything out of the ordinary.

Fear coursed through my veins. That was the reaction Vera wanted to cause, and I hated giving her the satisfaction.

Maybe she ran like last time, Egan suggested, but we both knew it was wishful thinking.

She couldn't get out of here without a harpy, and none were missing. She planned on using her disappearing act to kill us.

She had the desperate, crazy gleam in her eyes, the kind there was no turning back from. Vera was here to finish this.

To achieve her ultimate revenge.

To kill every last dragon shifter tied to her ex-lover.

Something sharp stabbed into my leg where the arrow had been. The piercing pain caused my stomach to roil as the wound deepened and bled more.

I roared, my dragon angry and hurt. She was eager to attack, but we had no target.

Egan breathed rapidly as smoke trickled from his nose.

Aiming for her opponent's recent injury was a sound strategy, I had to give her that, but I refused to sit here idly.

Egan slashed his claws at the area around me, trying to hit Vera, but all he hit was air.

For all we knew, she could have been standing right behind him.

She tried to appear strong and confident, but these were the actions of a weak coward. It proved she feared us even if she pretended she didn't.

Her cowardice should have encouraged me or made me feel like we were on equal ground, but it did nothing. I couldn't fight an enemy I couldn't see. My dragon didn't understand how to fight or handle this situation. Her senses had never let her down before.

My dragon roared loudly as flames bubbled in my stomach. She had no clue where to spew the fire. Nothing indicated or even hinted at where Vera could be. Absolutely no scent or sound. My dragon felt useless, adding to our rage.

Mom stumbled back, her eyes so wide I didn't think she'd ever be able to shut them again. The sour scent of fear swirled around us.

I couldn't spew the flames haphazardly, not with Mom this close. I'd risked my life to save her, and I refused to hurt her because of my terror. Acting irrationally would give Vera the advantage and hurt God knew who else.

We had to stop playing her game. *Calm down.*

I can't, he growled. *She's going to attack you again.*

We have to be smarter than her. This is what she wants. I took a deep, calming breath, following my own advice.

My dragon hissed against my mind, but I ignored her. She had to learn to trust me. I was already beginning to trust her.

Something prodded my arm. Nothing too painful but more like Vera was trying to scare me.

As I'd expected, the ghost-like apparition stood several feet away from my injury. Her blurred face was barely visible, watching Egan attack nothing. She wanted to startle me and make me injure myself even more.

Refusing to give her what she wanted, I forced my body to not respond. My dragon hissed inside my mind, but I ignored her again. I would stay in control.

After inhaling and exhaling slowly several times, some of my panic dissipated, and I pushed a fraction of my calm toward Egan. He needed it more so than I did. If our situation had been reversed, I wouldn't have been able to handle seeing him get hurt, unable to do anything. This was both a physical and emotional game the bitch—I meant, witch—played.

I forced my eyes shut, even though it was the most unnatural thing to do, but my martial arts training was kicking in. Sometimes, taking your sight out of the equation could heighten your other senses. I hoped it would do a whole lot more in dragon form.

My dragon roared unhappily, but I mentally brushed her like she often did against my mind.

I projected reassuring thoughts toward her, and somehow, she understood. Warmth spread throughout me as she took a small step aside, granting my request.

With my eyes closed, the surrounding sounds grew

louder. I could hear the fighting in the village as well as every breath Draco and Ladon took as they fought the two harpies.

Kayda chased the harpy that held on to Mindy.

Mom breathed raggedly as silent sobs racked her body, and her footsteps grew farther and farther away as she ran away from us.

Little did she know that wouldn't do her any good. She was only running toward more violence, but on foot and at human speed, she wouldn't reach the village for half an hour.

The ground quaked with each step Egan took. He stood protectively in front of my injured leg, ready to attack at the first sign of an assault. Even though he'd calmed, he was still on edge. We both were.

I tried to home in on Vera's presence, knowing she'd be near me.

A sharp edge dug between two scales on my arm—much like the tip of a knife. My arm twitched to jerk away, but I held it still. This was my opportunity to find her.

She dug the sharp tip deep into my arm, piercing the skin. The tip stung, similar to a bee sting, but I didn't react. I focused on where she had to be standing to dig the knife into my arm.

As the pressure increased, the overwhelming urge to react clawed inside me. The moment I felt as though I couldn't take any more, I noticed a warmer spot next to me. That had to be her. Her body heat wasn't hidden, only her scent and body.

I found her, I alerted my mate as she jabbed the sharp edge deeper, my excitement overriding my urge to react.

Delight flowed through our bond as Egan asked, *How?*

You won't like this, so please don't react. I hadn't told

him what she was doing for this very reason, but I couldn't leave him in the dark. *She's stabbing me in the arm. It doesn't hurt too badly, but since I didn't react, she's staying close to taunt me. I can feel her body heat.*

He tensed, annoyance wafting through our bond, but he didn't move like I'd asked. *We can work with that.*

She dug the sharp edge deeper, and I winced. A low scream confirmed what I already suspected: she was enraged that I hadn't moved.

Good, that was the entire point.

I swung my other hand at her, talons extended. I hit something solid and tossed her twenty feet away. She landed with a loud thud. I opened my eyes and saw blood dripping onto the grass. *She's bleeding. She can't hide that.* I couldn't suppress my excitement.

Egan's gaze found the blood that trailed toward us. *When her blood leaves her body, it appears. The magic must be for her actual body. Anything outside it shows.*

It was a small win, but I'd take it.

Vera charged at us without any hesitation. She must not have realized that we could spot her. Whether it was reckless, I didn't care as long as we kicked her ass.

Every three to four steps, another drop of blood landed. I had to time this perfectly. When blood dripped only two feet away, I breathed the flames that had been building inside me.

Her screams of agony confirmed I'd hit the mark. Within seconds, the smell of burnt skin hit my nose. Thankfully, in dragon form, my stomach was much sturdier or I'd have emptied its contents. I continued to push the fire out as Egan charged at her.

Before he could reach her, her cries ended.

Hope that she was dead sprang inside, but her body was still invisible. *Is she dead?*

No, her magic wouldn't be working anymore if she was. Egan lowered his head right where she'd been, opened his mouth, and chomped.

Did you get her? I doubted it since no blood poured down his chin, but I didn't fully understand how magic worked yet.

No, he growled and scanned the area. *She got out of the way.*

Dammit, maybe scorching her hadn't been smart. Now the surrounding air was warmer, and I couldn't gauge her location anymore. *She couldn't have gotten far.* Between bleeding and getting burned, she had to be moving slower.

No, but she'll be more desperate, which doesn't bode well for us. Egan stood protectively in front of me again like that had worked out so well.

I bit my tongue, not wanting to hurt his feelings. He was doing what he could to protect me. The best thing I could do was get off my ass. I slowly stood, gradually putting weight on my leg. It hurt, but I could walk on it, so the muscle wasn't damaged. If I'd been in human form, that would have been a different story.

The ground shook, and the intensity of the vibrations increased. My teeth rattled as the earth quaked and groaned under our feet like an earthquake.

Is that Vera or an actual natural disaster? I asked.

Vera. A natural disaster you'd know. There's a change in the atmosphere before it happens. This is all witch. She's using magic.

That was odd. Why did she wait until now?

My dragon surged forward, flapping my wings. We

hovered just above the ground to keep the magic from affecting us.

Egan followed suit. *I don't understand what she's doing.*

Join the club. I didn't understand a damn thing she'd done yet.

A cry of frustration sounded behind us. We turned around to see a flashing Vera standing a few feet away. She flickered in and out of view, and I kind of preferred the out.

Her face had taken the brunt of my flames, and her arms were a little crispy. My scratch marks were visible, but the flames had cauterized the wound.

So that was why the blood loss had stopped. I hadn't thought my plan through at all.

"How can you see me?" she snarled and looked at her hands.

The ground stilled as her eyes locked on me, her breathing hard. "If you would've kept your distance from him, everything would've been so much easier." Egan's nostrils flared, and her face contorted into rage. "I could've hurt you and had him begging me to save you, but no. Ever since you came into the picture, you've been nothing but trouble."

Her anger was completely channeled at me as if Egan wasn't even beside me.

"You freed the falcon. You brought Egan to the restaurant the night Ollie was there to kidnap you. You let the dragon into our dorm room." She wielded her knife at me, swinging it from side to side with every point. "You found the girl he was meant to find in the woods that day, and you burned me, forcing me to use a significant amount of my power to survive. You've ruined everything."

She dropped the knife she had in her hands and pulled out a dagger from a sheath on her calf.

The blade was a dark silver, and the slender handle was rounded at the top with two golden jewels side by side. Black wings sprouted from the handle, and I realized the shape looked like a dragon. The blade was six inches long with smooth edges, and I could tell it could cut through anything ... even scales.

"Not only will I enjoy killing you, but he'll also get to watch you die." She raised the dagger over her head and charged, screaming.

The sun shone into the cave, slanting bright light onto us. The edge of the dagger reflected the light into my eyes, half blinding me.

I blinked and squinted, watching her approach us. Did she really think this would work? She was completely insane.

The fire churned in my stomach, ready for release.

When she was five feet from us, Egan and I channeled our flames at her. Before they could reach her, she raised her other hand, forcing a strong wind in our direction.

The flames blew back against us. I braced myself for the pain, but luckily, the flames didn't hurt. *How the...?*

It's because we're soul mates, and they're our flames, thus part of our dragons. Our bodies have to be resilient to produce it. But anyone else's flame can burn you. Egan grunted as he flew higher.

I trailed after him, but I moved too slowly. Vera was only inches away and swinging her arms downward.

When I winced, bracing for impact, Egan grabbed Vera with his feet and dug his sharp, thick talons into her shoulders. He flapped upward, lifting her off the ground. The dagger tumbled from her hands and landed a mere two inches from my feet.

She screamed in agony as he lifted her higher.

"Please, don't!" she cried, reminding me of Mindy. "I'm sorry. Just let me down."

The fact that she'd even contemplate that we might let her go offended me.

He was a mile in the air when he dropped her. Her face transformed from pure terror to a cocky smirk.

She had something up her sleeve.

CHAPTER THREE

As Vera fell, she held her hands in front of her and sneered. A strong gust of wind sprang to life and blew upward, pushing against her body. Her descent slowed, and my heart sank.

No. How could we fight against someone with magic on her side? If she could prevent herself from falling to her death, there was no telling what else she could do. We had no clue how strong she was.

Egan roared and plunged toward the witch's body. He weighed so much that the wind blowing into him didn't affect him other than maybe slowing him a tad. Within seconds, he reached the witch, whose sole concentration was on slowing her fall.

He opened his sizable mouth, his sharp teeth on display, and chomped into her middle.

Blood poured from her torso as her eyes opened in horror. Her arms dropped to her sides, and the whirlwind she had created weakened with her life force.

My mate jerked his head to the side, tossing her.

She didn't put up a fight or struggle. Blood trickled from

her mouth, and her body slammed into the ground with such force that it bounced.

Needing to make sure the bitch was dead, I flew the short distance to her body. I landed gingerly beside her, and the sound of silence comforted me like never before. There was no heartbeat or air filling her lungs. Blood oozed from her body, and her open eyes glazed over as death welcomed her.

Under most circumstances, I'd have said that her soul was free to go to its final destination, but I was sure she'd lost it or used it up during her very long lifetime. Only anger and hurt existed inside her—the essential ingredients of fostering hatred into the world.

Good riddance. I hope you experience the pain you inflicted on everyone around you for all eternity. It had been hard for me to look at every other dead body I'd seen, but not hers. Her mangled body made me want to rejoice, and I wasn't sure what that said about me.

Egan landed beside me, and he breathed flames over her body.

Part of me wanted to look away, which eased some of the concern about my mental wellbeing. At least, I didn't enjoy watching her entire death unfold.

With witches, their bodies need to be burned or their energy will connect back with the earth. Egan continued a steady flow of flame. *We don't want any of her vengeful and spiteful spirit hanging around.*

Ashes flaked from the fire and floated in the slight breeze.

But she used the ashes of the falcon feather to control him. We didn't need someone gathering her ashes and using her power.

Yes, his feather. His body was still intact. Her body and

energy are being unleashed into the world. There won't be anything to anchor to her.

Egan's parents and Draco landed beside us. I found Mindy standing in human form, her chest heaving with each breath she took as she watched the scene unfold. The worry on her face smoothed over as relief overtook it.

She thought she was safe, but she was far from it. She'd helped Vera find my mother and revealed who the dragon royal family was. If she thought there was any comeback from that, she was dead wrong.

But I'd let her have her moment. The calm before the storm.

It irritated the hell out of me that our group couldn't speak to each other, but these were the cards we'd been dealt. I'd have to get over it.

As the ash thickened, Egan's flames lessened. When the flames stopped, even her bones were gone. Every ounce of her was ash, the charred ground the only thing marking the location of her death.

Ladon glanced at us and nodded toward the village. He held the dagger Vera had dropped.

Good, it looked special, though I didn't know why. Part of me felt connected to it, though.

He nodded again, ensuring that the message was clear. We needed to check on the others. I turned to look for the harpies they'd been fighting and found three similarly charred places flaked with dust. Maybe burning the dead was a dragon thing.

"Oh, God." Mindy sniffled and placed a dirty hand against her mouth. "I'm so relieved."

I bet she was. She thought there was no one left that knew she worked with the witch to get rid of me.

Unwilling to stay here and feeling the need to check on

Mom, I took to the sky. My leg twinged with pain but nothing too horrible. My shifter healing was already kicking in. That perk of my new form was pretty damn nice.

The others followed behind me, and I glanced over my shoulder to see Kayda's eyes filled with annoyance as she gently held Mindy with her dragon feet, carrying her toward the village.

Mindy could've shifted into her dragon form to help us fight, and she could have shifted to help the rest of the thunder if things weren't going our way, but she wanted Kayda to carry her. Maybe to show the thunder that their queen cared enough about her to chauffeur her back home. Who the hell knew?

How's your leg? Egan asked as he caught up to me.

I spotted Mom running toward the houses. *It's already healing, so hopefully, I'll be back to normal soon.*

I'm so sorry I couldn't protect you. Defeat wafted off him.

I hated that he put so much pressure on himself. He couldn't be held responsible for my health and safety. He was only one person. *You did protect me. You killed her before she could hurt me or anyone else again. If it weren't for you, she'd still be alive.* I pushed my love and adoration for Egan toward him.

He needed to realize how I felt and thought about him. He was the best person I'd ever met, and I would've felt that way even if we weren't fated mates. Hell, Sadie and the others thought extremely highly of him too. *You fought alongside Sadie and your friends when it was never expected of you. You protected them because you care. You treat everyone with respect and kindness, which is so damn hard to find in this world. You are the absolute best person I've ever had the honor of knowing.*

Something shifted between us, and his wings gently brushed against mine. He turned his huge head and stared into my soul as he said, *I'm not nearly as perfect as you make me sound, but you make me want to be the man you see me as. I've given you such hell about fighting and defending yourself ...*

I'm thinking it's a shifter quality over their mates, I teased. *But I'll take it. Besides, you only did it while trying to protect me.*

If I can use that excuse, then ... He tilted his head and his teeth appeared in a dragon smile.

Nope, no take-backs.

A loud scream broke our moment. Mom had turned around, and she was looking at us. Her bottom lip shook in pure terror as she watched the five of us approach.

We probably looked scary from her point of view, and having Mindy dangle from Kayda's talons probably made things worse since that was how the harpy had carried her.

Did Mindy want to be carried just to cause Mom more distress? Surely not, but I couldn't shake the feeling. She loved manipulating people and wanted to cause me pain.

Draco flew beside us and waved us on to the village. He patted his chest and gestured to Mom.

He was going to get her. I hated to do that to her, but we didn't need someone else finding her, and they'd have no clue who she was. With the way the dragons were attacked, they might think she was a witch or another threat.

Maybe I should get her, I suggested.

The best thing you can do is get back to the house and shift into your human form. That'll be the only way to calm your mother down.

I hadn't thought about that. Whether it was Draco or

me getting her, the outcome would be the same. *Okay. Standing around here naked would just make things worse.*

As Draco flew down to get her, Mindy yelled and patted her shoulder. "That hurts. Please stop."

Between Draco flying toward her and Mindy's comments, Mom ran backward. She stumbled over her own feet and landed on the ground. She placed her hands in front of her face and cried, "Please. Don't. I haven't done anything. Leave me be."

That psycho bitch was going to die. I faced the crazy dragon girl, ready to hurt her like she was trying to hurt me. She wasn't much different from Vera, meaning she was a bigger risk than we'd ever realized.

Don't. Egan flew slightly in front of me, blocking Mindy from my view. *If you attack her, it'll only upset your mother more. That's what she's hoping you'll do.*

Egan, I can't do this with her anymore. Not only had Mindy worked with Vera and tried scaring my mother more, but she'd also purposely tried to keep me from connecting with my dragon under the guise of training me, and she wanted Egan to leave me for her, despite us being fated mates.

Don't worry, we won't. Egan sounded as pissed as me.

What Mindy had failed to realize was when I hurt, so did Egan. He and I were bonded in a way she'd never understand unless she found her fated mate. She wasn't just pitting herself against me but the man she wanted as her own. Talk about backfiring, and Mindy was clueless enough not to get it.

I should've known Egan would feel the same way. He was trying to ensure we didn't scare Mom more than we already had. He always had my best interest at heart.

Ignoring Mindy's antics felt impossible, but I kept my eyes forward and my wings flapping steadily.

Okay, that wasn't true. The only way I was able to do that was with Egan by my side. I was beginning to learn how much stronger I was with him firmly beside me.

Mom cried over and over as Draco grabbed her, and not being there for her was one of the hardest things I'd ever had to do, but I would only make things worse for her, kind of like Aunt Sarah.

When Dad had been alive, we'd been a happy family. Mom and he had been so in love, but my aunt Sarah had always interfered with her controlling, abusive ways. After my dad had died, my life had truly changed. We'd moved in with Sarah, who'd controlled my every movement and would smack me whenever I got out of line. Of course, that had only happened when Mom hadn't been around to see.

It'll be fine when she sees you, Egan reassured me.

I wasn't so sure about that. Some things people could never get over.

The village came into view, and the dragons were on the ground, not in battle. Humans and dragons were dragging dead harpies to the grassy edge outside of the village and throwing the bodies on top of one another.

Uh ... is that normal? It wasn't like we were staying here.

Egan grimaced. *They're easier to burn that way. This is how we handle death when we can. Even though the harpies don't pose a threat, it's just a respectful way to treat the dead.*

The more I learned about dragons, the more I admired their race. They had a distinct sense of right and wrong, except for the few crazies in their midst.

We landed right in front of Egan's parents' log cabin home at the center of the village comprised of around a hundred buildings, and Egan and I hurried into the large entryway and to the shifting room on the left. It was big enough for both Egan and me to enter and change at the same time. Our bag was still there from earlier, and I was glad Egan had encouraged us to bring several changes of clothes in case something like this happened. I'd be shifting right back into my dragon form after I talked to Mom.

Within minutes, we were both on two legs and dressed.

Back outside the house, Mom was beating Draco in the chest with her fists and hands like she expected it to accomplish something.

Mindy stood between an older man and a woman she resembled. The woman had her ash-blonde hair pulled into a bun and stiff shoulders. She laid a hand on Mindy's shoulders, but her milk chocolate brown eyes were tight. Her features were sharp, probably similar to her heart.

The man had short, golden hair, but his striking honey eyes were the same shade as Mindy's. His chin was lifted and proud as he tugged on his navy-blue blazer like he was the most important man there. Clearly, neither he nor the woman had fought. Their clothes were in pristine condition.

Any other time, I'd have laughed, but there was too much going on. Their audacity was completely unnerving.

"What kind of monsters are you?" Mom yelled, bringing my attention back to her.

I cringed. That wasn't a very smart thing to say when you thought you were being held captive. "Mom," I said softly, trying not to spook her.

She stilled and spun around to face me. "Jade? Baby?" She ran over and threw her arms around me. "Are they holding you prisoner, too?"

"No." I shook my head, unsure where to start.

Egan stepped beside me and placed a hand on my

shoulder. He didn't say anything, allowing me to handle this the way I wanted.

The problem was I had no clue. Should I just blurt out, "You're calling me a monster too"? At least, my awkwardness wasn't running away all on its own.

"Then how are you here?" Mom blinked, trying to make sense of the situation.

"Here, I'll help you." Mindy's voice was soft like she cared. "Your daughter is a dragon and the very one who killed the witch and who knows how many countless others."

Mom's mouth dropped, and rage flowed through my body. This girl had no boundaries, but dammit, I would give her some.

CHAPTER FOUR

"Wait." Mom stepped away from me, wringing her hands. "You've killed people?"

Her reaction hurt so damn badly. She looked at me like she didn't know who I was and as if I might actually hurt her.

"No, she hasn't," Egan growled and glared at Mindy. "Are you trying to make this worse?"

Kayda and Ladon shook their dragon heads, and Mom screamed again. She was all worked up, and the last time I'd seen her far from sane was the day we'd learned that Dad had been in an accident.

Kayda must have said something to Ladon because they headed toward the house, leaving Egan and me to handle Mindy by ourselves.

I wasn't sure if I was thankful or upset. They trusted us to do what was right, but they were king and queen. Our words might not have as much authority without them beside us.

"Just trying to help." Mindy laughed in a high-pitch voice and attempted to flip her hair over her shoulder, but it was so dingy that it flopped back down where it was a moment earlier. She either didn't realize it or chose to ignore it as she continued, "Jade seemed at a loss for words, which is kind of strange for a future queen, but whatever. I just thought that as her teacher, I should help her."

No, she couldn't have said what I thought she did ... surely.

"You view yourself as my teacher?" I barked out a humorless laugh. I couldn't let something like that slide. Most of the thunder surrounded us, and I couldn't let Mindy treat me like this. If I did, it would help her assertion that I wasn't fit to be Egan's mate.

"Of course, I do." Mindy placed a hand on her heart and looked from her father to her mother. "Jade really struggled, but with my assistance—"

"You mean sabotaging me from connecting with my dragon." I was sick and tired of dealing with manipulative assholes. Between Sarah, Vera, and Mindy, I'd had my fill.

"It may have appeared like sabotage," she said condescendingly, "but I was preparing you the best way I knew how for the supernatural world. I—"

"Shut up," Egan said low and deep.

Mindy's mouth dropped open. "What? How can you talk to me this way? If you had a mate who could—"

No, he couldn't fight this battle for me. "Let me help. You were working with a witch? You told her who the royal family is? Or how about bonding with a witch over the death of a fellow thunder member?"

She blinked, completely caught off guard. Her cocky smile faltered, but she kept her shoulders and back straight. "I ... I didn't ..." She trailed off, scrambling for words.

"You didn't what? Maybe it's just me, but I couldn't

hear you." I pointed to my ear, letting my own smugness peek through.

She would have to lie to get out of this or think up some half-ass truth to scrape by. Either way, I'd force her to admit everything. It was my turn to taunt her ass.

"Honey, what were you saying?" her mother asked tightly, her eyes narrowed at her daughter.

Mindy's body shook, and she let out a fake sob. "I ... I don't know. It's been a horrible past few days. With everything I've gone through, I don't even know what I'm saying anymore."

"Are you sure about that?" Kayda's regal voice asked as she stepped from the house.

"Yes. Vera was obsessed with finding you. And when those harpies came ..." She stopped and shuddered.

Ladon took his wife's hand, and they made their way beside me. Egan was on my left side, and they were on my right.

"Others could come at any second." Mindy's dad rubbed her shoulders. "We should continue this later and focus on finding a place to go."

Ladon arched an eyebrow. "As everyone now knows, we're the royal family and will be giving the orders. We have already chosen a spot, but it is necessary that we address this before leaving, especially if we have a traitor on our hands."

Mom ran her fingers through her drying, bloody hair. She turned around slowly until she faced me again. "Is this some elaborate joke? Please tell me there's a camera hidden somewhere. I don't know how you all did this, but this doesn't seem real."

I wasn't sure who to address first. I wanted to be there for my mother, but Mindy and her family had to be dealt with before we could leave. And I needed to be part of that. Unfortunately, Mom could wait. "Mom, it's not a joke, but just give me a few minutes, and we'll talk about everything."

Kayda gestured to their log cabin. "If you would like to wait in our home, you're more than welcome. There isn't anyone inside there."

"Yeah." Mom nodded and took off toward the house. She glanced over her shoulder, eyeing all of the dragons still in their beast form. Everyone had stopped carrying off the harpies to watch the scene unfold.

Mindy leaned into her mother and whispered, "See, she isn't fit to be queen. They'll all see."

My hands clenched into fists, and I stared Mindy down. Why in the world would she say something like that when we could all hear her?

Egan tensed beside me, his eyes glowing. "She is fit to be queen, unlike you."

"What?" Mindy squeaked. "I don't know what you're talking about."

Her mother stiffened. "She was just telling me something she didn't think anyone else should hear. There's no need to overreact."

Now they were trying to make us look ignorant. "We could hear everything you said."

Mindy laughed uncomfortably.

Ladon and Kayda glanced at us out of the corner of their eyes. Their foreheads wrinkled, but they didn't say anything.

I'm over this. We don't have time for their games. Egan took my hand and lifted his chin, looking down his nose at Mindy and her parents. "It's obvious you somehow found out that we're the royal family, and we want to know how."

"Now listen, it's a little more complicated than that."

Mindy's dad lifted a hand, almost in surrender, as his face paled. He knew they were in deep shit and there was no easy way out of it.

"Then enlighten us, Rex." Ladon crossed his arms and stared the man down. "We've been best friends since childhood. You found your mate only a few years before me. How long have you known?"

The older man had the sense to look ashamed. He hung his head and averted his gaze. "Since we were young children. My father told me. I don't know how he knew."

There wasn't the stench of a lie, which was problematic. There was no telling who else knew, but I guessed it no longer mattered.

"Rex," Mindy's mother hissed.

"Oh stop, Susan." Rex waved at her. "They know. There's no salvaging it."

Susan? I almost laughed. I hadn't heard a normal human name, other than Mindy, for a dragon thus far. But Mindy wasn't as common as Susan.

Egan chuckled in my mind. *Don't forget she was human before transitioning into a dragon like you.*

But your mother has a dragon-sounding name.

It's actually a nickname Dad gave her after they mated. It means "little dragon," but the others started calling her that too. Egan squeezed my hand lovingly. *The name took on a life of its own.*

It fits her.

"So that's why you pushed for Egan and Mindy to be betrothed despite us learning that two dragons can't have offspring." Kayda sounded hurt.

"Wouldn't you do whatever you could for your son?" Susan crossed her arms and looked indignant, unlike her mate. "Mindy deserves to rule and have everyone worship her. All these years, you've hidden like cowards instead of embracing what you could be."

"Excuse me." Kayda paused as she closed her eyes to center herself. "We were hiding for survival. The fae dragon king has been searching for our thunder. He would torture each one of you because you live on Earth. We hid to be happy and create our own community. We hid so no one would worship *anyone* and everyone could be treated as equals."

"Honey, it doesn't matter." Ladon kissed his wife's forehead comfortingly. "We don't have time for this, and now we know that our best friends wanted to use us. We have to leave before the fae dragon king sends reinforcements. Egan and Jade will make the final decision on how to handle them going forward."

"Okay, well, we can talk later when things are settled." Susan pulled at her white shirt and rolled her eyes. "We do need to get to safety."

She grabbed Mindy's shoulders and turned in the opposite direction.

They'd taken a step away when Egan said, "There won't be any safety for you."

What are you doing? I had no clue where he was going with this.

Making sure we all remain safe, especially you.

Susan slowly turned around and looked at him. "Excuse me?"

"Let me say it another way. You're not coming with us." Egan's pupils turned to slits as his dragon peeked through.

Don't do something you'll regret. I agreed that they shouldn't come with us, but I didn't want to encourage him. If I did and something happened to Mindy and her parents, I didn't want him blaming himself or resenting me.

"But we're part of this thunder." Mindy blinked rapidly like she was holding back tears.

"Not anymore." Egan placed an arm around my waist. "You sabotaged my mate and helped the witch try to kill her. You've shown no remorse, insulting Jade, your future queen, repeatedly, in front of everyone. You and your parents will go live in the human world on your own and not contact any of us again. You are hereby banished!"

"Ladon, do something." Rex looked at Egan's father. "You're the only one who can make the call."

"You heard me. It's his and Jade's decision." Ladon's golden eyes found mine as he asked, "Do you agree with Egan's decision?"

Even if I said no, they'd smell the lie. Mindy and her mother couldn't be trusted, and by default, Rex couldn't either since they were his fated mate and daughter. I hated to put anyone in harm's way, but Mindy would jump at the chance to hurt me. "I do."

"Then it's settled." Ladon gestured toward a house that had to be theirs. "Get your stuff and leave immediately."

"We've been best friends for as long as I can remember," Rex pleaded.

"I would have made the same call." Ladon pointed at Susan as he continued, "As your mate admitted, you two were willing to do what was best for your child, and I'm willing to do the same thing for not only Egan and Jade but our entire thunder. You don't have the thunder's best interest at heart and are only out for your own self-interest. You have five minutes before we force you out." He glanced at Draco, still in dragon form. "You and the guards escort them out and then come back to help with the harpies. Everyone be ready to leave in the next twenty minutes."

I felt bad for the three of them, but I agreed with everything Ladon had said. He was on the same page as Egan and me, giving me a sense of peace. Banishing them couldn't have been easy if they'd been close friends for as long as it sounded.

"Egan, please." Mindy's voice cracked.

For the first time, I had the feeling she wasn't being manipulative. She was actually scared.

Egan took my hand, turning his back on her. *Come on. We need to go check on your mother and calm her down before we have to shift and carry her again.*

Great, I hadn't even considered that. There was no other way to get her out of there. This was going to be a fun conversation.

We entered the house with Kayda and Ladon right behind us.

"Mom?" I called, wanting to let her know it was just us. At least, I hoped that would provide her some comfort. Who knew with the way she looked at me moments ago?

Silence greeted us, but I could smell that she'd gone through the normal-sized doorway. She'd probably run in there as soon as she'd realized the other room was meant for dragons.

I stepped into the huge living room and found her sitting on the couch, staring at the dead harpies on the staircase. Arms wrapped around her body, she was gently rocking back and forth.

The room didn't have a homey feeling anymore. The loveseat and recliner still looked unchanged as did the ceiling-high bookcase filled with books, but dead bodies had a way of sucking the life out of a room.

Dammit, I'd forgotten about the dead bodies in the house. Kayda and Egan had shot all the harpies charging down the staircase toward us.

Give me a second. I released his hand and slowly walked over to her. I didn't want to spook her, but I needed her to pay attention to me. "Mom?"

She stopped and turned her head a smidgen toward me. Her eyes remained locked on the dead bodies. "I haven't seen a dead body since your father."

I hadn't expected that was where her mind would go. She hadn't spoken about someone dying since God knew when. "I'm sorry." I didn't know what else to say.

She pulled her attention from the bodies to look at me. "Have you really killed?"

At least, this was an easy answer. "No, I haven't. That girl was just messing with you."

"Thank God." Her face fell. "I knew that didn't sound like you, but after seeing you in that crazy form. I mean ... was that really you?"

"Yes, it was." I couldn't lie to her even if it would be easier. I'd learned early on that my life would never be easy.

"But how? For how long?" Her brows furrowed, and she started rocking again.

"Only for a few weeks, and it was after I met my soul mate." I pointed at Egan, who stood slightly in front of his parents. "When we cemented our connection, I became like him."

Mom inhaled sharply and spat, "You three ... I should've known it would be you."

Wait ... Mom knew them. How was that possible?

CHAPTER FIVE

Mom acted like she knew who Egan's parents were, but they'd been hiding here for over a hundred years. That couldn't be possible. She was being pretty rude to my ... hell, what was I supposed to call them? Mate-in-laws? Either way, the entire situation wasn't ideal. "Mom, you don't know them."

I cringed, realizing that wasn't the wisest thing to say to someone who was irrationally upset.

"Like hell, I don't." Mom stood and placed her hands on her hips. "But it's crazy. You don't look a day older than that day on the beach."

The beach? "What are you talking about?" But I knew. I spun around and stared at Egan. Then my focus shifted to his parents. Dad had been desperate for us to move away from Sarah and had found a job in Florida. Those few days down there, with no negative influences over us, had been the best we'd had. On our last day there, we'd gone to the beach. That day had been amazing. We'd played together, jumped the waves, and I'd met a boy close to my own age whom I'd connected with. The very next day when we'd arrived home, Dad had run out to do some errands, and he'd been killed in a hit-and-run accident, so I'd suppressed most of the memories until now.

The little boy I vividly remembered morphed into the man standing right in front of me. "You saved me on that beach."

"You're the girl I pulled from the water," he said with surprise. He glanced at his parents. "Why didn't you tell us?"

"Son, we were going to, but many things were going on, and even though I suspected that it was the same girl before you got here, I wanted to confirm it first." His dad slowly stepped toward us in the same way he would approach a rabid dog.

This nugget of information didn't worry me. In a way, it reassured me. Even when we were young, we'd felt this connection. It hadn't magically happened at random. We'd always been drawn to each other even when we didn't understand it. *This is a good thing. Everything makes sense, but your dad is right. We can talk about this later. We need to focus on calming my mom down and getting out of here.*

Egan's shoulders relaxed, and he turned to me. *You're right. I just can't believe I didn't put it all together before now. All these years, I've been haunted by the memory of you until that day you walked onto Kortright's campus. I thought you'd replaced the girl I'd dreamed about for years, but you didn't at all.*

You do realize that sounds creepy? Please don't say you were dreaming about a little girl in your twenties. People will get uncomfortable.

The corners of his mouth twitched upward.

"So you've been orchestrating this ever since we met on

the beach." Mom jabbed her finger at them. "Between the way that little boy catered to Jade and how you were talking about future visits, you freaked out my husband and me. That's why we cut our trip a day short, and now my daughter is suddenly involved with you and has become a dragon. I should've known you were in danger when you ran off the way you did."

We didn't have time for this, but she wouldn't willingly leave unless we had this out. The more we forced her to do something she didn't want to, the harder this would be. "They had nothing to do with me leaving."

"Don't you lie to me." For the first time in over ten years, Mom reminded me of the woman before Dad had passed. "You beat the shit out of your aunt then vanished into thin air. Of course, a man would be involved."

"Stop it. You sound just like Sarah." I was done treating her like a child. It was time for her to open her eyes and see things for how they truly were. "There is no conspiracy theory. I left because I couldn't breathe. Sarah not only emotionally abused me, but she would hit me as often as she could. When she took college away from me, that was the final straw."

"What?" Mom's mouth dropped, and she shook her head. "I ... I don't understand. I saw the bruises."

"Yes, I hurt her, but she attacked me first." I'd never struck first with her. "I left to go to college to make something out of myself. I was so damn tired of not being able to do anything without her permission. She caught me leaving and tried to beat the shit out of me. Even had the neighbors call the cops. I met Egan at the university, not before then. He went there the prior semester. Fate intervened and brought us together."

"This is crazy." Mom took in a sharp breath. "The way

they acted and how you just happened to run into him. Are you sure it wasn't a setup?"

"Mom, he's my soul mate. My other half." I patted my chest where my heart beat. "Fate made sure we found each other twice. If we weren't connected, I wouldn't have become a dragon shifter like him."

"Ma'am," Egan said softly and respectively as he wrapped an arm around my waist. "Your daughter is the most important person in my life. Even that day on the beach, I felt a tug to the deepest section of the water and found her drowning. I'd give up my life for hers."

"Oh, God." She collapsed back onto the couch. "This is too much, and it's crazy."

"I get it." Boy, did I. "I almost walked away from Egan when he told me everything, and it was another reason I didn't want to tell you where I was. I wanted to keep you far away from ..." I trailed off, unsure what else to say, so I threw my hands up. "All this."

"There's much to say, and I understand that, but we need to get moving." Kayda grimaced, unhappy to interrupt this moment. "We can take you back home or wherever you want to go, but the fae dragon king could send others this way when he doesn't hear back from the witch or harpies."

"God, more creatures could come?" Mom jumped to her feet again. "We need to get out of here." Fear shone through her eyes.

"I can take her back to my aunt's and meet back up with you." I wasn't sure what else to do. Egan was the only one who knew where Sadie's mom's pack was located and where Lillith and Katherine's nest was, so he couldn't go with me.

"No!" Mom shouted then cleared her throat. "I mean ...

I would really like to go with you if humans are allowed there."

"Really?" That shocked me. With how poorly she was handling the situation, I'd thought she'd be screaming to head back home.

"If that's ..." Mom glanced awkwardly at the wood floors. "If that's okay with everyone."

The problem was I didn't know. I turned slightly into Egan and asked, *What do we do?*

I don't know either. He breathed. *Do you want her to come with us?*

Yes. The magnitude of what I'd said rattled me. She hadn't wanted to spend time with me in years. The last time we'd even laughed together had been on the beach. If she wanted to come with us, I'd hate to turn down the opportunity. Who knew when it would present itself again, especially when Sarah got her clutches back on her? *I really do.*

Then we'll make it work. Egan squeezed my waist. "There are other supernatural races where we're going, and it must be kept a secret. If you can't guarantee that, you can't come."

"Other supernaturals?" She shivered and closed her eyes. "You know what? Don't answer that. Of course, I'll keep it a secret. I wouldn't want Jade to get hurt or worse. After what I just saw, I wouldn't want that to happen to anyone."

"Then I guess that means you're joining us," Kayda murmured. "After all, we're family now."

It meant a lot that his parents didn't give us a hard time. Family was important to them, and they were welcoming Mom into the fold. No wonder Egan had grown into such a kind and considerate man.

I almost asked about Sarah but bit back the words. Her

name would come up again soon enough, and I didn't want to push it. "You do realize there's only one way out of here, though?"

"What do you mean?" Her jaw twitched, one of her nervous tics.

"You were carried in here by a harpy." My gaze cut to her shoulders. Her dark green shirt was torn where the talons had sunk into her arms. Blood still seeped from the cuts, and we needed to clean those injuries sooner rather than later. Harpies weren't the cleanest creatures.

She shuddered. "Don't remind me."

"Did you pay attention to how you got in here?" The only way inside the valley was through an opening in the cave ceiling. With no rocks providing hand and footholds, the mile-high drop would kill anyone who attempted to climb up the entryway. The opening was wide, allowing the sun to shine through most of the day, and inside the mountainous cave were rolling grassy hills with the village located on one side. It was a gorgeous place that wouldn't be a terrible place to live. Near the hidden second entrance was farmland with some livestock. They'd set everything up to be self-sufficient.

She pulled at her lip uncomfortably. "No, not really. Why?"

This wouldn't go over well. "There's only one way in and out, and that's flying."

Mom's eyes popped wider. "Are you going to bite me and turn me into a dragon?"

Her words took a second to sink in, and when they did, I burst out into laughter.

Egan chuckled silently beside me, trying to keep a straight face out of respect for her.

"Mom, vampires are the only race that actively bites to

change people." Apparently, wolves could too, but it was frowned upon because the human often ended up with horrible defects. The only two exceptions were when Sadie and Roxy had bitten their fated mates, Donovan and Axel. According to Sadie, she, Roxy, Egan, and her vampire friends had been worried Donovan and Axel would wind up the same way, but since they had shifter blood, they'd transitioned just fine. "Someone will have to carry you out of here."

"Oh, thank God." She sighed and rubbed her temple. "Not that there is anything wrong with dragons. I just don't want to be one."

Now I understood where I got my awkwardness from. It was clearly hereditary.

Ladon chuckled. "Nope, we can't turn anyone into a dragon unless they are a dragon's fated mate. I'll head out and make sure everyone is ready to go."

"Okay, we'll be right there," Kayda reassured me, making it clear there was not any discomfort talking with Mom.

Mom pursed her lips. "Can Jade carry me?"

"Sure, I can do that." If it made her more comfortable, I was all for it. "But no yelling in my ear."

"That I can't promise," she joked back.

I hated to bring up bad memories, but I needed to know. "How did the witch find you?"

"I'm not sure." She scratched her nose. "Sarah had to run out somewhere for work and asked me to pick a few things up at the grocery store. While I was shopping, the witch came right up to me and started talking. After a few minutes, she asked if I was your mom. I figured she was a high school friend and didn't find it very strange. When I checked out, she asked if I needed help loading the car. I thought she was a sweet kid and took her up on it. I was leaning into the backseat, putting the last bag in, when she hit me on the head. The next thing I knew, I woke up in a small cabin in the middle of nowhere."

If Mom had paid attention to my high school days at all, she'd have known I didn't have friends. But I bit my tongue. Vera would've done whatever was necessary to trick her. "I'm glad you made it out okay." It'd been damn close, but we'd survived.

"We aren't out of the woods yet." Kayda sighed. "Ladon is heading back. Everyone is ready. We have our bags in the center, so everyone shift and get ready to fly."

"Can I wait in here until Jade changes?" Mom asked. "I'd rather stay close to her if possible."

"Of course. We'll shift first; then you two can." Kayda headed to the doorway, leaving Egan and me alone with Mom.

The front door opened, and Ladon joined his wife in the shifting room. It wouldn't take long before it was our turn.

Mom watched Kayda walk off and whispered, "Does it hurt to turn into your dragon?"

I'd expected it to, at first, so it was a good question. "It's strange, but it doesn't hurt. It's more like your senses are sharper than ever, and it's a little disconcerting, but there's no pain."

"And you've been a dragon your whole life?" Mom asked Egan.

It warmed my heart that she was talking to him. She might be scared and uncomfortable, but she was trying to get to know him.

"We don't shift until we're seven or eight." Egan smiled.

"But ever since then, yes, and I was born with my senses more dragon-like, so I didn't have to adjust like Jade."

"Interesting," Mom breathed.

Dragon footsteps sounded, and the front door opened again. Egan's parents had already shifted and were in a hurry.

We'd stayed here longer than we should've. "Egan and I are going to go shift. Are you ready?"

She hesitated. "As ready as I'll ever be, but I don't want to be here to find out what shows up next."

Yeah, me neither. The image of the harpies alone would take a lifetime to dull. "We'll just be a moment."

Egan took my hand, and we entered the shifting room. We stripped down and put our clothes in the bag. He grabbed our bag, and within minutes, we were walking out into the entryway in dragon form.

Mom's face turned slightly pale when she saw us. Even though she'd known we'd be walking out in this form, it had to be unnerving to see us like this.

I wanted to comfort her, but there wasn't an easy way to do it in this form. Instead, I opened the front door and waved her out. She slowly followed after me, hiding behind my bulky frame as we met all the other dragons ready to leave. Each dragon carried two large bags of personal belongings.

Ladon looked at his son and motioned for him to lead.

He linked with me. *Get your mom, and let's go.*

Ready to get the hell out of here, I lowered myself and opened my arms to Mom. She stepped slowly inside, and I gently wrapped them around her so I didn't alarm her.

Draco stepped beside us, and the three of us took to the air. We flew around the thick smoke trickling upward from what was left of the harpy bodies. Mom coughed. I pushed away the thought of what we were breathing in.

As we flew out of the cave, the silence of the once brimming woods wasn't lost on me. The saying of the calm before the storm echoed in my head.

A loud cry of pain cracked through the sky, ruining any thought of getting out of here without issue.

CHAPTER SIX

My heart pounded in my ears, and if it hadn't been for Mom in my arms, there was no telling what I would've done. But I couldn't risk hurting her, so I kept my head on straight. *What is that? More fae creatures?*

That's what it sounds like, but the barrier spell is working. They're fighting against the spell and crying out in discomfort. Egan flew in front of me, following behind Draco.

That spell had been brutal, so hopefully, it would help keep the enemy creatures distracted. I glanced over my shoulder and found more dragons exiting the cave.

Mom snuggled deeper into my chest, either needing comfort or trying to comfort me. Either way, I appreciated the gesture.

More cries echoed throughout the woods, putting us on edge. Luckily, they were grouped together, coming in from our right.

Draco flew forward, keeping clear of the noise as the thunder flew hard through the channel.

I focused on the feel of the wind against my scales to

keep my anxiety at bay. Nothing good would happen if we reacted out of fear.

The sun shone down on us, and the smell of spring flowers hit my nose. On any other day, it would have been enjoyable, but the fae creatures could breach the barrier at any second.

Waving us on, Draco slowed and moved to the right. He had his tense warrior-dragon face cemented into place, his mouth firm and his nostrils flaring. His gray-green eyes deepened to black, but unlike Vera and the harpies, they weren't soulless. Pure determination and anger shone through.

Numerous stone figures flailed in mid-air. They looked like the gargoyle statues I'd seen in a haunted house Dad had taken me to once. But these were about half my size and bulky. Their faces were scrunched in chiseled stone, and their jagged stone teeth were scary. They were entirely gray except for their bright red eyes.

Gargoyles are real? The more I learned, the more things astonished me about this life. I never would've thought that these creatures existed. But why the hell not? Half-naked old ladies and reptile combinations were real, but I hadn't expected stone to come to life. Would the trees start dancing or attacking us next?

Egan kept his gaze locked on the strange creatures, but he didn't look as concerned. His wings beat steadily. *They're from Fae. They live near the dragons and are born of the stone from the volcanoes there. From what we've been told, every eruption causes a new batch of gargoyles to be born.*

Fae had to be one strange, messed-up place. I'd pass the opportunity to visit in a heartbeat. My ass was staying firmly in this realm.

We passed by all of the gargoyles and flew into a cloudless blue sky, but I refused to get too comfortable. Every time I thought we had a small win, we were attacked, or something equally horrible happened.

I could still hear faint screams, but the thunder was no longer under threat.

Egan took the lead, and we ascended higher into the sky.

No one can see us, Egan explained. *We'll be passing by cities and towns on the way there.*

Trusting him completely, I situated my mother and followed right behind.

A FEW HOURS LATER, my arms were getting tired from Mom's extra weight. The first hour, I'd gotten a little cocky since carrying Mom hadn't gotten to me, but I'd been too cocky too soon. My arms were aching, and each time Mom moved, holding her became harder.

From all of the fidgeting she'd been doing the past little while, I had a feeling she felt as uncomfortable as I did.

How much longer? I officially sounded like a whiny child, but if we didn't reach Lillith's home soon, I'd need a break.

Egan examined me. *We're almost there. Do I need to take her?*

No. If we're close, I'll be fine. Besides, I wasn't sure how Mom would react to someone else carrying her.

Hints of the green mountain greeted me. At this altitude, we probably looked like an enormous flock of birds flying over.

We flew past a small town, and after a few more miles,

Egan started a slow descent. He said, *Just a few minutes now.*

The others followed closely behind. We flew beyond the small country roads and over a stretch of thick woods. It reminded me of Trixie's, the witch who'd thought she'd blocked Vera from tracking me. We'd flown over a large section of nothing before landing in the middle of a vast clearing that held a small cabin that had seen better days.

I hoped we would have better conditions here, but I didn't have a dime to my name since quitting Haynes Steakhouse, so I'd have appreciated any kind of shelter.

We hadn't seen any cars driving on the roads for miles, and Egan descended farther, only a mile above the trees. I kept my eyes forward, afraid that if I looked down, I might drop Mom accidentally. It was an irrational fear.

After a few more minutes, a huge mansion appeared a mile away. It was a symmetrical, three-story brick building with brick steps leading to the tall red door at the center. It looked well kept.

Wow, Roxy had called it a mansion, but I'd figured she was being sarcastic. *Is that it?*

Yes. Egan sounded relieved. *Between the vampires and wolves, there are miles and miles of land. With so much space, I'm hoping we won't struggle to find room for everyone.*

That seemed like wishful thinking. Huge homes usually had more rooms for entertainment and stuff than sleeping space ... or so it always seemed in stories and movies. *How many bedrooms and bathrooms are there?*

Fifteen bedrooms with sixteen full bathrooms. However, between Sadie, her pack, and the vampires, there are only about seven bedrooms available. But they have a living room with two L-shaped leather couches that should sleep four and a few blow-up mattresses. And then we can talk to Titan and see how many homes they might have to offer us.

We had a lot to figure out, but we were better off than I'd dared hope for. *Where will we stay?*

I have a bedroom there with how much time I spent here last semester.

Despite our parents being nearby, I hoped that there wouldn't be a problem with me staying in the same room with him.

When we landed in front of the mansion, the front door opened, and Sadie and the others ran outside.

"Thank God, you're okay." Sadie jumped down the stairs, her rose-gold bob bouncing. Her light blue eyes found Egan then me. "We've been so worried about you." She placed her cell phone in her back jeans pocket, and her coral top inched upward, revealing some of her tan, smooth skin.

"She's been calling you nonstop." Donovan stepped up beside his mate and pulled her shirt down. His cobalt eyes locked on Mom as he ran his free hand through his shaggy dark hair. His muscles contracted, outlined in his white polo shirt. He was huge, but only half the size of Egan. In general, dragons were stronger and more built than wolves.

"Holy shit." Roxy's hazel eyes widened. She fluffed her vibrant red hair and clicked down the stairs in her hunter-green platform heels. She wore a matching green designer dress that accentuated her breasts and small hips. "They brought a human."

Now would be a good time to shift into human form so I could explain why.

"That won't go over well." Axel scratched his buzzed head, and his dark eyes deepened to an obsidian.

"What won't go over well?" Lillith asked as she came

out the front door. Her dark brown eyes had a deep crimson ring around the pupils, telling me she'd recently fed. Her jet-black hair was cut like Sadie's, but that was where the similarities ended. Where Sadie normally wore clothes in varying shades of color, Lillith did not. Her outfits were all black, the same color as her hair. The only part of her that was a different color was her pale vampire skin.

She wore trendy black Chucks, so her steps were silent when she walked down the stairs. But she stopped short when she saw Mom. Her hands went to her waist, as a slight breeze made her black skirt rise above her knees and her lace shirt crinkle. "Why is there a human here?"

I wasn't thinking, Egan said slowly.

What's wrong with Mom being here? Someone needed to let me in on the crucial piece of information I was missing.

"Uh ... I'm Jade's mother," Mom said feebly as she tried to get out of my arms, but I held firm. I wasn't letting her go until I knew what the hell was going on.

Katherine's family was turned about ten years ago. Her brothers aren't great around humans yet. Egan winced even in dragon form. He stepped in front of me, blocking Mom from their view.

"Really? You think that's going to hide her smell?" Lillith snapped.

"Hide what smell?" Katherine asked as she ran out the door. Her lighter brown eyes held the dark red center, and her long hair blew behind her. She rushed toward us but stopped short. She sniffed so hard that her chest expanded, making the pink word "Believe" on her black shirt legible. Her hands fell at her sides, brushing against her blue jeans. "Oh, that one."

Lillith turned toward the house. "We need to keep Luther and Athan inside."

"I can leave." Mom leaned forward and glanced at me. "I don't want to cause problems."

"You aren't," Katherine assured her. "My brothers have been practicing, so they won't pose a threat to you."

"Pose a threat to me?" Mom's brows furrowed. "I ... I don't understand."

"You know what?" Sadie cleared her throat and gestured to the entire thunder behind us. "How about you all set your stuff down and shift back to human form so we can figure out sleeping arrangements. After your long night, I know you three," she said, pointing to Draco, Egan, and me, "must be exhausted."

Until she'd mentioned it, I hadn't noticed, but between the crazy fighting, the all-nighter, and seeing Mom, fatigue had caught up.

"Come on ... Jade's mom." Roxy tapped her lip. "What is your name? Or do you wanna go by that?"

"Oh, it's Liz." Mom nearly sounded like herself answering a normal question.

Sometimes, normal was underrated. I almost missed things being as I expected them to be. Not that I would give Egan up.

Roxy sashayed over to Mom and pried my arms from her. "All right, Liz. You can hang out with me. I don't bite, unlike the vampires here."

"Vampires?" Mom's voice skyrocketed to glass-breaking levels.

Things were going swimmingly. She probably regretted wanting to come with us.

"Don't worry," Roxy said, brushing off her concern. "The guys just drank several pints of blood, so they aren't hungry, and the decaying blood smell you got going on in your hair would make even the hungriest vamp think twice before chomping down on you."

"Decay?" Mom parroted and touched her crusty hair. She gagged and wiped her fingers on her jeans.

"Yeah, that's going to help." Roxy rolled her eyes at Sadie and Katherine.

"Dude, sometimes I worry about your mate." Donovan shook his head. "Does she really think that's comforting?"

"Nope, you're not getting me in trouble again." Axel took a few long steps away from his best friend. "Roxy does what she wants. I've learned to stop trying to reason with her."

"See." Roxy pointed at me. "I finally got him trained. I'll teach you the ways with that big lug right next to you."

"Okay." Sadie clapped her hands. "You all go shift, and I'll stay here and protect your mother from them." She waved her hand at her pack and the vampires.

Mom's shoulders relaxed some.

I didn't blame her. Sadie had a calming presence about her, unlike Roxy and Lillith.

Come on. Egan nodded toward the trees. *Let's change and get back to your mom before they make it all worse.*

That sounded like a solid plan.

We rushed off to the woods as the other dragons followed suit. We all spread out, giving each other ample space. Egan dropped the bag and unzipped it awkwardly with his huge, scaly dragon hands, and we pulled out our clothes.

Back in human form and fully clothed, we hurried back to the others. Mom and Sadie were talking a few feet away from the rest.

As we walked up to them, Sadie and Mom stopped, and the group turned toward us.

Egan asked, "What's the plan? We have a hundred and twenty with us."

"How many families does that break into?" Donovan placed his hands into his pocket.

"Around fifty." Egan rolled his shoulders.

Sadie gestured to the mansion. "Between the bedrooms, couches, and the three blow-up mattresses, we can take in fifteen couples easily."

"I'm the youngest here," Egan said. "One reason why I got to leave and look for a mate. Only Mindy and I have been born in the last fifty years."

"Wait, she said she trained younger kids." That was the whole reason she'd been sent to train me.

"She has a handful of them. Kids who came from other thunders. She was given the task to train the young for when we would start having children of our own again." Egan shrugged. "We stayed hidden and mostly traveled from thunder to thunder on rare occasions. Usually, only the leaders of the thunders did it because they already knew where we were located. They brought their kids, the next leaders of the thunder, to meet the others and learn about all the locations."

"The next best news is that Titan's pack has about thirty homes open since a majority of the younger families relocated to our pack." Sadie glanced toward the woods where the other dragons had begun filing out. "As long as a few don't mind bunking together, we should have plenty of room until we can figure out our next move."

Wow, this was a much better plan than we'd realized. It just sucked that we would have to split up.

The front door opened, and a guy around our age

popped his head out. His blond hair was a shade lighter than Egan's, and his gray eyes seemed friendly until they landed on Mom.

Fangs descended as he hissed and leaped at her.

"Athan!" Katherine screamed. "No!"

CHAPTER SEVEN

The next few seconds blended together. I hadn't expected an attack, and Athan had stunned everyone.

Egan stepped in front of Mom as the vampire reached her, his teeth ready to sink into her neck. Egan placed his hands on Athan's shoulders and shoved him to the gravel driveway. Rocks bounced from the impact, and a puff of dust surrounded us.

Needing to help protect Mom, I ran over to her and wrapped my hand around her arm. When I tugged, she hardly moved. She was frozen in fear.

I would have to use my supernatural strength to make her budge. I hated to do it, but this was a life or death matter. I yanked on her harder, and her feet stumbled, but she stayed upright. She was now behind Egan and me.

Wings flapped as Draco sped past me, half shifted and racing toward the vampire.

Athan jumped up with a loud, crackling hiss, desperate to get to Mom. He blurred as he tried to go around Egan, and I prepared myself to fight the vampire off. Egan lowered his body and threw the vampire over his shoulder.

The whole point of coming here had been to find safety, not be threatened.

"Stop it," Sadie commanded as she raced to stand beside me. Her light blue eyes glowed brightly.

I'd never heard or seen her like this before. She really was an alpha, not that I hadn't believed it before. She had a strong presence, but she never used it. Everyone naturally gravitated to her and wanted to hear what she had to say. She led by caring about people and encouraging them to embrace her views and thoughts. A leader like that could decimate armies because of the morale they instilled in others.

Despite her words, Athan's eyes turned red as he desperately snarled and struggled. I refused to cower. If he got to her, he'd kill her.

The vampire clawed at Egan's back and shoulder.

"Do not injure the prince," Draco rasped and fisted the vampire's head, holding him up.

His legs dangled, and he cried in pain like a puppy in trouble.

Egan reached to take the vampire back from the warrior and winced, dropping his hand to his side. "He's not used to humans, and he's a friend. Don't hurt him."

"I won't, but he can't be trusted." Draco stared at the vampire, his nose wrinkled with disgust.

That only agitated Athan more. He swatted at Draco, but the dragon was too huge and held him a safe distance away. He rocked, his eyes locked on Mom.

He was completely out of his mind. All the vampire needed to do was reach over his head and slash into the dragon's hand.

"I said stop," Sadie growled and punched Athan in the face.

His head snapped back, and his body went limp, dangling like a wet noodle. Draco dropped the vampire on his back, knocking the breath out of him. His face crumpled in pain as he panted.

I might have felt bad for the vampire if he hadn't tried to eat my mom.

"Athan." Katherine kneeled beside him. "What's gotten into you?"

"You said he'd eaten." Lillith glanced from Athan to Roxy. "He wouldn't be acting like this if he had. Sure, he might be tempted, but that was a full-on hunger attack."

Roxy cringed. "About that. I might have been misinformed."

"Misinformed?" Lillith narrowed her eyes. "You were the one with Ollie, him, and Luther, playing that stupid video game."

"Well ..." Roxy blew out a breath and chewed on her green fingernail.

Axel rubbed his forehead. "Babe, come clean."

The words spilled from Roxy so fast they were almost unintelligible. "The game got intense, and I wasn't paying attention to them, so I don't know if they were drinking the blood. I assumed they were."

"Then why did you tell us that?" Katherine moved the hair out of her brother's face.

Roxy lifted a hand in surrender, her face lined with remorse. "I honestly thought they had and didn't expect them to leave their game. When I saw his reaction, I realized they may have gotten caught up in the game too." She leaned over to see Mom. "I'm sorry, Liz."

My anger deflated even though I didn't want it to. Roxy

was usually confident and vibrant, and for the first time, she looked remorseful. She obviously felt terrible and was beating herself up.

"We need to get him inside," Egan said and bent to pick up the vampire.

"I'll get him." Draco cut his gaze to Egan's bleeding shoulder. "You're injured." He picked the vampire up and headed to the front door.

Roxy opened the door. "Here, I'll help—"

"No. You've done enough," Lillith said. "I'll go with Draco and make sure he and Luther drink. We don't need another vampire going crazy." Lillith scowled at Roxy and walked past her.

The look on Roxy's face was devastating. Her head flinched backward, and her cheeks reddened. If I hadn't known any better, I would've thought she'd been slapped.

In a way, she had been. Lillith hadn't held back her words.

Draco marched past her like he was on a mission. Granted, that was his normal disposition, seeing as he was prepared to protect Egan and me at a moment's notice.

When the front door shut again, Mom peeked around me and whispered, "Is he gone?"

"Yeah, he's back inside." Axel rubbed his mate's shoulder, comforting her. Roxy's face reminded me of a tomato, and she frowned even more.

"How can he hear me?" Mom asked louder, not bothering to lower her voice.

I pointed at my ear. "Supernatural hearing. They could hear you clear as day in the woods."

My eyes went back to the tree line where all of the dragon shifters stood. They all wore troubled expressions after watching what had gone down.

If I'd been in their situation, I'd have felt the same way. Hell, I mirrored their expressions now. I didn't need to feel like there was a constant threat lurking in the background. Maybe Mom should go back to Sarah, but I didn't want to encourage that. Mom needed time away from Sarah's influence.

"Is everything all right?" Ladon asked and stepped out from between two trees. His gaze locked on his son's injured shoulder, and his eyes turned dark gold.

Kayda shoved past her husband, rushing to Egan. "Of course it's not all right." She gingerly reached for his shoulder. "We need to clean this."

"And Mom's too." They had near-identical wounds. Egan had the better end since the vampire looked clean and he had shifter healing abilities. Mom's injuries would become infected without treatment and take weeks to heal. I wanted to check on Egan myself, but Mom was buried against my back. The irony wasn't lost on me that she acted more like the child in our relationship.

"There is no way in hell I'm going in there." Mom stepped away from the door.

"You know what?" Sadie casually strolled over to Mom and wrapped an arm around her waist. "Why don't I take you and the other dragons staying with my stepdad's pack over there to get settled?"

Mom rubbed her hands together, her lips drawn. "Are there vampires?"

"Nope, only wolf shifters." Sadie beamed. "And the dragon shifters who want to stay there as well."

"Of course. Wolf shifters." Mom winced. "I guess nothing should surprise me anymore, but I'm down as long as someone doesn't try biting me."

"I can go too," I volunteered, wanting to comfort Mom.

"We were hoping that you, Egan, and his parents would stay here with us," Donovan said slowly. "There's a library here filled with old books. We were thinking you could assist us with research."

I stiffened, hating for Mom to feel abandoned.

"It's fine, honey." Her focus landed uncomfortably on Egan. "You stay here with your ... uh ..."

"Fated mate," Katherine suggested gently. Her kindness knew no bounds, and she was one of the few here, like Donovan, Axel, and me, who understood what it was like to get thrust into an unknown world that made no sense.

"Right." Mom's brows furrowed, and she tilted her head. "Fated mate and his parents."

Sadie tugged Mom toward the back of the house. "She can stay with Mom, Titan, and Torak. They'll keep her busy and on her toes."

"As long as I'm safe there," Mom grumbled, eagerly stepping away.

A small smile spread across my face. She was handling this better than I'd expected, especially after how she'd reacted back in the cave valley. Maybe she wanted distance between us to process everything. She and I were similar like that.

"Son, how do you propose we split up?" Ladon asked, throwing me off guard.

Ladon was the king, not Egan. Shouldn't that be his call to make? I almost linked with Egan but figured this was something he should handle on his own. Maybe his father was preparing him now that Egan knew his future.

Egan surveyed the group and cleared his throat. He squared his shoulders as he stood beside me and took my hand, presenting us as a united front. "Draco and the oldest dragons should stay here. The remainder of the thunder should go with Sadie and the others to the wolf pack. They have thirty homes available for us to use, so families can choose who they want to double up with for the time being. The fae dragon king will not stop, and our time of hiding is over."

A few dragons close to our age cheered. They could have been in their mid-thirties for all I knew, but the younger generation liked the thought of joining the rest of the world.

The thunder split into two groups without fighting, and everyone obeyed based on age. *Are there a few leaders who will qualify for the pack houses? We don't need the younger ones going and acting wild because of their newfound freedom.*

I'd seen what my fellow classmates had done once they'd arrived at college. Their social media pages contained drunken pictures of them doing embarrassing things I couldn't believe they'd post in the first place, and a few even had friends posting pictures of them vomiting into toilets, clearly too drunk. We didn't need crazy dragon shifters getting loose in the world and drawing unwanted attention here. Sadie and the others had made it clear that their families enjoyed living in a place few knew about. We would respect their wishes and ensure they remained hidden.

Okay, maybe "world" was a stretch, but they surely were new to the supernatural community.

You're right. Egan squeezed my hand lovingly. "Rose and Thorn, will you please go to the pack homes and make sure those from our thunder pulls their weight?"

That was code for behaving respectfully but in a more politically correct way. He had a knack for leading without making others feel insulted.

Rose's stern face transformed with a proud smile. Her

amethyst eyes glowed slightly at the request, making her plum-brown hair stand out. She was over six feet five inches tall, one of the tallest women, and even in her jeans and shirt, she looked perfectly put together. "Of course, my prince."

Now that I wasn't expecting, Egan grumbled, not thrilled about the prince part.

She took her husband's hand and broke away from the group destined for the mansion. Her husband had a few inches on her, and where she was bright and colorful, he looked pale. His eyes were a light silver, and he had white, ash-blond hair. His skin tone looked more vampiric than the golden shine of normal shifters.

An older couple from the previous group replaced them.

"Okay, let's do this," Roxy said, still sounding defeated. She hurried to catch up with Mom and Sadie, likely to apologize again.

Were those two an arranged marriage? They acted like natural dragon shifters, unlike Kayda and me. We had more of a human way about us. Not so noble ... or rigid.

Egan nodded and tugged me toward the house. *Yes, they are. How'd you know?*

Between learning about arranged marriages among your kind and the way those two move like dragon-born shifters, I put two and two together. Being observant was the main way I'd survived living with my aunt all those years. I'd had to figure out her moods and what to expect based on how her face was set or the way she stood to know how to proceed with her.

By the time we entered the house, the adrenaline of the vampire attack had worn off, and my feet dragged against the pristine wood floors as we walked down a long hallway.

Egan led us into a huge living room where two L-shaped leather couches were set across from each other with a wooden coffee table in between. Everything was positioned in front of an eighty-inch, flat-screen television, and remote controls for a gaming console littered the floor. The vampire young man sat on the couch, his face in his hands as a teenage boy sat next to him. The teenager looked exactly like a male version of Katherine, except a few years younger.

Standing right in front of them with his arms crossed, Draco glared down at the two of them.

Egan stopped, and I leaned against his side, barely able to stand on both feet.

"I hate to do this, but Jade and I have been up since yesterday afternoon, and we need a long nap." Egan turned to his dad. "Do you mind if we rest for a few hours and rejoin you later?"

"No, but I'm not sure who these people are." Ladon looked a bit uncomfortable.

"That's where we come in." Lillith stepped into the room. "I can introduce you to everyone. Egan already knows them anyway."

"We'll be fine," Kayda interjected. "Go get some rest. You two deserve it."

Even though I normally couldn't sleep with so many people around, I had a feeling once I got comfortable on that couch, sleep would crash over me. I nearly sighed with relief as I moved toward the couch, but Egan's arms slid around my waist.

He asked, *Where do you think you're going?*

To get some rest.

He tugged me toward another hallway and rasped, *You're going the wrong way. Our room is up there.*

Together? In front of your parents? Thank God he planned on us sharing a room. I'd figured we would, but I didn't know if his parents expected us to do whatever ceremony dragons did before staying together. I had no clue how this worked in their world.

He picked me up and kissed my lips gently as he climbed the stairs. *Yes. Did you think I'd let you out of my sight? We're mated. I won't spend a night without you right next to me.*

Despite my exhaustion, my body warmed at his kiss and touch. Of course, his words didn't hurt either.

At the first door on the right, he paused and turned the doorknob.

All thoughts of sleep abandoned me as I wrapped my arms around his neck and slipped my tongue between his lips.

He stumbled into the room and barely regained his balance. He growled as he matched each stroke of my tongue. *If you keep this up, we aren't taking a nap right away.*

I'm okay with that. My hand slid under his shirt.

Someone cleared their throat. I went still and buried my face in his chest like a coward.

CHAPTER EIGHT

I wished the floor would open up and swallow me whole. The sweet scent of vampire hit my nose, but it was more male. A hint of a bitter undertone counterbalanced the smell slightly. Still, his scent reminded me of cotton candy at an amusement park.

"I'm sorry for interrupting," Athan said. "But I ran upstairs, hoping to catch you before you got into your room so I could apologize to you since your mom isn't around."

Yeah, there was no getting out of meeting his eyes. At least, he was similar to his sister and nothing like Lillith or Roxy. They'd have been using this opportunity to embarrass me.

Hey, there's nothing to be ashamed of, Egan reassured me. *Even though vampires don't have fated mates, they have high sex drives like any other supernatural.*

I rubbed my head into his chest, and my shoulders sagged. *Not helping.*

"I guess I'll leave you two alone." Disappointment dripped from each one of Athan's words.

Not only was I a scaredy-cat, but I was also hurting the

poor guy's feelings. He obviously felt bad, which, in all fairness, he should, but sometimes forgiveness went a long way. Or that was what I was hoping for.

Inhaling sharply, I forced myself away from the safety of Egan's arms to look at the vampire. He already had his back turned to us, heading for the stairs. His head hung, making him appear smaller than during the attack.

"I'm being silly." My face warmed, but I tried to be casual. "We were just about to get it on, and you caught us. That's why I was hiding, not because you almost killed my mother."

And here I thought I'd overcome my awkward mouth-diarrhea.

Athan's brows furrowed as he tilted his head. I could see his brain spinning, but I wasn't sure why. "Are you trying to make me uncomfortable as punishment, or did you not mean to say that?"

Egan snorted and broke out into loud laughter. He placed a hand on the base of my neck as he faced the vampire. Between his bouts of laughter, my mate said, "She didn't mean to. She's not like Roxy and Lillith, who thrive off embarrassing and shocking people."

Now I was being laughed at. Great. I might as well have been back in high school. "You two can kiss my ass." Egan could find somewhere else to sleep or think I didn't want him in here with me.

"Hey, wait," Athan called out, and I stopped short. "I'm not laughing at you. You just caught me by surprise."

And I'm not either. Egan wrapped an arm around my waist, pulling me back against him. He rasped, *I think it's adorable and refreshing. I can tell exactly what you're thinking.*

Deciding not to make the situation worse, I ignored

Egan's words, trying to stay annoyed, and turned my gaze on Athan. "You came here to say …" Dear God, please redirect the conversation. I didn't want to say anything else, afraid of what might fall from my lips.

"Right." He rolled his shoulders like he was either preparing for a fight or a long speech. "Of course, I'll say this to your mom … if she'll let me near her again." He grimaced like he realized he might never get a chance to tell her directly. "But I feel awful about attacking her. I didn't realize a human would be part of your group, so I didn't gorge myself to make sure I wasn't the slightest bit hungry. Between that and not being mentally prepared for a smell that delectable—" He stopped and licked his lips at the memory.

I had no clue what to do. He'd come here to apologize, but he was licking his lips at the thought of Mom's scent. *Uh … what do I do here?*

Give him a second. Egan's thumb rubbed against my neck. *He really is a good guy. With him and his brother being turned younger, they don't have as much self-control, and the bloodlust is hard for them to overcome.*

Isn't he our age, though, like Katherine? Katherine hadn't batted an eye at Mom.

Women, in general, can control their urges better than men, but when she first attended Kortright, she wasn't very comfortable around humans. She's grown a lot in a semester, being around humans constantly. They've taken Athan and Luther out around humans, but it's very controlled. Obviously, they still have more work to do. Lillith was born a vampire, so she grew up learning how to control her urges.

Born a vampire. Who knew? *Does that make her a purebred?*

Yes, but those who are turned aren't viewed as much less. Egan coughed to snap Athan out of it.

"Right, sorry." Athan put his tongue back in his mouth and rubbed a hand down his face. "This isn't going like I hoped. It's just, I really am sorry, and Luther and I will do everything possible to make sure an attack like that doesn't happen again."

"Please do." I wouldn't tell him it was okay, because one, it wasn't, and two, they'd all know I was lying.

"Promise." Athan placed his hands in his jeans pockets and rocked back on his heels.

An awkward silence descended among us, and Egan pushed the door to our bedroom wider.

"Right." Athan lifted his hand and snapped, "You two were busy. I'll let you get back to it."

This couldn't get any more uncomfortable. Boy, I really hated that he'd proved me wrong.

"So ... see ya." He saluted Egan and raced toward the steps.

Once he'd rounded the corner and was out of sight, I leaned against the doorframe and banged my head against the wood. *Is he going to run down there and tell everyone?*

No. He isn't Lillith or Roxy. Egan pulled me into the bedroom and pressed my back against the wall. His hands trapped me, turning me on more than I'd thought possible.

Egan surrounded me, and even if I'd wanted to get away, I couldn't. The sense of him overpowering me should have pissed me off, but the alpha mood had me primed for him.

He kissed my lips and gently bit my bottom lip. My hands wrapped around his neck as I hooked a leg around his waist.

Any sense of fatigue was gone, my body fueled by a desperate need only he could fill.

What's gotten into you? He was normally gentle, almost too much so.

He stilled. *Am I being too rough?*

Oh God, no. You better not stop. I sucked on his bottom lip hard and grazed my teeth against his tongue.

His hands cupped my ass, his fingers digging into my skin. He groaned as he tore his mouth from my lips and kissed down my neck. When he reached the base, he tasted my skin then gently bit.

I bucked against him and slipped my hands under his shirt. My nails scratched his back as my breathing turned ragged.

His mouth went back to mine, and he kissed me so thoroughly my mind grew dizzy. He spun me around and headed toward the bed.

"No, stop." Of course, this was when my germophobic ways would come in handy. "We're both nasty, and your shoulder needs to be cleaned."

"Then it sounds like we need to hit the shower." He walked across the room, through another doorway, and sat me down on the tile next to a sizable, light gray, stone shower.

I almost whined when he pulled away to turn the shower on inside but was tempted by the water falling from a double shower head like rain.

The bathroom was dark compared to the rest of the house. A dark-gray double sink sat to the right of the doorway with a matching tub to the left. Between the tub and the shower was a closet full of fluffy white towels. I'd never been in a house this luxurious before.

He pulled out two towels and placed them on the stand next to the shower door.

"Come here." He removed my shirt as he kissed toward my breast. I leaned my head back as his lips released some tension from my body.

His tongue flicked my nipple as he rasped, *God, you taste so good.*

The tangy scent of our arousal killed every single one of my brain cells.

He pulled my crotch right against him and ground against me. Even with our jeans on, the friction built, and my body almost exploded when he nipped at my breast.

There was something primal about him. Something raw. Something I'd never seen before, and it was thrilling. My hands shook with desperation as I unfastened his jeans and pushed them, along with his boxers, to the ground. My hand stroked him, and he shuddered at my touch.

I loved having that much power over him.

He grabbed my arms and pinned them as he quickly removed my pants. He paused midway and grimaced. "Did I hurt your leg?"

Shit. I'd forgotten all about that injury during the flight here. Begrudgingly, I untangled myself from him and glanced down to find the wound had scabbed over. I moved my leg from side to side, and there was absolutely no pain.

"I'm fine." My eyes went to his shoulders. "Let's get you in the shower and clean before yours heals too much like mine." I hoped I didn't get an infection, but the skin wasn't red around the scab. Maybe shifters were immune to infections?

You don't have to tell me twice. He winked and moved to pull his shirt off.

If I hadn't been watching him so closely, I might have

missed the grimace that slipped through as the shirt tore over his head.

But my eyes didn't stay on his shoulder wound for long as his naked body pulled my attention away.

His six-pack was damn lickable, and his pecs were defined, each muscle clearly lined. He was four times my size, all muscle, and damn sexy.

He opened the shower door, making me walk backward inside. The water felt like a warm caress. It felt magical and fueled my hunger for him.

Water poured down our faces as he captured my lips and positioned himself between my legs. With one swift thrust, he entered me, and I raised my leg higher, causing him to hit where I needed.

A low, deep groan escaped, and he leaned over my body, slamming inside me over and over again.

Wrapping my legs around his waist, I moved in rhythm with him. He captured my nipple in his mouth again.

My vision hazed as utter lust overcame me. The back of my head hit the tile, triggering discomfort, but the pleasure magnified. I didn't want him to stop and moaned, "Faster."

He groaned as he quickened his pace. He pounded harder, and the pressure built quicker than ever before.

His lips landed on mine, and he used the wall for leverage. His citrus scent surrounded me, mixing with his vanilla taste. I opened myself up to him, needing him to feel how much I cared for him. I loved him more with each passing moment, so much so that sometimes all the emotions he caused actually hurt.

I love you too, he whispered inside my head, letting me not only hear but feel the emotion behind it.

An orgasm ripped through me, and he groaned, releasing at the same time. Our bodies convulsed together as we went over the edge. When we were finished, he didn't move, the water like a barrier keeping the outside world at bay.

He stared straight into my eyes, piercing my soul. *I didn't hurt you, did I? I'm sorry. I don't know what came over me. But both my dragon and I were desperate for you.*

I kissed him and replied, *That was amazing. I want it like that more often, in addition to your usual sweet ways.*

The desperate, alpha side of him was a sight I'd never get tired of, especially when sex was involved. *You can dominate me here anytime you want as long as you let me be my own person in a fight or when threatened.*

I'm trying. He kissed my nose and stepped back. He picked up the shampoo and motioned for me to turn around.

Unable to deny the sweet request, I turned, and his fingers worked the shampoo through my hair. The orange smell that was part of him hit my nose. Ahh, so that was partly due to his shampoo.

After he was done, I quickly washed him, cleaning the claw marks well. By the time we were clean and drying off, fatigue hit hard again, but I didn't feel on edge. I was completely sated.

"Ugh, I'm going to have to put the dirty clothes back on." We'd left the bag in the woods for Draco, and he probably had it downstairs.

"You can wear one of my shirts." A sexy smirk spread across his face. "I've been waiting for that to happen anyway."

We stepped into the room, and now that I wasn't sex-crazed, I looked around. The room was even bigger than my dorm room. A king-sized oak bed sat in the middle against the far wall with matching oak end tables on both sides.

Across from the bed was a dresser, and a flat-screen television hung right above it. A door stood open to the left, leading into a huge closet. There was a chest of drawers in the corner, next to a double window that overlooked the woods. I felt like we were staying in a mansion.

Oh, wait. We were.

The room had light gray-blue walls that were popular at the moment, and a navy blue comforter was spread over the bed.

Egan strolled into the walk-in closet and came out carrying two shirts and a pair of flannel pajama bottoms. He handed a shirt to me and put on his clothes.

We both crawled into bed, and he wrapped his arms around me, pulling my back right against his stomach. I drifted off to sleep.

A LOUD POUNDING on the door startled me from my dreams. Strong arms left my waist as Egan stood. He rushed to the door and opened it only a crack. He said quietly, "Jade is sleeping."

"I'm sorry to bug you, son, but we have a problem," Ladon said with remorse. "This can't wait."

CHAPTER NINE

My body protested, but I forced myself to sit up in bed. I kept the covers over my legs since all I had to cover me was one huge shirt. The last thing I wanted was to flash my vag at my mate's father. Some things couldn't be unseen.

Believe me, I knew.

"Is Mom okay?" She'd been oddly resilient after Athan's attack, which wasn't like her. Usually, she'd break down, and Sarah would have to fix everything for her. I had a feeling my aunt would often orchestrate the whole thing, but I'd never been able to prove it. Sarah was smart. I had to give her that.

Ladon's face smoothed into a gentle smile. "This isn't about her. There haven't been any more attacks."

A weight lifted from my shoulders. I hadn't realized I was waiting for her to have a meltdown until this moment. *Can you run and get a change of clothes for me? I love wearing your shirt, but I'd like to get dressed before heading downstairs to see everyone.*

Yes, I'll go grab our stuff now. Egan winked at me before

turning back to his father. "Okay, let me find something for Jade, and we'll be right down."

"Okay." Ladon stepped back so Egan could walk past him.

When he didn't follow his son, discomfort grew inside me. I felt comfortable around his parents—well, as comfortable as I ever had around new people—but I didn't know what to expect. Since meeting them, we'd been thrust into nonstop action, and we hadn't had a chance to formally meet. In a way, that had created a bond between us, but we still didn't know each other, and we definitely hadn't talked without Egan around.

Also, my refusal to stand because I was Porky Piggin' it made the situation even more unsettling.

Oh, God. Roxy's sayings were rubbing off on me. I'd had no clue what that meant until she'd informed me about her time in the woods with only a shirt on. She'd been buck naked from the bottom down—no pants or panties—dragging her dying mate toward a van to get him to safety.

"Are you okay?" Ladon asked, his brows furrowed. "You seem perplexed."

Yeah, I wasn't touching that one with a ten-foot pole. "Just some internal ramblings. Sorry. Are you and Kayda okay?" If I'd been the praying kind, I'd have been down on my knees, thanking God that for once I'd contained my awkward mouth-diarrhea.

He stepped into the room and leaned his shoulder against the doorframe. He rubbed his right wrist and rotated his other shoulder. "I just wanted to say I'm very glad that you and Egan found each other. Egan has always been strong, but I've noticed a difference with you by his side. He's always done the right thing, and he's always been loyal —it's the dragon way—but there's a light in his eyes that wasn't there before. He finally understands his greater purpose, and you two will need that to get through what comes next."

That sounded daunting, but maybe that was just me. We all had to get through what came next, not just the two of us. Egan would die before he allowed anything to happen to his loved ones.

The sheer truth of the thought rattled me. The idea of losing him made it hard to breathe. If just thinking about it hurt this badly, what would actually losing him feel like? The concept petrified me.

"We'll all get through it together." I had to believe that.

Egan's footsteps grew closer as he climbed the stairs. He entered the room, and his eyebrows rose when he saw his dad still standing there. "Everything okay?"

"Yes, I just hadn't had an opportunity to talk to Jade alone." Ladon shrugged and stepped out the door. "I'll see you two in the kitchen." He walked away, leaving Egan and me alone.

That was super awkward. I was here in bed with nothing on. My ass always wound up in uncomfortable situations like these, and I had no clue why.

Egan chuckled as he shut the door and placed our bag on the floor. He pulled out a pair of jeans, underwear, and a light gray T-shirt and laid them on the bed next to me. *He didn't realize that. He thought you were in your pajamas. If he'd known, he'd have been embarrassed and run out the door.*

At least, there was that. It had only been awkward on my end.

I pushed the covers off me and changed. My reflection in the dresser mirror caught my attention. My dark brown hair appeared more lush and vibrant, and my eyes seemed lighter, like they had a tad of gold in them. I ran my fingers along my face, surprised that my skin appeared sun-kissed—more shifter-like. My muscles were more defined than ever, and I'd always been in good shape. Even though I was recognizable, I didn't look quite the same. Maybe a more glamorous version of my previous self. "Do I look different to you?"

"When you connected with your dragon, she was free to be part of you. You're the same, only with her influence over you." He stepped behind me, placing his chin on the top of my head. "But you're still my Jade and just as beautiful as the first day I met you."

"Thanks for calling me beautiful, but I'm not your property." Even though we were mated, I was still my own person. He hadn't hovered over me too much during the last few attacks, and I didn't want to do anything to discourage him from the small progress we'd made. "I can take care of myself."

"Yes, I know." He placed his hands on my shoulders and gently rubbed them while exhaling. "You've made that clear." The spot between his eyebrows creased with displeasure.

"I love you." I spun around, laying my hands on his chest. "But I need to make sure you see me as a person ... an individual. I need you to know I can take care of myself and that I'm not some liability."

He bit his bottom lip and nodded. "I know I've been super protective of you. I wish I could say I'm sorry, but I'm not. I just found you, and the thought of something happening to you ... well, I can't fathom it. But you're right. You are more than capable of handling yourself, and even in human form, you could've taken out several dragons I know."

Smooth talker. I giggled as I stood on my tiptoes and kissed him.

A rumbling moan sounded from the back of his throat as he tried to deepen the kiss.

I pulled away before I lost my mind. Something was going on downstairs that they needed us for. We couldn't be irresponsible and act like horny college kids—even if that's exactly what we were. *They're waiting on us.*

He leaned his head back dramatically and looked at the ceiling. "For once, it almost felt like things were normal."

"I have a feeling this has been your *normal.*" Between them handling Sadie's issues last semester and this, maybe this was what our future looked like. One battle after another.

"No, we were in hiding, so this didn't happen. Now that we're not hiding anymore, we have to deal with the centuries-old stuff we've been avoiding. It'll get better." He took my hand and led me to the door. "It has to."

I sure hoped he was right. Always waiting for the next fight was already taking a toll, and I hadn't been part of this world for long.

We entered the kitchen. It had so many white cabinets running along the wall that I couldn't easily count them while a gas stove that had a double oven was placed in the center. The gray island sitting in the middle of the room held the sink, and it jutted out several inches and turned into a bar surrounded by four bar stools.

The dark gray countertop complemented the cabinets and island perfectly as did the dark oak floor. A rectangular oak table sat against a section of glass windows and next to a glass door that led out to a back porch and the woods beyond.

Athan, Lillith, Katherine and who I assumed to be Luther were at the bar, each with a glass of blood.

"Are you okay?" a man asked, sitting cross-legged at the end of the table, and I noticed his khaki pants pulled up an inch above his ankle. He appeared to be in his late fifties. His jet-black hair was cut short, and his dark brown eyes reminded me of Lillith's. Unlike her all-black attire, he wore a light green shirt.

Pulling my attention from the vampires, I said, "Yes. It's just seeing the blood in a glass caught me off guard."

Whenever I'd seen the vampires drinking blood before, they'd used coffee cups to hide it. The metallic smell had alerted me to what it was, but I hadn't seen the crimson. "Girl, same," Roxy said, forcing my focus on her.

She sat between Axel and Sadie and was back to her normal self. She'd either gotten over the situation from earlier or Mom had forgiven her.

The man sitting at the other end of the table caught my interest. He was shorter than the other men here, but his haunting, lavender eyes locked on mine. His matching lavender hair was longer, hitting right at the chin, but his sharp features resembled Sadie's.

This had to be Naida's older brother Rook, Sadie's fae father.

Naida turned in her chair, and her teal eyebrows, which matched both her hair and eyes, rose high. Her long hair was pulled into a low ponytail and contrasted starkly against her white clothing. "Wow, you look good for a former human."

Out of Sadie's crew, Naida was around the least. Apparently, there was a civil war happening in the fae realm. I wasn't too surprised to see her here, but it had been a few weeks since I'd last seen her at Kortright University. "Uh ... thanks?"

"Forgive my sister." Rook stood, revealing his stark-white clothing that matched his sister's. "Even though she's spent time on Earth, her social skills are very lacking. She needs to spend more time here to adapt better."

"Yes, because things are going so well back at home." Naida crossed her arms and turned back around in her seat. "It's not like people are trying to kill either you or Murray."

Wow, maybe things were worse over there than they'd let on.

I took in Kayda sitting next to Naida and Ladon, with Ladon beside the dark-haired man on the end. Donovan was nowhere to be seen. Odd.

A woman with dirty blonde hair and light brown eyes lifted a hand, reminding me of a peacemaker. Other than her eye and hair color, she could pass as an older version of Lillith. "Let's all take a deep breath. We have enough fighting going on without us turning on each other."

Lillith spun around in her chair and muttered, "Mom, that's so cliche. That sounds like something Dad would say." She pointed at the man who'd asked if I was okay.

So my gut hadn't been wrong. They were her parents.

"I'm Jade." That was random, but I hadn't met a quarter of the room here.

"See, that's what normal people do." Lillith's mom pointed at me. "They introduce themselves instead of jumping straight to war talk." The lady placed a hand on her chest. "I'm Dawn, and this is my husband, Cassius. We're Lillith's parents."

"I'm pretty sure she figured that last part out." Lillith sighed dramatically, but the corners of her mouth tipped up.

"And I'm Rook." The lavender-eyed man smiled genuinely. "Sadie's father."

"Do all fae have matching eyes and hair?" I paused. "Well, other than Sadie."

"You gotta remember I'm a hybrid." She chuckled, comfortable with that fact. "But, yes, full-blooded fae have matching hair and eyes."

"Oh, so all the other half-bloods mix it up?" I had to learn these rules so I'd have an idea of who I might be talking to. The only other tell that Naida and Rook were fae was their floral scent. Sadie's was a musky floral, but that was her shifter part bleeding through.

"Sadie's the only halfling. If there are others, they'd be killed upon being discovered," Naida said matter-of-factly.

"Then how are you alive?" Wow. That sounded rude. "I'm glad you are, but how are you the exception?"

Sadie waved my apology off like my question wasn't a big deal. "No, it's a valid question. The only rule stronger than no hybrids is no one of the royal family is allowed to be killed."

"And Rook should've been king." Naida tapped her fingers on the table. "Half of Fae is demanding he take the throne."

"Which is why we needed you down here," Kayda said and placed her hand on Naida's.

Axel placed his arm around his mate and asked, "Should we wait on Donovan to get back first?"

Egan glanced around the kitchen and sniffed. "Where are he, Julie, and Paul?"

"They ran out to get more clothes for you and the others and a ton more groceries," Sadie explained. "I didn't want to tag along since Dad and Naida showed up. We have a lot to discuss."

"Wait." I couldn't have heard her right. "They went shopping, and Lillith and Roxy stayed here?"

"We don't always have to go shopping." Roxy shook her head, lifting her chin high. "There are more pressing matters to attend to."

"Yeah," Lillith agreed and lifted her glass toward Roxy. "We didn't want to go."

The smell of rotten eggs filled the kitchen as it wafted off them.

"Oh, dear God." I dry-heaved. "Just stop."

"They wanted budget items, especially for the amount of clothing needed." Axel scooted away from his mate like that would make the smell go away. "These two high-end fashionistas weren't allowed to go because they'd double, if not triple the bill."

"Exquisite taste is not a bad thing, and stop using the word 'fashionista.' You know that term annoys me," Roxy grumbled and moved her chair closer to Axel. "And I'm your mate. You must be near me even when I stink."

Ladon glanced over his shoulder at Egan.

I could only imagine what he and Kayda were thinking. They'd been hiding away from everything and were now in a kitchen full of loud, diverse supernatural races.

"I've opened the pack link to Donovan," Sadie said, attempting to calm the chaos. "We can talk, and he'll hear it through my ears."

"Good. We don't have time to waste," Rook said, focused on Egan and me. "Tell me everything."

We filled them in on every detail we could think of. The falcon attacks, the bracelet in our room that controlled Ollie, Vera, Trixie, the witch who tried to remove the tracking spell, Mindy working with the witch, and all of the attacks between the harpies and gargoyles. To think about what we'd gone through in such a short time was crazy.

"Wait, gargoyles and harpies?" Naida rubbed her temples and closed her eyes. "Are you sure?"

"Positive." Ladon sighed. "Over the centuries, we've kept up with fae creatures in case a day like this ever came."

"Then this is all worse than we expected." Naida glanced at her brother. "You know what this means, right?"

My breath caught at the dread in her voice. Whatever it was had to be worse than just the fae dragon king.

CHAPTER TEN

"Unfortunately, I know exactly what this means." Rook rubbed the inside corners of his eyes, and his shoulders deflated.

"I'm not trying to be rude, but would you mind filling me in on what you're alluding to? I'm new to this supernatural world, and most of the time, I have no idea what 'this' means." Starting off a sentence with "I don't mean to be rude" should've given me pause, but I was tired of always trying to fill in the blanks.

Roxy pointed at me. "Girl, you aren't the only one not picking up what they're putting down. I'm all for them spelling it out for us."

Sadie's normally friendly face morphed into a deep frown.

I wasn't the only one who suffered from resting-bitch face. Although this was the first time I'd seen hers, and my face was stuck in that form.

"That's exactly what it means." Naida placed her elbows on the table and steepled her fingers. "You and Murray have to do something. Turning your back on the peoples' protests is allowing the other fae races to make moves."

"The other races working together has just been brought to our attention, Nads." Rook huffed. "It's not like we've been sitting on this information."

Nads? The fact that Naida didn't get upset spoke volumes. She seemed okay with that nickname.

"Yes, her nickname is actually Nads." Roxy beamed, watching my reaction.

Apparently, my face reflected my inner horror.

Egan tugged me to the wall behind Cassius. We leaned against it since all the seats at the table were taken. He linked with me. *I'm pretty sure that doesn't mean there what it means here.*

Naida's gorgeous eyes landed on me before flicking to Roxy. She pursed her lips. "Why does everyone react that way to my nickname?"

Roxy shrugged so over the top that her shoulders reached her ears.

Poor girl. Sadie probably didn't want to embarrass her while Lillith and Roxy enjoyed the situation. Yeah, I had to tell her. "Nads is slang for balls."

"Balls?" Naida asked, seeming even more perplexed.

A loud snort left Lillith, and Roxy's shoulders shook with unshed laughter.

Great. She'd been staying here on Earth and didn't know any of the vernacular. "Uh ... family jewels? Nut sack?"

Her face remained blank, and she blinked, not catching on yet.

Maybe I should stop? I asked.

Egan's chuckles wove through each word. *You've already gone too far. Just finish the job.*

Okay, then. "Brass clankers? Nuggets?"

Laughter erupted from everyone but Naida. Her face turned slightly pink.

I hadn't meant to embarrass her. Maybe I shouldn't have said anything and followed Sadie's lead. "Testicles?"

"Oh my God." Naida's jaw dropped, and I was afraid it'd hit the floor. Her eyes zeroed in on Rook. "You call me that, knowing what it means?"

"Whoa. Whoa. Whoa." He lifted his hands in surrender. "I only learned what it meant. Besides, Mom and Dad gave you that nickname, so don't blame this on me."

Naida turned to Sadie and hissed, "And you didn't pull me aside to tell me?"

"Dad's and Murray's faces are filled with adoration when they call you that. It doesn't mean that over there, so I didn't want to ruin it for you." Sadie sighed. "But I'm relieved Jade explained it. Roxy and Lillith get way too much enjoyment out of it."

"I always wondered why they'd get so happy." Naida pouted and waved her hand. "But we have more important things to address than Earth's odd humor."

"That I can agree with." Cassius cleared his throat, the corners of his lips still tilted upward. "What exactly is everyone split on over there?"

"Half the fae want me to take the role as king since I'm the firstborn, despite Murray being crowned." Rook glanced out the window, deep in thought. "And the other half support Murray since I don't want to rule and they already view him as the king."

"It's similar to the wars you've had here over personal freedoms." Naida gestured behind Cassius. "The stuff all your books talk about in the library. We've never had something like that happen in the fae realm, but because of the odd situation we've found ourselves in, now is our time."

"Fae is all about rules and order," Egan explained. "A civil war like that is not a good thing. If they turn away from the rules, that means that they could attempt to kill Sadie for being a hybrid even though she has royal blood."

Katherine placed her glass on the bar top. "Maybe if they turn away from the rules, they'll allow hybrids to exist."

"That wouldn't happen." Rook rubbed his chin. "Fae are elitists. If anything, they wouldn't care that she's from the royal family and would attempt to kill her. We don't get to choose our destiny."

Wiser words had never been spoken. The weight of the truth punched me in the stomach.

Axel nodded and smiled at his mate. "You're right. Even when what's chosen for us is exactly what we want, sometimes it doesn't matter. You're just lucky it all worked out." He kissed Roxy's cheek lovingly. "Even when she may be the death of me."

"You're trying to get into trouble." Roxy waggled her eyebrows. "I kind of like it. I'll start thinking about your punishment."

Smelling someone else's arousal wasn't nearly as appealing as when it was Egan's and mine.

Sadie waved her hand in front of her nose. "And you used to say I was bad."

Conversations always swung wildly from one topic to another. Sometimes, it changed so fast I got whiplash.

Rook's face pinched, and he clearly wasn't thrilled with whatever thoughts were running through his head.

I had a feeling I knew what they were. Despite just meeting him, I could tell he loved Sadie unconditionally. If the only way to protect her was to become king, I had a feeling that was exactly what he would do. "When I found Egan, I fought it as hard as I could."

The banter went quiet at the table as every pair of eyes turned to me.

Ignoring the uncomfortableness of being the center of attention, I continued. "I mean I pushed him away. I'd tell him I needed space and accused him of only being nice to me to get into my pants, and when he finally told me the truth, it petrified me. He was telling me a world I'd never known about existed and I was destined to be part of something I didn't understand."

Kayda tilted her head as she listened to me. Her poker face was unreadable, making me nervous, but the truth was the truth, whether she wanted to hear it or not. I already knew Egan deserved better than me.

"But when I tried to really step away from him after everything had come out in the open, I couldn't. Like you, fate forced my hand even though I thought it was the last thing I'd ever want." When I'd told him I was all in, I'd meant every word, but I'd been so damn scared. "And hands down, this is the best thing that has ever happened to me. Fate knew what I didn't then. Maybe being the king won't be as bad as you're afraid it will be."

"She has a point." Naida nodded, respect shining through as she stared at me. "If you want to end the civil war, you'll have to step up and convince the half that is okay with you not being king that you want it. Otherwise, you taking your rightful place will be for nothing."

The best thing that ever happened to you? Egan rasped sexily as he placed an arm around me. *You've almost died and been attacked more times than I can count on one hand. I find that hard to believe.*

You are worth it. I lifted my head to see his golden eyes. *If you keep doing what you did in the shower earlier.*

His gaze landed on my lips. *That can definitely be arranged.*

"You got on us and aren't saying anything to them?" Roxy said, pulling my attention to her. Her bottom lip stuck out in a pout. "Why is it okay for them to be horny in front of us, including his parents, but not for me?"

I closed my eyes and buried my head in Egan's chest.

"They aren't having verbal foreplay." Lillith downed her drink. "Not that I enjoy the smell, but at least they're doing it in their mind link and not subjecting us to their kink."

"This is the third time this conversation has come up." Ladon pulled at his shirt collar and shifted in his seat. "Will this continue to be a common theme?"

"Yes." Naida motioned to Roxy and Lillith. "These two always bring up this topic. I can understand the vampire since she doesn't have sex, but Roxy perplexes me. It's like the more she gets, the dirtier and more aggressive she becomes with him."

It shocked me that Naida would speak so bluntly about sex. She seemed so reserved. *Is she okay?*

Egan's thumb gently brushed my side. *Naida doesn't mind openly discussing sex. We earthlings are prudes since we don't have loud, wild sex. Or that's what she told Sadie a few weeks after she and Donovan completed their mate bond. This group has a way of shocking you from time to time.*

Good to know. I'd lock up that useful tidbit for later.

"Hey!" Lillith crossed her arms and scowled. "I might not be getting any, but I guarantee that sometime soon, I'll get a guy to clean out those cobwebs."

"Lillith Rose!" Dawn exclaimed. "Do not talk like that in front of your parents. It's hard enough listening to it from everyone else, but you've gone too far."

"What?" Lillith nodded at Naida. "She started it."

Cassius whispered to Ladon, "See, it always comes back to this."

"All right," Rook said and kissed Sadie's cheek. "Nads and I need to get going."

Roxy giggled.

"Stop it." Naida pointed at her. "Do not laugh at my nickname."

"Come on ..." Rook paused. "Sis. That's a safe one, right?" His attention landed on me.

I gave him a thumbs-up. "That one is good."

"See." Rook stood and touched his sister's arm. "The whole nickname thing can be worked out. But we need to return to the fae realm to warn Murray about our problems and come up with a plan."

"You two, be careful." Sadie hadn't lost her displeasure. She moved between Rook and Naida, pulling both into a hug. "And make sure Murray stays safe too. I can't lose any family."

"Neither can we." Naida returned her niece's embrace. "We'll be back soon, but if we're gone a little longer than normal, don't be afraid."

"And contact us if you need us." Rook patted his daughter's cheek. "You know how to talk to us when we're there now."

"Well, for a few seconds." She stepped back, giving them space. "Love you both."

"Love you," Rook and Naida replied at the same time, and their bodies began to flicker. Then, they vanished.

It reminded me of Vera right before she'd died, even

though I was sure they'd left Earth instead of becoming invisible.

The room descended into silence, which I couldn't allow. "Uh ... how are the other dragons and Mom settling in?" Mom had been on my mind since I'd woken.

"We haven't checked in on them yet." Sadie pulled out her cell phone and typed out a message. "Do you want to head over there and meet Titan and his pack and check on the others?"

"That's a great idea." Egan nodded. "And where are the rest of the dragon shifters staying here?"

"After they got settled, they decided to take a nap." Ladon climbed to his feet and rolled his shoulders. "They grouped together in rooms so no one had to sleep in the living room; they should be out around dinner."

"Which will be ready in a couple of hours." Sadie headed to the back door and unlocked it. "We have time to explore the woods so you can get a feel for the area and check on everyone."

"Let's go," Kayda agreed and faced Dawn and Cassius. "Do you need us to do anything before we head out?"

"Nope. You helped us get the rooms ready and blow up the air mattresses." Cassius smiled. "You two go on back, and we'll send Donovan to get you when they start dinner."

"Sounds like a plan." Roxy jumped to her feet. "Let's go see the others. I could use a run."

"Wait, we've got to get Draco first. He'll be upset if we leave without him." Ladon headed out of the kitchen, moving down the hallway in the opposite direction.

He'd probably be upset that we'd had that entire conversation without him, but we could fill him in on the way to the pack.

Draco and Ladon reappeared, and our group, consisting

of Draco, Ladon, Kayda, Egan, Sadie, Roxy, Axel, Ollie, and me, headed outside.

I'd been surprised that Ollie had abandoned the video game, but he'd said his feathers needed air, whatever the hell that meant.

All of the vampires had opted to stay back and give the shifters time to get acclimated, and Athan and Luther had visibly cringed at the thought of seeing Mom again.

I couldn't blame them. The thought of them seeing Mom didn't appeal to me either.

We walked through the thick woods while the sun was setting. The entire day had gone by so quickly. We must have slept longer than I'd realized.

The animals ran, and the forest thrived. It felt like we were separated from the world yet still part of it, unlike at the cave where, once you entered, you were confined to a small part of the world.

As we approached the pack homes, I heard my mother's voice nearby.

"But Sarah, I'm fine." She paused. "I can't. I'm sorry."

She was talking to my aunt away from everyone else. I didn't know why, but I'd thought she wouldn't contact her.

"Sarah, please." Mom sobbed. "Fine. I'll tell you."

No, she'd promised. She wouldn't betray me ... would she?

CHAPTER ELEVEN

If I thought she'd hurt me before, nothing compared to this moment. She'd promised me she wouldn't tell Sarah anything, and in her first conversation with my aunt, she was throwing us to the wolves ... and no, I wasn't trying to be funny.

And who the hell had given her a cell phone? I'd figured she wouldn't have the means to call anyone unless she was with me.

Egan growled and took a hurried step toward Mom, but I snatched his arm.

Let me handle this. She was my responsibility, and I'd allowed her to come here. If anyone was going to confront her, it was me, even if I wished Egan could do it for me.

Inhaling deeply, I forced my legs to move. "I'll be right back," I told the others.

"We can come with you," Sadie offered, sympathy lacing her words.

I hated pity. Always had. "No, I'm fine," I bit out. "Just give me a minute." Maybe I was overreacting, but I had to shut Mom's conversation down and get to her before she blew our cover.

Even though Sarah knowing where we were wouldn't mean much to her, it could to others. If Vera could find my mother, then someone could figure out Sarah's relation to me. Not that her impending death would have the same effect on me, but it would on Mom.

My aunt didn't like losing control, so if Mom blurted out our location, Sarah would be in her car and on her way here to regain it. It didn't matter if she didn't know the exact location; Mom knew enough to get her close to us. If anyone followed her, she'd lead them right to us. Hell, if they told her they wanted to cause me pain, she'd probably let them ride shotgun the entire way.

"Someone jumped me at the grocery store." Mom blew out a breath. "She had stringy caramel hair and lifeless eyes. That's all I've got."

My feet halted, and hope sprang in me again. Maybe she wasn't betraying me after all.

Egan touched my arm, startling me.

That was how worked up I was. I hadn't noticed he was following behind me. What a great dragon shifter I was turning out to be. I needed to be more aware of my surroundings.

He stepped up beside me. *I was hoping we'd misunderstood their conversation.*

Me too. But the situation reaffirmed something. *The problem is Mom always caves to my aunt. We need to get close and monitor their call.*

Ideally, I'd have wanted Mom to hang up, but the more I tried to come between them, the more Sarah upped her game. I didn't need her harping on Mom more and weaving a stronger web of manipulation around her.

I took his hand, glad he'd decided to come with me. My gut still told me to do everything alone, without considering the fact that I didn't have to any longer. So for him to come without me asking him meant so much to me.

We quietly passed through the trees and came to a small clearing. It led into a series of homes that must have been Titan's pack.

Mom paced in the center, her eyes jumping around her like she expected someone or something to jump out. The slightly acidic stench of fear wafted from her.

"Liz, just tell me where you are," Sarah demanded on the other end of the phone. "This is ridiculous."

"I ... I can't." Mom grimaced and stared at her feet. "I'm sorry."

"Then when are you coming home?" Sarah pressed. "And who are you with?"

No, please don't tell her you're with me, I thought. That would make her more adamant about finding us. I ran forward to intercept the conversation.

"I'm with Jade." Mom rushed the words, still unaware I was only a few feet away from her.

The trees hid me from her human eyes, but annoyance bubbled within me. Why in the world would she tell Sarah that?

"You're with Jade!" Sarah's voice rose several octaves. "Who else is with you?"

"Her boyfriend." Mom hesitated. "He seems nice," she added randomly.

"So, she ran off to be with a guy? Were they the ones who jumped you and you're covering for her?" Sarah laughed without humor.

"No, it wasn't Jade," Mom replied. "They saved me."

"It doesn't matter," Sarah replied swiftly. "Either way, it's time you both came home. Now."

"I don't think there's any way Jade will come back home." Mom sounded upset. "But I'll come back soon."

Of course, she would. I'd hoped she'd decide to stay with us, but it was clear that wouldn't happen. The rancid stench of a lie didn't swirl around her.

In a way, I didn't blame her. Her entire world had been stuck in limbo for ten years, but I'd hoped that she'd see life in a different light—one without the parameters she'd believed for so long were in place.

"If you would just tell me where you are, I could come get you," Sarah said, dropping the suggestion again.

"I know, but I ... I can't." Mom's shoulders sagged. "Not yet." Mom turned toward the tree I was behind.

Deciding not to hide any longer, I stepped out from the shadows.

Her eyes widened, and she stumbled back until recognition flickered in them. "I've got to go. I'll talk to you soon." She hung up the phone and placed her hands behind her back as if I would forget the phone existed.

Trying to stay calm, I forced my body to relax. For the past few minutes, I'd been so tense that my muscles were tired. "Already called Sarah?" I tried not to sound accusatory but fell short.

"She hadn't heard from me in a week." Mom bounced the heel of her tennis shoe on the ground. "What did you expect me to do?"

If Sarah had been a normal sister, then Mom's point would have been valid. "I don't know. Realize you two have a very codependent relationship and maybe you could find happiness again if you would just gain some distance from her."

All I'd ever wanted for Mom was for her to be happy, but she was the complete opposite—horribly miserable. She deserved to find another man and fall in love. Not that I wanted her to replace Dad, but she shouldn't have to go through the rest of her life alone.

"You sound just like your father." Mom raised her head to look at the darkening sky. "But Sarah was all I had after our parents died, and I don't want her to be alone either."

The more you push her, the more likely she won't want to stay. Egan stepped from the woods, appearing right beside me.

This time, Mom didn't act surprised or scared.

Mom smiled, but it didn't reach her eyes. "I figured you weren't too far behind."

"Staying apart from your daughter is something I never want to consider." Egan kissed my cheek lovingly. "But if you two need some alone time, I'll go with Sadie and the others to see Titan and the rest of the pack."

"No, I think we're good here," Mom interjected eagerly. "I need to give Winter her cell phone back. She only let me borrow it to call my sister."

Yeah, she didn't want to continue this conversation with me. Maybe that wasn't a bad idea. We would only argue anyway, and at least, she hadn't told Sarah where we were, which was what had concerned me the most.

"We need to check on the other dragons." I looped my arm through Egan's and nudged him toward the homes. As we got closer to the clearing, Sadie and the others came out from the woods where they'd been waiting.

"Everything okay?" Sadie asked as she glanced between Mom and me.

I didn't want to lie, so I said the only thing that popped into my mind. "She needs to give Winter her phone back."

"Sure, let's go find them." Sadie's look of concern smoothed into a mask of indifference.

Not sure how to take it, I brushed it aside. I could talk to her later.

Now that we were closer, I focused on the neighborhood. There were at least one hundred simple, two-story, log cabins with two larger houses in the center. The design was similar to the dragon homes back in the cave, but these were smaller and newer.

Smoke billowed from behind one of the bigger homes, and the scent of cooking meat hit my stomach hard.

My stomach gurgled, and Roxy snorted.

"I'll admit it smells good." She tipped her face toward the smoke. "But Julie's cooking is like vanilla icing on a chocolate cake or peanut butter and chocolate. It's pure orgasmic even for us red meat lovers."

"Orgasmic?" Mom shifted away from Roxy and closer to me.

She wasn't comfortable with loud, outspoken people. That was probably one of the main reasons I tried to not make a fuss. Mom hated it. She'd rather appease everyone and live in a compromise than stand up for what she needed or believed in.

I'd been like that for far too long until I'd had enough, but it had been difficult to break the cycle. The longer you remained complaisant, the harder breaking free had to be.

Roxy either didn't register Mom's discomfort or didn't care as she continued. "Something so good that your legs convulse in pleasure."

I caught up to Sadie and said, "Please tell me that Roxy will eat in her room. I don't want to hear or smell what she's describing."

"You think that's bad." Axel sniffed. "Her legs have never quivered for me."

A peal of laughter tumbled from deep in my stomach. I hadn't realized how badly I'd needed to laugh.

Egan's eyes turned a lighter gold as he watched me. He linked with me. *I need to see you like this more often. You don't smile nearly enough.*

With those two, I've laughed more than I have in the last ten years combined. Axel was more serious than Roxy, but I sometimes saw how her playfulness affected him. He'd spit out something unexpected, sounding more like his mate every once and a while.

"That should tell you we need more practice." Roxy winked and kissed him. "I'm about my legs shaking as often as I can get it."

Mom's face darkened to a deep crimson, and I realized she must have bathed as her brown hair looked normal again.

"Every time you're in wolf form, you're always scratching at something," Egan teased. "So your leg shakes plenty. I'm pretty sure you have fleas."

"Oh, there's the dog jokes." Roxy stuck her tongue out at him. "You could at least try to be original."

"Why would he need to?" I couldn't help but join in. "Those jokes are always around."

Two men headed our way. The older one had alpha power radiating off him, which was somehow enhanced by his short brown hair and full goatee. Both he and the younger shifter were built like Donovan—tall and thick. They had the same forest green eyes, but the younger one had his long black hair pulled into a low ponytail.

"You'd think a dragon would know better than to enter into a pack home, making jokes like that." The older one's voice was deep, but a grin peeked through as he walked over and smacked Egan's shoulder hard several times. "It's good to see you again. I haven't seen you since we took on Tyler at that godawful house of his."

Egan placed an arm around my shoulders and pulled me closer as he responded, "It has been too long, but my mate here was making me chase her."

"This is the notorious Jade that the girls have been talking about." The younger one's eyes twinkled as he held his hand out to me. "I'm Torak, Sadie's brother."

"Brother?" I hadn't expected that. "I didn't realize Rook had two children."

"Oh, he didn't." Torak wiggled his fingers. "There's no fae magic here. Technically, I'm her stepbrother, but that sounds cold." He arched an eyebrow at Sadie. "But I can't say I'm not hurt. You didn't tell her about me?"

"In Sadie's defense, they were too busy pining over each other and being dramatic," Roxy stepped in. "And when they finally got their shit together, we were being attacked left and right. Oh, then there was this jealous ex ..." She trailed off. "I don't know what to call her. She wasn't an ex-girlfriend, but she acted like she was—"

"I think he got the gist." Sadie chuckled and hugged the younger man. "And I would've told her about you when things got more settled. You're the best brother a girl could ever have or want."

"Oh, you're good." Torak ruffled her hair. "I guess I can't stay mad at you when you sweet-talk me like that."

"Well, it's very nice to meet you," the older man said and shook my hand. "I'm Titan, Sadie's stepfather."

"I'm Jade." Every supernatural I'd met had been so nice and welcoming—well, except for Vera and the other crazies.

The door to the other bigger home opened, and a

woman stepped out. She strolled over to Mom, her shoulder-length, ash-blonde hair bouncing from side to side. She took the phone and placed it into the back pocket of her blue jean shorts then pulled Sadie into a hug. The two of them were the same height. When she pulled away, her sea-blue eyes found me. "It's nice to finally put a face to the name. It's so nice to meet you."

Anger pulsed through me again as I thought about how Mom had called Sarah already. It wasn't this woman's fault, but my frustration leaked out anyway. "You must be Winter since you took the phone from Mom." I crossed my arms and lifted a brow, staring directly at Mom.

"Oh, was I not supposed to?" Winter asked and looked at Sadie. "I didn't realize—"

"No, I can call whomever I want." Mom's eyes flashed with anger as she spun to face me. "You need to remember that I'm the adult here—and your mother."

Was she being serious? This had to be a joke. "I hate to tell you, but I'm an adult as well, and you haven't acted like my mother in ten years."

Her head jerked back, and she glared. "What did you just say to me?"

This fight had been a long time coming. All of the feelings and resentment that had been bottled up inside me bubbled up. I hated that we would have it out in front of everyone, but I couldn't calm down. I'd felt like I might have a chance of connecting with Mom, but at the first opportunity, she'd called Sarah. "You heard me, or should I repeat it again?"

CHAPTER TWELVE

I steadied myself for her retort. I wanted her to say something back to me. I'd never seen this side of her before. Instead, her face crumpled into a look of pure despair.

"You're right." She sniffled, tears trailing down her cheeks. "I've been a lousy mother."

No, she was supposed to fight me, not fall apart. Sarah made her break down. I didn't want to be like my aunt.

Kayda cleared her throat and looked at Titan. "Do you mind taking us to the others? We want to check on them before turning in for the night."

"Yeah, sure," Titan agreed eagerly. "We can show you to their homes right now."

If their escape wasn't proof that we'd made everyone uncomfortable, I wasn't sure what else could be. At least I wasn't the one feeling awkward for once.

The group hurried off, leaving Mom and me behind; our eyes locked on each other.

Egan stepped toward the others, then stopped. *Do you want me to stay?*

This was a conversation Mom and I had been teetering on for a long time. *I do, but it's probably best if you don't though. I won't be far behind.*

If you need me, let me know. Egan pecked my lips. *I'll be back in a flash. You will always be my priority.*

Sometimes, fate still amazed me. How could someone like him be destined for someone like me? Things didn't add up. I was hard around the edges, had so much baggage dragging behind me, and pushed people away, afraid to get too close. Through all my downfalls, he'd stood unwaveringly beside me. He'd patiently waited for every barrier I'd ever put up to shatter.

I love you, I told him, but those three little words seemed insignificant.

When he'd said I was his Jade, he hadn't meant it possessively. It had been the only way to even partially convey his feelings for me. And at that moment, Egan became mine. Mine to love, to hold, to lean on. Not in the way of him being my property but rather my rock.

The magnitude of what he'd meant crashed over me, and I'd responded so coldly ... defensively ... like he would ever view me in a way I didn't want him to.

I should've known better.

He brushed his fingers across my cheek. *And I love you.* He glanced at Mom silently crying and gave her a small, sad smile. "I'll give you two some privacy." He hurried to catch up with the others.

Everyone had cleared. "Want to take a short walk to get a little privacy? Supernaturals and their hearing ..."

"Yeah, okay." She nodded and strode toward the woods.

We walked in silence, following a worn path through the trees. Neither of us was eager to begin the conversation, so I mustered the initiative.

She hadn't deserved me talking to her like that, but she needed to realize how much she'd hurt me too. "I'm sorry for being so abrasive, but in the past ten years, I've harbored a lot of resentment toward you." Resentment was the perfect word to describe my emotions. "It's like when Dad died, I lost both of you."

"You're right." Mom's head drooped, and her hair fell over her shoulders. "But losing your father, it was like a part of me died too."

That was how I imagined I would feel if Egan passed. "I understand that." Now more than ever. "But I was so young and needed my mother. We moved in with Sarah, and things got worse."

"I know that you and my sister don't like each other." Mom twirled a piece of hair around her finger. "But she gave us food and shelter when we needed it."

"Is that what you think?" Maybe she really was clueless. I'd always thought she was, but lately, I'd begun to doubt that. "That she did all that out of the kindness of her heart?"

Mom's head jerked up, and she met my gaze. "She's never asked us to repay her."

"She manipulates you all the time, and yes, she has asked us to repay her." Between that and taking a college away from me, that was the whole reason I'd run to Kortright. "Remember, I was supposed to go to a local community college last semester, but I had to withdraw and get a waitressing job at an Italian place to pull our weight with expenses."

"You're right." She blew out a breath and averted her gaze. "I forgot all about that. But we'd lived there for over ten years, and I couldn't hold down a job."

"That's because she made sure you were late and guilted you into calling in sick all the time." I had to wake her up. It was time for her to see my aunt for the horrible person she really was.

Mom rubbed her hands over her arms. "Look, I know she's not perfect, but she's all I have, especially now. You have Egan, and he's crazy about you. I just hope you don't get destroyed like I did."

Even though losing him would kill me inside, I would never wind up like her. Not after seeing what it had done to her and me. "I still need my mother." My voice cracked despite my efforts to keep my emotions in check.

"Oh, honey." She stopped and pulled me into her arms. "I'll always be here for you. I wanted to come here and be with you before going back to Sarah."

My heart fractured. I'd hoped she'd want to stay with us permanently, but her admission confirmed my fears. "So, you're going back?"

"I have to." Mom shrugged. "I don't know how to explain it, but she's been there for me for so long. I can't turn my back on her."

"But, Mom, she treated me horribly. She hovered over me and made sure I didn't even go outside to get the mail without her permission. And when I did something she didn't like, she'd beat me." I felt like this was a losing battle.

"'Beat' is a strong word." Mom lifted a brow. "If that happened, I would've seen it. And we were living under her roof. We had to follow her rules. I know it doesn't always seem fair, but life isn't fair. That was what our parents taught us, and Sarah is exactly like our mother. Besides, even if I wanted to get away, I don't have anywhere to go."

This was how Mom had been raised. No wonder she didn't see a different way. Whatever connection Dad and she had must have been stronger than her relationship with Sarah. Mom leaving her for Dad must have infuriated her.

"Yes, you do." I lifted my arms out. "You can stay here with us. There is another way."

"Oh, baby girl." She hugged me. "I'd love to, but this isn't my world. I'm not a vampire or shapeshifter. I need to go back home."

If I wanted to have a relationship with her, this was how things would always be unless something drastically changed. A coldness settled in my blood, but I couldn't do a damn thing to change her mind without resorting to my aunt's tactics. "Okay."

"Okay?" Mom stopped and faced me. "What does that mean?"

"This is something we'll have to agree to disagree on." Those words hurt, but I had to accept that this was the relationship she and I had. I'd rather have a connection with her than lose her. At one point, I thought I'd have to cut ties with her, but Egan and Sadie were showing me that you could love someone and maintain a relationship with them even if it wasn't the exact one you wanted.

"Jade, I love you." Mom touched my arm. "But sometimes it hurts so much to be around you. You remind me so much of him, but you're right. I haven't been fair to you, and I want to do better."

Her acknowledgment that things were shitty between us, even if she wasn't willing to examine her relationship with Sarah, was a start. Maybe time would fix the other.

"I miss him too." I did so much, especially those nights when Sarah would take out her frustrations on me. Mom and I could share memories of Dad. She had no one else but me to talk to about him.

"I loved when he'd play guitar and sing me to sleep each night." I hadn't let my mind wander back to those precious memories that only appeared in my dreams.

While sleeping, I couldn't protect my mind like I did when I was awake.

Mom laid her head on my shoulder. "Or how he'd wake up and make Mickey Mouse cinnamon rolls for you."

"I still love cinnamon rolls." That was a habit I could never break. It was comfort food I sought out when I felt alone.

"Wow, this is nice." Mom wiped her nose with the back of her hand. "I'm a snotty mess, but it's been so long since I've talked about him or remembered him this way."

"Me too." My mind raced with memories. "Do you remember when that girl in first grade told me I wasn't important enough for her to be my friend all five days of the week, so Dad came to school and brought cupcakes for all my friends?" Dad had eaten with me and asked if a few of my friends would like to join us at the special table. When she'd tried to suddenly be my friend, he'd informed her it was Tuesday and not one of her days. The rest of my friends had sat with me and eaten cupcakes. After that, she'd apologized, and Dad had given her a cupcake. He'd told me that forgiveness was key and to never lose sight of it.

But obviously, I had.

The two of us strolled through memory lane for a while longer until Egan's citrus scent tickled my nose. My breathing picked up like it always did around him.

Mom tensed. "What's wrong?"

"We have company." I glanced over my shoulder and found him standing there with a tender grin. "Are you guys already done?" Now I felt bad. I'd told him I would join him but wound up spending time with Mom instead.

"We are, and everything is fine." He came to stand beside me and kissed me. "It looks like you two are having a good time."

"We're reminiscing about Dad." Speaking of memories, I hadn't been able to ask him about that day on the beach. Between that and my exhaustion, it had slipped my mind.

"I hate to interrupt, but we're heading back." He gestured over my shoulder at the musky smell of wolf shifters. Then Egan's parents' scents hit my nose. "Donovan linked with Sadie a few moments ago. They'll be here soon."

"Good. I'm famished." My stomach gurgled again.

"Girl, we got you loud and clear." Roxy snapped her fingers. "And I feel you. Ollie's been whining to go back to the mansion. He must be having withdrawals from the video games."

Ollie shrugged. "I hadn't played since the whole Vera thing. I wanted to do something normal. It's not withdrawal."

Sadie stood between Ollie and Roxy, and when her focus landed on me, her face morphed into a frown.

I needed to make things right with her and might as well do it tonight since I already had my heart on my sleeve.

"Don't let her give you shit." Axel rolled his eyes. "She plays just as much as Athan and Luther when we're there."

"Speaking of vampires, I'm going to head back to the wolves." Mom hugged me. "But I'll see you in the morning?"

"Of course." I hated to end my time with her, but I had other responsibilities as well.

"Good night, everyone." Mom waved and headed back toward the pack.

I didn't want to make her feel weak, but after Vera had captured her and almost killed her, I wanted to keep an eye on her. I waited until she was several feet away so she wouldn't hear me.

"Hey, Sadie," I said quietly. "I'm going to keep watch until she gets to the pack. Do you mind coming with me? We can catch up with the others later." If I didn't get her now, Donovan wouldn't let her out of his sight since he'd been gone for a few hours. I hadn't understood it at first, but being away from your fated mate wasn't fun.

Not me? Egan teased.

I need to apologize for snapping at her earlier. I hope you understand.

Pride wafted off him. *I figured that was the case. I'll give you some privacy.*

Sadie's eyebrows arched. "Uh ... sure. We'll catch back up here in a second."

The group headed toward the mansion as Sadie and I followed slowly behind Mom. She was several yards away, unaware that we were near.

I needed to get this out before I changed my mind. "Look, I'm sorry I snapped at you earlier. You were looking at me with so much pity, and I hate that. That's how everyone has looked at me since my dad passed away."

"You think it was pity?" Her mouth dropped. "Girl, that wasn't it at all."

Wait ... "It wasn't?"

"Jade, I get that you've had a hard life." Sadie patted her chest. "Believe me, I do. I had a hard childhood too, but I had two advantages you didn't."

"A winning personality and good looks?" I quipped, feeling uneasy.

"Well, yeah." She nudged her shoulder into mine. "But you have that too—" She winced. "Well, the good looks part."

I almost said "hey," but she was right.

"But seriously, I had Roxy and a pack." She touched my

arm, her warmth easing some of my anxiety. "And I wasn't looking at you with pity. When people love you, they worry about you and want to be there for you. I don't pity you. I want to support you."

The weight of her words slammed into me. I hadn't considered that alternative. "I love you too."

"I know." Sadie tugged me to a stop. "And that's why I'm willing to forgive you so easily."

Mom's scream penetrated my ears, and I took off running. No, I couldn't lose her now. Not after we'd bonded.

CHAPTER THIRTEEN

"Wait!" Sadie called out, but I ignored her.

I needed to get to Mom. Maybe the fae dragon king had found us. *Egan, I need you. Mom screamed. I'm afraid she's in trouble.*

Something unreadable passed through our bond as he replied, *I'm on my way.*

Pushing my legs hard, I felt my dragon brush my mind. Before I realized what was happening, wings sprouted from my back, ripping my shirt. My body lurched skyward, and I flew over the trees.

I found Mom plastered against a tree, a look of pure terror on her face. Her body convulsed as she let out another blood-curdling scream.

A wolf stepped from behind the trees, confirming my worst fear.

We were under attack. Again.

As I swooped downward, the strumming of other wings headed my way. I turned to find both Draco and Egan half shifted like me. They were all human except for the massive, scaly wings protruding from their backs.

Thankful they were so close, I focused on Mom, descended, and grabbed her in my arms. Channeling my dragon strength, I lifted us into the sky.

"The wolf was trying to get me!" Mom screeched as she wrapped her arms around my neck, almost choking me.

A loud roar sounded behind me as Egan and Draco flew past me and lowered to the ground. The wolf stumbled back with the prickly scent of fear.

Yeah, I bet having two dragons coming at you would make anyone feel threatened. Both Egan and Draco were huge.

Draco landed first, stepping in front of Egan.

We had to drive the poor guy crazy since Egan and I didn't like sitting on the sidelines. It wasn't right to ask others to do something we weren't willing to do ourselves, but that made the royal warrior's job harder.

The wolf whined and lowered its head.

A howl from the pack homes pierced the air, and several people ran toward us, including Titan, his face lined with worry.

Sadie raced to join us, her eyes cast skyward at me. She said, "Stop. He's my pack member and means no harm."

Neither dragon heard since their attention was on the wolf while also scanning the area for a veiled threat.

I hadn't considered that another witch could be involved and hiding others, waiting for the right time to attack. But this was a false alarm, and I needed to end this before someone got hurt. "Stop. He's one of Sadie's," I shouted to make sure they heard.

Egan paused and turned to me. When my words soaked in, he relaxed, but Draco remained tense, staring down the wolf as if it might lunge. Draco's chest heaved as he unclenched his hands at his sides.

Mom sobbed uncontrollably as I lowered us to the ground. Warm tears spilled down her cheeks and splattered all over my chest.

"Hey, the wolf isn't a threat. He's part of their pack and must have been out on a run. There's nothing to be scared of."

As soon as my feet touched the ground, Mom pulled out of my arms and stumbled away from the group, almost falling. Titan and a few pack members rushed into the clearing, three in their wolf forms.

Mom screamed again and covered her eyes. "I'm sorry, but I can't do this. I ... I thought I could, but I want to go home."

Her words fractured my heart. I thought we'd have more time together before she asked to leave. Then there was the whole complication with her actually going back to Sarah's. We'd have to monitor her so she wouldn't get hurt.

How are we going to handle this? I tried not letting my hurt bleed through, but it was pointless. We had our mate bond, and I couldn't hide it from him even if I'd wanted to.

We'll figure it out, Egan reassured me as he faced the wolf pack. "I'm sorry. I didn't recognize his scent, and the fae dragon king has sent wolves to attack us before."

A chestnut wolf beside Titan stepped forward, his teeth bared and growling. He pawed the ground, pulling out clumps of grass. He wanted to attack us because of how we'd treated his friend.

"No, I get it." Titan lifted a hand and glared at the aggressive wolf. "Stand down." Alpha will laced his words. "Remember, he fought alongside my daughter when she needed help. They meant no harm."

This could have gone horribly wrong, but these people

surprised me time and time again. "It's my fault. Mom screamed, and I reacted. I'm sorry."

"There's nothing to apologize for. No one got hurt." Titan nodded at me. "When you're always under attack, it's hard to tell who's friend or foe, especially when you haven't met everyone in Sadie's pack. How could you have known? Tomorrow, we need you all to meet everyone in my pack. We don't need someone from either side attacking each other."

Egan hurried over and pulled me into his arms.

When his warm hands touched the bare skin on my back, I glanced down. Just like him, my shirt was ripped to shreds and barely covered my breasts. My bra was still intact, but I was almost giving a peep show.

"We need to get you some clothes," Egan growled and turned me toward the mansion. He frowned at the young wolf. "I'm sorry about that. We're a little skittish, and you scared her mom, and we didn't recognize you. We should've realized you weren't a threat when you cowered, but we've had a witch messing with us. We won't make the same mistake again."

The wolf nodded, and his mouth dropped open in a wolfish smile.

Sadie walked over to the wolf and patted his head. "He said he understands."

"That's enough excitement for tonight." Draco kept his attention on the pack around us. "Let's head back before something else happens."

"I'm going with you," Mom insisted. "I need you to take me home." She walked over to me and touched my shoulder. "I can't stay here. I'm sorry."

"But how do we protect you?" I didn't want to force her

to stay here if she wanted to leave, but I didn't want something horrible happening to her either.

"Where do you live?" Titan asked as his pack peeled off back to the houses.

"Indianapolis," Mom answered. "Please tell me that's close by."

He tapped his chin. "It's about four hours away, but I know a pack there. I'll make a call and see if they won't mind keeping watch. If they're up for it, I'll text Sadie."

Egan kissed my cheek. *I'm sorry she's leaving, but at least, Titan knows someone who might be willing to keep your family safe, and we won't have to worry about anyone hurting her for our location.*

As long as Mom doesn't get hurt, I'll be fine. Sarah deserved some pain, but Mom had enough her whole life.

"All right. Talk soon," Sadie said and hugged him.

Our smaller group began the trek back to the mansion. Mom walked silently beside me, her heart was still racing from the encounter.

I couldn't blame her for wanting to leave. Her introduction to this world was being kidnapped by a witch and carried by a harpy. That hadn't done me any favors.

Egan took my hand, his lips turned down. He wasn't pleased with my outfit. I, however, was more than ecstatic over his. He stood next to me shirtless, and his muscles contracted, making my mouth water. If it hadn't been for Mom walking beside me, scared, I'd have sweet-talked him into a quickie in the woods.

Draco cleared his throat and cut his eyes to me, making it clear he smelled where my mind had traveled.

My face burned. Being called out like that was the equivalent of a cold shower. I needed to get my mind on a different track. *So, what's the plan?*

Once we hear back from Titan, we'll take her home. He squeezed my hand gently. *I'm sorry she's leaving. I know you enjoyed your time with her and hoped she'd stay longer.*

There was no point in lying. He'd know. *You're right. I knew losing Dad broke her, but I hadn't realized the depth of their love. She talked like they were fated mates.*

Your parents must have been soul mates. Not *quite the same as fated mates, but it's a human form that's just as strong. Some say that a child from a union like that is almost as resilient as supernaturals, which is required when the human mate transforms into a dragon.*

The thought comforted me. My parents had given me the best gift in the world as a result of their relationship. They'd allowed me to have a fated mate and find a love similar to theirs. It was beautiful. *I didn't realize how much pain she's been in. Losing you ... it would almost kill me.*

I feel the same way about you. Now that you're my mate and a dragon, our life is interconnected. If one of us dies, the other will follow soon after. It's morbid but another thing that's different with dragon shifter mates. Because your body changed with our bond, and the two halves of our soul fused together, our lifespans are attached. His voice was low with so much feeling.

Honestly, it's romantic. I stepped closer to him, feeling naked with how his skin brushed against my bare skin. I couldn't wait to get home and take out some of this sexual frustration. *Also, I wanted to say I'm sorry.*

For what? He wrapped an arm around me and pulled me closer like he knew I was cold.

Maybe my bluntness would come in handy here. I wasn't one for long romantic speeches like him. *When you called me your Jade earlier, I wrongly bit your head off. I now understand what you meant and that you weren't acting like a possessive, dominating male.*

His golden eyes glowed. *You understand now?*

Earlier today, when you left me and my mom alone to talk, you became my Egan. I allowed my feelings to flow into him. I wanted him to feel my sincerity. Words were easy to say, but feelings and actions—that was a whole other ball game.

Yes, I am, he rasped, overcome with emotions. *When you linked when you thought your mom was in danger, telling me you needed my help, that made me realize you're embracing who we are to each other. You've always tried to take care of yourself and kept me at arm's length like I had to beg you to allow me to be the mate beside you.*

Wow, I did suck at this relationship stuff. I'd always known it, but I hadn't realized how bad I was. Seeing me from Sadie's and Egan's points of view stung. *Well, I'm done with that. As long as you continue to treat me like an equal, we're a team from here on out.*

I really like the sound of that, he replied, not missing a beat.

Something dinged, and Sadie pulled her phone from her back pocket. She swiped the surface a few times and glanced over her shoulder. "Titan said the pack agreed. We just need her address."

Mom rattled it off eagerly, and I took a deep breath to keep my emotions level. I despised allowing her to go back to that horrible woman, but Mom was right. She was an adult and could make her own decisions.

The mansion came into view, and Roxy, Axel, Donovan, Kayda, and Ladon waited for us.

"I heard you had a false alarm." Roxy smirked, finding the situation funny.

"They didn't know George," Sadie said, standing up for us. "And they've been attacked by witches, wolves, harpies, and gargoyles. You can't blame them for being cautious. Remember how we were when we were attacked wherever we turned?"

"As if we could forget." Donovan rushed over to his mate and kissed her.

I glanced into the kitchen and saw two new people. A petite, middle-aged woman with light blonde hair stood in front of the stove, cooking something in a pan. From the smell, it was garlic and ground beef.

A middle-aged man grinned with adoration at the woman that warmed his pale face. He had the same dark brown hair as Katherine, but his eyes were more gray than brown.

They had to be Katherine's parents, Julie and Paul.

"Is that a new look?" Axel chuckled as he glanced from Draco to Egan. When his gaze landed on me, he quickly averted his eyes, and his shoulders tensed, clearly uncomfortable.

"We all half shifted," Draco said strangely.

"Wait." Kayda tilted her head. "Jade half shifted?"

All of the unwanted attention made me feel uneasy. *Why is that such a big deal?*

Only the strongest dragons can do that, Egan said proudly. *You're the only woman I know who's done it.*

That built up my confidence. "I'm going to go change." This would give me a chance to avoid Egan's parents' attention.

"Got you covered." Roxy tossed me a shirt. "Sadie told me you ripped through your shirt too." Then she lobbed a shirt at each guy also.

That was convenient. "Thanks."

"Wait." I hadn't considered needing to shift to take Mom home. "Shouldn't we change into our dragons to take her home?"

Egan shook his head. "Indianapolis is heavily populated. We'll have to travel human style and drive."

But if we do that, Mom will know exactly where we are. I trusted Mom, but the more she knew, the more danger she'd be in.

Egan put on his shirt, his stomach muscles contracting. *The wolf shifters won't let anything happen. Titan is a good guy, and he wouldn't contact this wolf pack if he didn't trust them.*

"We're taking a car." Mom beamed. "A normal car?"

Roxy chuckled. "Yeah, we don't have any that can sprout wings or fur ... yet."

Mom's face turned a shade lighter. "But you're working on it?"

Yep, this was the moment I learned my mom was gullible, and if I didn't stop Roxy, she'd have Mom believing that it would be on the market for the hot price of one hundred dollars in the next year. The girl was insane.

"The car is out front." Donovan handed Egan the keys. "Do you want me to come with you?"

"No, I'll accompany them," Draco said formally, but there was a hint of anxiety.

He didn't like us leaving either. When someone who trained in war and strategy didn't like a plan, it usually meant it wasn't a good one.

THE ENTIRE WAY to Sarah's home, Egan and Draco watched the rearview mirror, making sure no one was tailing us. I sat in the backseat with Mom, right behind my mate, and snuck glances over my shoulder at every opportunity. Nothing seemed out of the ordinary, which unnerved me.

As we pulled into the neighborhood, a shadowy figure lingered behind nearby trees. The glow of their eyes followed the car.

They were supernatural.

CHAPTER FOURTEEN

We have a problem. I linked with Egan, not wanting to freak Mom out any more than she already was. *Someone is hiding behind that tree on the right.*

Egan slowed the car and pulled over to the side of the road. The moon was beginning its descent, and the clock on the stereo flashed two in the morning. There was no traffic, and our presence wouldn't alarm anyone except for the person watching us.

"What's going on?" Draco asked softly so Mom's human ears wouldn't hear.

Not bothering to respond verbally, Egan tipped his head toward the trees.

Mom stiffened and looked out the window but remained calm. "Why did we stop?"

She must not be able to see the supernatural. *He has glowing eyes. Does that tell us anything?*

Not really. Egan unlocked his door. "Before taking you to the house, we need to make sure no one is waiting for you. We don't want anyone hurting you for our location."

"I would never tell." Mom rested a hand on her heart. "I

wouldn't put Jade in harm's way. But do you think someone else could find me?"

"Not at all," Draco said, and when the sulfuric smell of a lie didn't hit me, some of my nerves calmed. "The witch who knew about you is dead, and to keep her leverage with the fae dragon king, she wouldn't have told just anyone. But we want to be diligent before taking you home."

If we didn't believe she would keep our location a secret, we wouldn't have brought her back here. Correction, Egan and Draco wouldn't have. Egan loved me so much that he would never put me in danger, even if he had to hold my mom captive at the mansion.

In the past, that would've pissed me off, but I'd do the same thing for him. Granted, our parents would be locked inside a mansion with food, water, and a place to hang out. They wouldn't be living in any discomfort or enduring hardships, but being forced to stay somewhere against your will wasn't fun for anyone.

"We know you won't say anything." Egan smiled at her tenderly. "Just making sure you'll be around for the birth of your grandchildren is all."

"Your children." Her voice caught, and she fanned her eyes. "Are you?"

"What?" She couldn't possibly think that. "No!" I'd never thought about having children before. I wasn't opposed to the idea, but I'd never been interested. Given my childhood, who would want to bring anyone into the world to suffer like that? But with Egan, the idea was strangely appealing.

Draco opened the door and stepped out of the car. "I'll take a look around."

"I'll go with you." Egan opened the door as well.

Draco paused like he might argue but reconsidered.

If more men were waiting, he'd be outnumbered. Whether he liked it or not, Egan going with him was his best bet.

Do you mind staying here with your mom? Egan asked. There was so much hope flowing through our bond that I knew exactly where he wanted me: safe inside the car.

Any other time, I'd have demanded to go, but I needed to stay with Mom, and Egan had asked instead of demanded. *No, but if you need me or something goes wrong, let me know immediately. Please.*

His eyes turned liquid gold. *I will.*

They shut the doors, leaving the car running. The two of them walked briskly to the tree line while Mom sat with her eyes forward, a small smile on her face.

"Grandchildren," she whispered. "Do you think you'll have them soon?"

Wow, she was a little too eager. "Mom, I'm in college. Can I at least get through that first?" And through whatever war we were in. My brain knew to keep that last part to myself. I almost patted myself on the back.

But realization settled over me. With Egan's family having him so much later in life, he hadn't gotten a chance to know his human grandparents. I'd like to give my children the opportunity to know Mom before she passed.

"Oh, of course." She placed her hand on my leg. "Egan is a good man, not that you couldn't be with him anyway. He's your fated mate, but even if he wasn't, I'd really like him."

"Even though he's a dragon shifter?" I lifted a brow as I watched him and Draco out of the corner of my eye. At the first sign of trouble, my ass would be out of this car to help them while I told Mom to drive far away.

"Despite it, yes." She chuckled. "At least he can protect

you. Your father always tried to protect us and provide for us. He was determined to give us the very best of everything we could afford." Her voice cracked with emotion.

If I hadn't been run through the wringer earlier, I'd be tearing up too. "Dad was a wonderful man and father."

She nodded. "He really was."

Draco and Egan stopped several feet from the tree line, and a few seconds later, the person I'd seen and three other men stepped out from the small batch of trees.

I hadn't noticed the other three. My blood pumped hard, pounding in my ears. How many others could be out in the woods?

Four to two weren't horrible odds. Dragons were strong, but I had no idea what type of creatures they were and if there were more hiding. *What's going on?*

They claim to be from the wolf pack Titan contacted. There was no alarm from Egan. *We're verifying it. Give us a minute. If anything goes wrong, get yourself and your mom to safety.*

Yeah, right. I couldn't leave him like that. But I kept my mouth shut. There was no point in arguing with him when he needed to stay focused.

"Jade, who are those men with Egan and Draco?" Mom turned her entire body toward her window, watching the exchange. Her leg bounced. "Are they supernaturals?"

"Yes, they're from the pack Titan talked to." At least, we weren't under attack. It was a good thing I'd stayed inside. I probably would've attacked without giving them a chance to explain themselves like back in the woods when Mom had freaked out. But that guy had been in wolf form. At least, these guys had known to stay human to communicate with us. Egan and Draco had a lot more patience than my hot head.

"Oh, they're already here." Mom sagged with relief, and her leg stilled. "I figured with it being so late, they would just show tomorrow."

Her assumption annoyed me, especially since we were being cautious and this pack had been willing to help without hesitation. "You do realize by coming back here, you'll be watched twenty-four hours a day, right? It's not like the fae and their helpers would only attack during daylight hours if they found you."

Mom's brows drew together. "They'd do that for us?"

"Yes, they would. I'm learning that the supernatural community is way more supportive and loyal than humans are." Every single one of them had welcomed me with open arms, except for Naida. But from what everyone had said, she was standoffish to everyone, except with Sadie. After she spent time with you, she thawed some, but she was still rigid. From what Egan had said, most fae were that way.

"What do you mean?"

Memories of Kortright flashed through my mind. "At the university, they accepted me before they realized my connection with Egan. And Titan and the vampires all helped without a second thought. They look out for one another."

Part of the reason Sadie and the others had accepted me could have been because I was destined to be supernatural. At first, I didn't feel like I fit in with them, but I didn't fit in with humans either. Finally, I felt secure, even though I was just realizing it.

"I have no interest in being part of this strange, scary world, but you look like you're at peace and happy for the first time since Dad died." Her gaze went back to Egan. "That day on the beach, you had a very similar look in your eyes, which petrified your father."

"Why?" I thought they would've wanted me to find happiness instead of feeling like I was awkward and didn't fit in anywhere.

She rubbed her hands across her upper thigh, over the new jeans she'd gotten from the pack. "Because you were too young to feel a tenth of what your father and I felt for each other, and we didn't want your heart broken. But it's clear we may have reacted too rashly. I wonder what might have happened if we hadn't left the beach that day and headed home."

"You can't play the 'what if' game." That was dangerous. I'd played it way too often growing up with Sarah. All it had done was add more angst and heartache to the guilt I already carried.

Egan and Draco turned back toward the vehicle with the four guys following behind.

They'll take your mom the rest of the way. Egan didn't seem tense, but he wasn't relaxed either. The vibes through our bond were hard to pinpoint, which made me nervous.

Why? Is something wrong?

No. He looked at me as he continued. *But the longer we stay out in the open, the likelier someone will see us. And your aunt is pacing around the house. I don't want her to see us or our car.*

Are you sure they are who they say they are? After everything we'd gone through, we didn't need to hand her over to the enemy.

Egan grinned as two guys spoke to him and linked with me. *That's exactly what Draco said. We called Titan, and he vouched for them. That's what took so long.*

I didn't like dropping her off like this, but I didn't want to see Sarah. And if she saw us and our tags, it meant she could locate the vampire nest. So, if someone showed up who was hunting me down, she'd offer me up on a silver platter, no threats or torture required. "Mom, those guys are going to walk you the rest of the way to your house."

"What? Why?" She picked at her nails as her anxiety peeked through.

I had to tread carefully. "Sarah is awake, and I think it's best we don't run into each other."

"But are they safe?" Mom's mouth quivered.

Now she was getting on my nerves. I'd seen her like this way too often to count, and it had made me determined to be a strong person.

To not need anyone.

But I realized that wasn't the way to be either. You could be stronger with the right people by your side.

I steadied myself before I snapped. I didn't understand how she was okay being this way. "Do you think we'd leave you with them if we thought they were a risk?" I couldn't prevent the hurt from leaking through. After almost dying for her, she should know I wouldn't hand her over to just anyone.

"No, I don't." She sucked in a breath and blew it out. "I'm being ridiculous like always. I wish I could be strong like you. That's why I pushed you into martial arts and everything. You can stand on your own two feet, something I've never been able to do."

She was stronger than she gave herself credit for. "Maybe if you tried."

Mom opened the door and climbed out, leaving me alone in the car.

I wanted to say, "See! You just shut me down. A weak person wouldn't do that," but I bit my tongue. No good would come from it. This was something she would have to work through herself, just like I'd had to.

Following her lead, I got out of the car and walked around the back of the midsize sedan to the others. Mom stood several feet on the outskirts, staring the four men down strangely.

"We'll make sure she stays safe," the one who was slightly older than the others said. He looked in his mid-twenties, but I'd learned you couldn't use appearances as any sort of guidance in this strange, wild world. He could be one hundred for all I knew.

I wasn't sure what to say, so I went with the best I had. "Thank you."

"You're welcome." The guy winked at me.

Egan stepped close to me, placing an arm around my waist.

I almost giggled but swallowed it down. At least, he didn't growl, but he was making it clear I was his, and I loved it.

"You three get on out of here," the wolf said with humor, finding Egan's reaction funny too. "If what Titan said is true, your enemies will be looking for you any way possible. It's best you get back out to the mountain where you'll be harder to find."

Draco frowned. "You know where Titan lives?"

"Don't worry, we don't," the younger one said as he shifted his weight to his right leg. "Just that it's in the mountains and well hidden. We see him from time to time when he visits my dad, the alpha of our pack."

Titan was a very well-respected wolf in the community. Sadie had told me he could have easily taken over Tyler's pack, but Titan was a much better man. He believed that one person ruling over everyone gave certain groups unfair advantages and other groups special interests.

If politicians had taught us anything, I'd say Titan was dead on.

"Your sacrifice is noted, and as my mate said, we're extremely grateful." Egan lowered his head slightly.

The younger one chuckled and took a few steps toward the neighborhood. "Making friends with dragons is always a smart move. We'll alert Titan if anything weird happens."

I hugged my mother so tight she groaned in pain.

Oh, snap. Supernatural strength. I had to remember that. I loosened my hold and took a deep breath of her jasmine scent. Musk laced it, probably because she'd borrowed clothes from a wolf shifter.

"You three head on back. It's late." She kissed my forehead and patted my cheek. "I love you. Call me, okay? I'll get a new phone tomorrow so you can reach me."

"Okay." I gave her a small smile as my eyes burned with unshed tears. "If you need anything, message me. I'll have my alerts on."

Mom then focused on Egan. "You better take care of my baby girl."

"I'll guard her with my life." The sincerity behind his words was evident with each syllable.

Mom turned, and two guys flanked her while the other two followed behind.

As I watched them walk away, an overwhelming feeling settled over me like something was wrong.

CHAPTER FIFTEEN

Everything inside me screamed to snatch Mom and run, but I had no clue why. Titan had vouched for the guys. Vera was dead, and there was nothing out of the ordinary going on. There was absolutely no reason for me to feel this way. Again, my panic had to be taking over.

Is something wrong? Egan asked and took my hand.

His touch calmed me, confirming that paranoia was the problem. When there was an actual threat present, his touch made me feel safer, but it didn't soothe me. My aunt had that effect on me. Every time I thought about her, my skin crawled. *Just wish she wasn't going back to Sarah.*

Me too.

"Let's head back to the mansion," Draco whispered. "They're right. The longer we stay here, the likelier we are to be found."

Why did they keep saying that? "How so?"

"There are many kinds of supernaturals that can track, like vampires, and there's no telling how many there are in Fae." Draco headed back to the car. "The farther we are from a city, the harder it'll be to find us. The larger the population, the more creatures could be nearby, already looking."

I couldn't argue with that. There was still so much I didn't know about this world.

Egan and I followed him, and Draco slipped into the backseat, leaving the front passenger seat open for me. He'd tried to do the same thing on the way here, but with Mom freaking out, we'd all agreed it'd be best that I sit back there with her.

Always the gentleman, Egan opened the door, and I climbed in and put my seatbelt on. By the time I buckled the seatbelt, Egan had slid into the car, and we were heading back to the mountains.

My eyes flicked to the side mirror, watching the neighborhood disappear as he turned onto the road back to the city.

I MUST HAVE DRIFTED off because my car door opened, startling me awake. Familiar sexy arms wrapped around my body, lifting me into a hard, muscular chest.

My eyes fluttered open to find Egan staring tenderly at my face as he headed to the front door of the mansion.

Hey there, sleepyhead. His voice was low and raspy.

I loved it when he used that voice. My body always responded, and already being cuddled right against his chest had parts of me warming. *Hey, you.* I licked my lips inadvertently.

A low growl rattled his chest. He could smell and feel what I wanted. His tangy scent of arousal hit my nose, increasing my own need.

The slight glow of the rising sun told me it had to be around seven in the morning. The light glowed behind Egan, adding to his allure.

"Well, okay. I'm going to go crash for a couple of hours on the couch," Draco said uncomfortably as he opened the door. "Uh, I'll see you two later."

Egan walked past him, his eyes locked on mine. There was no doubt what we'd be doing once we were alone in our room.

Seconds later, we entered our bedroom, and Egan shut the door quietly before lowering my feet to the floor and kissing me.

His tongue slipped into my mouth, and his hands slipped under my jeans, resting on my ass. He deepened the kiss, and all I could breathe and smell was him. His fingers kneaded my ass cheeks like he was trying to force himself to slow down.

I stumbled back toward the bed, dragging him with me. He removed his hands from my pants and wrapped them around my waist right as I fell backward and landed on my back on the bed. He caught himself with one hand while using the other to lift my shirt up. He pulled his mouth away from my lips and gently nipped at my breast. My back arched into him.

Closing my eyes, I slipped my hands under his shirt, feeling his abs. He felt so warm, and I loved running my fingertips along his defined muscles.

His hand slipped to the button on my jeans, and he unfastened them with ease. I lifted my butt off the bed, and he pushed my jeans and panties down. He stood and removed them completely. Then he lowered himself on the bed on his side and slipped his hands between my legs.

Between his mouth and touch, the friction built, and a low moan escaped.

He knew exactly how to work my body, and when he slipped a finger inside, I almost orgasmed.

I grabbed his hand, removing it from me, and he growled, *What do you think you're doing?*

If he thought that would make me listen to him, he should've known better by now. *I want to make you feel good too.* I pushed him off me and sat, removing my shirt and bra.

His eyes glowed as he watched me undress. *You're so damn beautiful.*

And he was the first person to make me feel that way. Before him, I'd felt ugly and unworthy. It was why I couldn't believe someone like him would be interested in me. But despite all accusations of him wanting me for just sex, he treated me with respect. *I love you.*

He cupped my cheek and smiled. *I love you too, my Jade.*

Unlike before, those words were like music to my ears. I unbuttoned his jeans and removed them and his boxers. I took a moment to gaze at him. He reminded me of one of those chiseled god statues.

I straddled him and leaned over, yanking the shirt over his head. He groaned and chuckled, helping me, and tossed it to the ground. He fidgeted, getting ready for our connection, but I wanted a minute. I rubbed my hand over his chest, enjoying how the thin golden hair on his pecs felt against my skin. Just devouring his body turned me on almost as much as his hands and mouth.

His eyes followed me as I lifted, drawing him inside me. As I lowered, he moaned and clutched my hips. He said, *I love watching you like this.*

Surprisingly, I liked him watching me too.

Our gazes stayed on each other as I rode him. His chest shuddered, and he moved in sync with me.

The speed increased, faster and faster, and he lifted his hands, cupping my breasts. The friction built as our bodies rubbed against each other, and when he pinched my nipples, the pleasure increased tenfold.

I closed my eyes as I spread my legs farther apart, allowing him to go deeper. The feel of him inside me and his hands on my body had me tumbling over. His body convulsed underneath me as we orgasmed together.

I swear it gets better each time. Egan lifted himself and kissed my lips, pulling me into his arms. He rolled us onto our sides, and I turned to face him, resting my head on his chest. My eyes grew heavy once again.

THE NEXT COUPLE of weeks passed by in a blur. March was upon us, and the weather was warming, even here in the mountains.

For once, life seemed normal. Well, as normal as it could get in a supernatural world, but the packs and thunder were getting along. Ollie was growing on all of us, and the vampires felt like family. There were no attacks, and Egan and I spent more time laughing than being broody and tense. If our lives could be like this every day, it'd be damn near perfect.

Roxy yawned. "What do you think we should do today?"

Sadie, Roxy, Lillith, Katherine, Kayda, and I were all lounging on six teal Adirondack chairs on the back porch of the mansion. Each mate sat on the ground next to us.

"We could always go for a run." Axel waggled his eyebrows. "It's been too long since I kicked your ass in a race."

"You did not kick my ass!" Roxy crossed her arms and wrinkled her nose. "I stumbled."

Lillith pursed her lips. "Not that it matters, but from where I was standing, you only stumbled when Axel got too far ahead and there was no way you could catch up."

"You bish!" Roxy bared her teeth. "Whose side are you on?"

"The truth." Lillith chuckled and lifted her head toward the sun. "They say it will always set you free."

"Humans are dumb." Roxy pouted. "They say stuff like that to make themselves feel better."

"I'm pretty sure you got that from Tyler." Sadie waved her finger. "Who wasn't the best role model."

"Even you?" Roxy's mouth dropped. "You're my bestie. What the hell is going on here?" Her hazel eyes found me. "Jade, I can count on you, right?"

I stiffened, and Egan placed a hand on my thigh.

"I'm like Switzerland," I gestured to the entire group. "Neutral."

"Katherine?" Roxy stuck out her bottom lip. "Please don't say no."

"I love you all equally, but you have to admit you might be a tad competitive." She put a small space between her thumb and pointer finger. "Just a smidge."

"Momma Kayda?" Roxy asked with defeat.

"Oh, no." Kayda stood and grabbed Ladon's hand, pulling her mate to his feet. "I don't get involved in disagreements unless I have a vested interest. This is one we won't be getting into. We're going to check on the dragons while you two do whatever this is you're doing." She and Ladon headed toward the back door.

"Sorry, babe." Axel kissed her arm. "It looks like they're all siding with me by not picking a side."

"Traitors." She looked at each of us. "All of you are traitors."

"Stop being dramatic." Lillith yawned and placed a hand over her mouth. "You're wearing me out."

"Oh, please." Roxy stuck her tongue out at the vampire. "You breathe drama."

"I do not," she gasped.

I think we need to go do something. Ever since things had calmed down, Roxy and Lillith had gotten snippy with each other, likely due to the amount of one-on-one time we had with everyone. There wasn't much to do out here except eat, watch television, scan library books, play video games, or hang outside.

Egan and I stayed in the bedroom as much as possible, but it felt too weird being up there as much as we would've liked with his parents close by.

The door opened and shut as Egan's parents walked back into the house.

You're right. Egan stood and raised his hands over his head, stretching.

His shirt crept upward, showing his abs. I enjoyed the view.

"Better wipe that drool off your face—" Roxy snorted. "—before it makes a puddle on your chest. I bet Egan doesn't like being stared at like a piece of meat."

"Don't speak on my behalf." His attention on me warmed my body. "She can look at me like that any time she wants."

"Oh, really?" Roxy turned toward the mansion and said more loudly, "Momma Kayda, you might want to come back out here."

"If you think Mom would give us a hard time, she wouldn't." Egan lifted me off the lounger and into his arms. "She wants grandbabies. Tons of them."

That was the second comment about children this month. *You keep bringing up children.*

Yeah, is that not okay? His forehead creased with confusion.

I had to tread carefully. I didn't want to hurt his feelings. *I want them too, but not now. I want to make sure we're on the same page.*

A grin peeked through. *The fact that you do is enough for me. But I won't say that the thought of having children with you doesn't thrill me. To have something we made together would be the second-best thing that ever happened to me.*

You sweet-talker. I beamed up at him. He made me feel so happy and safe.

Roxy bickered with the group, and I took Egan's hand, leading him behind a few trees several feet away to give us some privacy.

I stroked the stubble on his chin. *I still can't believe you were the boy on the beach. It makes perfect sense, but it's still surreal.*

And you're the girl who made me feel funny things I didn't understand. He kissed me as his voice deepened. *And you turned into a woman who owns me.*

I still hadn't asked him the question that had been burning in my mind for the past few weeks. At every opportunity, I got distracted by sex, which I wasn't complaining about. If everyone else hadn't been around, I'd have been on top of him, claiming him as my own again. *I thought you guys were in hiding. How did we run into each other all those years ago?*

We went to another thunder so I could meet the eldest dragon there at the time. Now I know why. The priest performed a ceremony on me, and Dad said every one of his family members had to go through the same rights. Now I realize it was because we're royalty. On the way back to our thunder, Mom asked to see the beach one last time. She always spoke of it fondly. Dad obliged but said it had to be quick. Little did we know I'd find my fated mate. Of course, I didn't understand that then, but my parents must have. I think that's why they pushed me to go to college ... to find you again.

I kept forgetting he was royalty. *Is needing an heir another reason you want children?*

Not at all. He pushed a piece of my hair behind my ear. *It might be beneficial for that reason, but I'd want this as badly if we were just plain ol' Egan and Jade.*

It would've been nice to be ordinary people—or dragon shifters.

Lillith stood and clapped her hands. "Okay, this is getting gross, even for me. I don't know what you're doing back there, but if we don't intervene, we're going to start hearing uncomfortable noises coming from behind the trees."

Roxy snorted. "Egan's huge. We'll see everything he's working with if that happens."

"Okay." Sadie cleared her throat. "Let's go for a hike."

They'd managed to embarrass us even when we'd tried to hide.

"That sounds good." I stepped from Egan's arms begrudgingly but moving around sounded nice.

Egan took my hand. "We should tell Draco or we may get in trouble." We joined them again before Roxy and Lillith could continue their tirade.

"I'll go tell him." Katherine jumped to her feet and ran inside.

Donovan frowned slightly. "She jumps at any chance to be around him. She does realize he has a human fated mate out there somewhere?"

"Don't worry," Lillith grumbled, "I'll remind her. We don't need her to get her heart broken."

That was something we could all agree with.

Ollie, Draco, and Katherine came back outside, and our group took off into the woods.

A breeze hit my skin, cooling my body down to a more comfortable temperature. The animals scurried as if they were excited for spring. The scent of budding flowers hit my nose, even though they hadn't bloomed yet. It was like they were preparing for the season, ready to pollinate the area.

We moved quickly and quietly through the trees in comfortable silence.

A few miles away from the mansion, I laid my head on Egan's arm as we walked at a slow, relaxed pace. The sun shone through the trees now that it was high in the sky. I hadn't been this relaxed in such a long time.

But then Egan tensed.

What's wrong? I lifted my head. We were in a thicker part of the woods with trees completely surrounding us. Then I realized the animal noises were gone.

He took a deep breath. *Something is near.*

Draco appeared beside us, spreading his legs into a fighter's pose. He'd recognized the same threat Egan had.

Panic surged through me as I tried desperately to figure out what we were looking for.

A roar sounded only a few feet away from us, and I spun around to see a huge brown bear stepping into view between two trees.

The animal threw its head back and roared again. Then it charged.

CHAPTER SIXTEEN

An awful decaying stench laced with musk hit my nose as the bear approached. The grizzly's ice-green eyes held a human-like quality.

Wait. Intrigue replaced my fear. *Is he a shifter?*

Yes, Egan growled as Draco stepped in front of us.

When this was all over, I'd need a flowchart or diagram of all of the shifters in the world. Hell, maybe even a detailed outline. It was beyond insane how much I didn't know.

"One bear thinks it can take us out?" Roxy chuckled and flipped her hair over her shoulder. "There are four wolves, two vampires, and three dragons."

Ollie jerked his head toward her and scowled. "And a falcon."

"Oh, please." She waved him off. "You don't count."

"In all fairness, he pecked through several girls' eyes and necks." Lillith shrugged, completely at ease like Roxy. "And he pecked through that wire net that held Jade."

They did have a point, but they needed to take the

threat more seriously. *I have a bad feeling about this. The bear doesn't seem worried.*

My thoughts exactly. Egan looked at the sky.

At first, I wasn't sure why. then I heard the flapping of several pairs of wings overhead like a synchronized beat. I couldn't tell how many. It could have been ten or hundreds.

"Ollie." I glanced at him, the hairs on the back of my neck raised. If I hadn't known any better, I might have thought I was a wolf shifter, not a dragon. "Go to Titan's pack and get them and the other dragons."

"What?" Katherine faced me. "Why?"

"Listen," Donovan growled. "The bear's not alone. Tell them to bring weapons. We have no clue what we're up against. If they're fae, the iron might help too."

That was all Ollie needed to hear before taking off. We might need backup and quick. Out of all of us, Ollie was the smallest when he shifted and could hide. Whatever was coming sounded huge.

"How is this possible?" Lillith's jaw twitched. "The witch is dead. How did they find us?"

"Mom." My voice cracked. "I need to check on her."

We will, but right now, we need to keep our heads in the game and hope Ollie gets back with everyone soon. Egan lifted his head, looking higher in the sky.

I followed his gaze, and my world stopped. The strangest animals I'd ever seen were flying toward us, which was saying something after the harpies and gargoyles.

Each one looked the same. Enormous, scarlet lions beat long, boney wings that sprouted from their backs. They each had a thick, long, scorpion-like tail tipped with a dangerous stinger as well as numerous stingers along its huge tail. Their red faces resembled an old man with a very long beard that matched the red shade of their bodies.

"What the hell is it with fae creatures looking like old people?" Sadie groaned as she returned her focus to the bear.

"Looking old is a strategic advantage." That was something they'd taught me in self-defense class. "You think of them as weaker and lower your guard around them. Apparently, the fae must think the same way, or they find the look sexy."

"Doesn't matter." Axel bellowed while his bones cracked as he called his wolf. "We'll kick their asses."

Wings sprouted from Draco's body. "It won't be easy. These are manticores. They are some of the toughest opponents. You can only kill them by piercing their bellies or injuring their mouths."

Great. Of course, they'd be straight out of Greek mythology. "We'll have to use branches and whatever else we have until the others get here."

Sadie, Roxy, and Donovan followed Axel's lead, shifting into their wolves. We all needed to be in our strongest forms.

"Do not engage until the others have arrived unless you absolutely have to," Draco commanded. "With our small numbers, they'll focus on eliminating the biggest threat first. Try to wait for our numbers to grow before revealing your strength."

The bear stepped back like he was going to allow the manticores to handle us. Once we kicked their asses, the bear was next on my list.

My dragon brushed against my mind, on the same page as my human side. I latched on to the flames, and the warmth flowed through my body. I took a few steps away from Egan and Draco as my body expanded.

My clothes stretched until they ripped from my body.

Egan and Draco had the same plan, and every one of us was now in animal form.

Draco's navy blue scales glistened as he gestured for Egan and me to head back to the mansion.

No, he couldn't be suggesting what I thought he was. *I'm not hiding in the mansion.*

Neither am I. I get we're part of the royal family, but I'm not leaving my friends out here to fight a battle that's happening because of our race.

It thrilled me that he wasn't begging me to go back to the mansion. If this had been a month ago, he'd be growling at me to go. *So, belly or mouth. That's what we aim for.*

That's the plan. He edged in front of me but not too noticeably. *Anything else before they get here?*

I counted the manticores flying at us. The sky was full of them, but I spotted an end to the group.

One hundred.

We had more people than that. We should be okay.

Yeah, I love you, and don't die. I flapped my wings, lifting off the ground. I didn't want to be sitting ducks and let them come to us. I understood not wanting to start the fight, but we didn't need to make it easy for them to clobber us.

Draco made weird noises that sounded between a growl, a groan, and a roar. I had a feeling he was cussing my ass out super creatively. I wondered what he might call me when this was over. He might teach me a new word or two.

What are you doing? Egan asked as he rushed to catch up to me.

We need to split them up. If they got to us before we had backup, it would be harder to hold them off. Maybe Egan, Draco, and I could make some of them chase us around in the sky.

The odd noises were still gurgling from Draco as he caught up to us. He hovered slightly in front of us as forty manticores split off from the main group and headed our way.

See, we're already splitting them up. My plan was working.

Sadie and the others must have caught on because her pink wolf ran into the woods, away from the others. The other three took off in different directions as well.

The remaining sixty split apart with ten taking off after each wolf, leaving twenty still heading toward Lillith and Katherine.

Now we just needed to play cat and mouse for a little while.

The three of us hovered in the air as the forty manticores headed toward us. Suddenly, the one in the front swung its tail around, despite still being a hundred yards away. Something snapped from its tail, and five stingers spiraled toward me like freaking arrows.

I froze, watching in both intrigue and horror as they darted toward my heart like it was a bull's-eye.

Jade! Egan yelled in my head, snapping me back to the present.

What the hell was wrong with me?

Something hard slammed into my side, and wings wrapped around me. Draco's ashy smell surrounded me. His wings unraveled around me after we'd dropped several feet.

We flapped our wings, catching the wind before we crashed into the trees below.

Egan reached me, brushing his wings against mine. *Are you okay?*

Yeah, but what the hell? I still couldn't believe what I'd seen, but as I looked at the forty manticores, I realized they were now closer, which meant we were screwed. Splitting them up wasn't as effective as I'd hoped it would be, but it was better than the full one hundred coming at us at once.

We could only hope that the others would arrive soon. We'd have to survive until then.

As the manticores grew closer, I noted a slight difference between them. Some had more blue in their eyes while others had gray.

When the closest one got within thirty yards of us, its mouth turned upward in a smile before it bared its teeth.

What I saw scared me more than anything I'd seen from them.

The creature had three rows of sharp, jagged teeth like razor blades. Between those, the lion body, and the stingers, the direness of our situation truly dawned on me.

Draco was always tense. Part of his job was continuously looking for threats and never underestimating the enemy, so in a way, I hadn't expected them to be worse than anything we'd faced before. Not anymore.

We had to fly fast and crazy or we'd be screwed if they fine-tuned their attack. *Move.*

I took off, flying as fast as I could away from Egan and Draco. I darted randomly in the sky, keeping my movements irregular with no hint of a pattern whatsoever.

I spun around and breathed a sigh of relief when I caught Egan and Draco doing the same thing.

Thank God. That was the only way we could all survive.

A stinger whizzed toward me, and I knew what to do. I darted hard to the right, causing the manticore to miss his target.

The one closest to me roared in frustration and flapped his wings faster.

Shit, he wasn't shooting at me anymore; he wanted to catch up. The thought of his teeth pushed me harder to get the hell away.

As I flew higher, bulky figures appeared in the distance.

Dammit, was that more of them? God, I hoped not. We might not survive, but that was the point. The fae dragon king wanted us dead, especially Egan, to eliminate any threat to his crown. It was exactly the kind of thing any power-hungry asshole would do. He wanted to hunt his own kind down to end them just so whatever magic could transfer to him.

What was it with asshole men? He had to be short. From every experience I'd had, the men dying for more power suffered from short man syndrome. It was a real condition.

I blinked a few times, and the figures flying toward me took form. They weren't huge lions but dragons. The thunder was on their way, which meant that the wolves had to be too.

Glancing over my shoulder, I saw ten manticores hot on my trail. That had happened quickly. They flew out in a line, planning to surround me.

If I got caught like that, it'd be hard as hell to escape. I ducked, letting my body drop toward the ground.

Just like back in the cave, my dragon wanted to abort and pull up, but I stayed in control. One backward glance confirmed what I'd hoped: those ten assholes were still almost on top of me and following my lead.

Could I pull it off and make a few of them crash? According to Draco, the impact wouldn't kill them, but I could knock them out or injure them somewhat.

Surely.

Something like arrows whistled closer, and I lifted my head to find Egan zigzagging, dodging stingers. The last one targeted the back of his tail. He jerked hard to the right, and the stinger missed him by less than an inch.

A growl of frustration came from a manticore behind me. A click sounded like earlier, right before they'd launched stingers at me.

I'd gotten so distracted by Egan's attack that I'd stopped focusing on a random flight pattern. I spun in circles as the wind rushed past my immense body. We were still seventy-five feet off the ground, but the trees were getting closer. I only needed to get close enough to one of the trees and stop short so the ten manticores behind me wouldn't have time to react before going splat.

Since the manticore still hadn't fired at me, my flight pattern must have been random enough to hold them off.

Forcing my eyes forward, I found an opening between trees that was large enough for me to fly through and get back into the sky. I darted to the right, needing to time this perfectly.

Leaves were budding on tree branches, again proving that spring was right around the corner. It would have been nice if they'd been in full bloom to hide us from these creatures, but at least it wouldn't be hard to find a good branch to use to stab them with.

Twenty feet off the ground, I sucked in a deep breath. There was no time to hesitate or lose confidence. If I let my nerves get the best of me, I'd slam into the ground like I hoped these manticores would.

The time had come.

I shifted my weight, going right side up again. Spreading my wings, I took flight between the trees like I'd planned. My bottom half was bigger than I'd realized, and as I squeezed through the trees, my body pushed them outward, bending them.

They didn't fall over, and I almost cried with joy when several bodies hit the ground.

At least, one thing had worked out. If they stayed down for longer than a minute, maybe I could find a stick to kill them with.

As I flew upward with confidence, I found myself staring at two manticores no more than twenty feet away. They must have realized my intentions.

One had its tail ready, and several stingers launched directly at me.

I didn't have time to move, so I closed my eyes and prayed.

CHAPTER SEVENTEEN

The stingers hit my scales one after another, jabbing like pinpricks. They fell to the ground, and I waited for intense pain to hit, similar to the harpies' arrows.

But the pain never came.

I opened my eyes as the manticore's mouth turned downward. Or I thought it did. Despite having a human face, the expression was pretty one-dimensional.

Angry and feral.

Are you hurt? Egan linked, letting his intense worry bleed into me.

These creatures were scary, but maybe they weren't as fearsome as we thought. *I'm fine. They sting, but that's it. The pain is already gone.* I flew upright, not bothering to fly in a random pattern.

The manticore that had shot at me roared like that would put the fear back inside me.

Nope. The teeth and huge-ass stingers were enough to frighten me, but I didn't need to worry about the small ones anymore. I flapped my wings, hovering in place while keeping my eyes locked on the manticores flying around.

Below me, five of them had hit the ground and appeared disoriented. Two lay completely still while the other three squirmed but couldn't roll back onto their feet.

At least they weren't smart. That was what I'd been banking on.

Egan flew closer, despite the twenty still on his tail, and linked with me. *It's almost time to fight. The others are only a mile away.*

At least sixty dragons were heading our way, and twenty or so wolves and fifty men were running toward us. The men each held two items: what looked like a sword and a metal pole.

Donovan had mentioned something about iron. It had to be fae related, and now we had multiple weapons at our disposal—or we would when they got nearer.

Our army rushed toward us, and I only prayed the wolves were resistant to the stingers too. Had I been in human form, those would've hurt, and the wolves' hide wasn't much thicker.

A wolf howled, and I spun around. The manticores had Roxy surrounded. Five landed on the ground, circling her so she couldn't get out. She hunkered, her vibrant red fur standing on end.

I had to help her. *It's time to engage.* We couldn't wait any longer. One of our own was in danger.

Not bothering to wait for Egan's reply, I rushed to Roxy. If anything were to happen to her when I could prevent it, I'd never survive it. The others should be here in minutes.

I swooped down with my own manticores chasing after me and almost froze in place when the creature closest to Roxy opened its mouth. The three rows of teeth looked as ferocious as before, but the amount of drool pooling from its mouth made its intent obvious.

These assholes weren't trying to injure us; they wanted to eat us.

One charged toward Roxy and reached her within seconds.

Pushing my wings even harder than I had before, I reached my friend just as the manticore's mouth was only centimeters from her head. From the angle of its attack, the creature was planning to eat her head first.

I opened my own mouth and attacked its neck. My teeth sank in, and its blood poured across my tongue. The creature roared and swung its scorpion tail at me. I released my hold and flew upward, the stinger barely missing my leg.

The manticore flew right after me, its gray eyes turning dark as coal. Between it and the others that were focused on me, I needed to do something. Unfortunately, Roxy wasn't out of danger yet.

Draco barreled past me, his focus on Roxy.

Wow, he's not focused on us? Not that I was complaining, but Draco always made it clear that Egan, Ladon, Kayda, and I were his priority.

Oh, he is, Egan replied tensely. *He knows you'll keep putting yourself in danger if he doesn't help Roxy. The others are here, and it's time to take it up a notch.*

A dark purple dragon roared as it flew past me and attacked a manticore. One dragon after another came to my aid and to help in the fight.

The fact that these people had come to help me without any hesitation made me realize they had accepted me as one of their own.

I'd been so worried because of Mindy, but she'd been the exception. And I had to protect them just like they were protecting me.

Pale pink lights lit the sky like fireworks. I followed the

trail to find Sadie running toward Roxy in wolf form and shooting magic from her paws every couple of steps. Every other burst hit a manticore. It would flinch back in pain, but not for long.

When Draco had said these guys were worthy opponents, he'd meant every word. They were ruthless and bounced back from attacks like they'd only stubbed their toes.

The men poured into the area, waving their swords around like the manticores would fear them. But the creatures barely batted an eye.

Egan appeared next to me, so stiff his dragon looked like a statute. If it hadn't been for his flapping wings, I would've thought he was frozen. *We have to figure out how to beat them.*

A manticore shot stingers at a chestnut wolf. I recognized him as the one who'd defended his friend, the wolf Mom had thought was attacking her. The wolf yelped in pain and fell with a loud thud.

I had to do something, but as I headed toward them, the creature rushed over to the wolf and swallowed him whole —bones and all.

No. That couldn't have happened. But no matter how many times I blinked, my eyes confirmed what I'd seen. My stomach lurched, and bile burned my throat.

Holy shit. The wolves were susceptible to the stingers.

Pure rage bubbled inside me, and I roared so loud some of the manticores stopped what they were doing to stare at me.

That's right, assholes. Pay attention to me. I had to save my friends and their pack members.

Lillith blurred across a small clearing with her vampire speed, carrying a sword in her right hand.

A manticore opened its mouth to attack Roxy, but Lillith thrust the sword inside it. The creature screamed as the metal sank in deep, and it sagged.

One down, ninety-nine to go.

We need something to use against them. We had claws, but with their tails and our size, getting close enough to use them was problematic. They could easily take any of us out. We needed to get a hold of a weapon or debilitate their stinger.

Egan nodded slightly. *My grandfather told me a story about these creatures when I was little. Before our thunder left for Earth, the fae dragon king sent these creatures to attack, but the true dragon ruler knew the secret to defeating them: dehydration.*

Babe, I love you, but I think it'll take a long time before these creatures get thirsty. Maybe after they eat all of us. That sounded like a horrible plan.

He chuckled, surprising me given the situation. *What's one way to dehydrate someone?* Some of his confidence clicked back into place, and smoke trickled from his nostrils.

Fire. I hadn't even thought of that. If we lit them up, their skin and bodies would lose their moisture.

A manticore flew near us, and Egan opened his mouth, blowing his flames all over the creature. It cried but continued to fly toward us, then began to slow.

Be careful. If we can light them up, the wolves can kill them. Egan continued his assault on the creature. Its wings slowed, and its elevation dropped.

That sounded like a solid plan. I raced toward Roxy, Sadie, and Lillith. Draco fought two manticores, but he was losing steam. One manticore shot its stingers at him while the other swung its tail.

As I channeled my anger, fire grew and bubbled in my stomach. I motioned for the girls to step back.

Lillith caught on as I opened my mouth and smoke curled over my lips.

"Get back!" Lillith yelled. Sadie and Roxy took several steps back.

When they were far enough away, I pushed the fire from my stomach, aiming at the manticore posing the most significant threat to Draco.

The creature growled and spun around. It charged at me, abandoning Draco. I gestured for Lillith to attack as the manticore took flight, trying desperately to get me.

She was a blur as she ran under the creature, using its body to protect herself from the flames, and swung the blade into its stomach.

A screech of pain left the creature, and Lillith rolled out of the way just before it collapsed.

"That's it!" Lillith yelled, counting on everyone's supernatural hearing. "Dragons, light those manticore asses up. The rest of us, jam the swords in their bellies or deep in their mouths to kill them."

Good, that was one way to spread the word. I didn't give a damn if the manticores understood our plan.

Re-energized, Draco turned on the one shooting stingers at him. He lit the creature up as Lillith rushed to help him kill it.

A low growl alerted me to the oncoming creature, its attention solely on me. He opened his jaws wide, his intentions clear.

But I refused to hesitate or freeze in fear.

Fire spewed from me, hitting the creature's mouth.

Sadie's pink wolf stepped up beside me, and she aimed

her magic inside the creature's mouth. Her magic held a continuous surge, similar to my flame.

After several seconds that felt like a lifetime, the manticore stopped struggling and crumbled. Its chest stopped moving, proving it was dead.

I looked for the next target, but the enemy creatures were already fighting with other dragons. Everyone had heard Lillith and were following her instructions.

Most of the wolf shifters hadn't shifted, so we had plenty of people in human form to wield weapons.

I took to the sky to check on everyone and watched as Ollie ran toward the mansion. After all this time together, was he really running to safety? Part of me wanted to follow, but I couldn't leave my people and the packs. We were already at a huge disadvantage.

I linked with Egan, looking for him. *Are you okay?*

Yes, I'm helping Donovan and Axel, Egan replied. *Several shifters in human form are here. Are you safe?*

For the moment. I didn't want to lie to him. None of us were safe with these strange creatures here. *I'm going to see if anyone else needs my help.*

One manticore flew high, stalking the area.

No, I wouldn't allow him to find a target.

Rushing toward the creature, my dragon prepared for the attack. A few yards away, I opened my mouth to hit the creature with flames, but it plunged abruptly.

My flames hit nothing, and I yanked the fire back inside as I chased after it.

I couldn't hit the manticore with my flames with the wind blowing back in my face. It wouldn't touch him.

The creature lowered its head, increasing its speed, reminding me of a bird tracking fish in the water.

I attempted to locate its target, but nothing came into

view. We flew past several dragons and other manticores engaged in battle, but they weren't its target.

As we neared the ground, Titan and Winter rushed from some trees. They were in human form, handing out weapons to whomever needed them.

They were the reason we were gaining the advantage. They were rushing to dole out a huge pile of weapons to anyone who lost a sword in the fight or to a straggler looking to help.

Placing myself right behind the manticore, I moved my wings and used my body to increase my speed. Tumbling to the ground, I arched my feet and hands to use my talons for as much leverage as possible.

I rammed into the manticore's back, and I dug my sharp talons into its rough skin. Even though it wouldn't kill the bastard, it would distract it.

Its head jerked backward as it tried to bite me, but I was far enough back that it couldn't reach me. I almost roared with victory, but something hit me hard and lodged into my back, and sharp pain erupted down my spine.

I'd forgotten about its scorpion-like tail.

My grip slipped, and I fell from the manticore's body. As the distance grew between us, the creature removed the stinger from my back.

Jade, what happened? Egan asked with concern.

But I didn't have the time or energy to respond because I was only forty feet from hitting the ground. Using every ounce of concentration and strength available, I channeled my strength to my wings. The stinger must have torn through muscle because when my wings moved, it caused sharp, deep pain. I couldn't flap them fast enough to ascend, but I slowed my fall.

I braced myself for the inevitable impact as my body

slammed into the ground. My dragon growled as a cloud of grass and dirt covered our entire body.

But the pain of the impact wasn't as bad as I'd expected.

"We need help!" Winter screamed, and adrenaline coursed through my body, numbing the intense pain from the stinger.

I climbed to my feet and found the manticore swinging its tail around, ready to launch a barrage of attacks on Titan and Winter. Pushing the flames from my stomach, I ran as fast as possible toward them.

The stingers launched before I could blaze the sucker, but I remained focused on the fight. I wouldn't allow it to attack again.

The creature spun toward me, opening its mouth despite my flames in pure rage. As it rushed toward me, a human wolf shifter ran over, using the flames to hide its approach, and threw a sword under the belly, plunging it hard in its skin.

Damn, I wished I had an aim like that.

With a half cry, half roar, the manticore sank. Although I watched the animal die, the crying sound remained.

What the hell?

Then the cry turned into pleading, and I realized it wasn't the creature.

"Help me, please!" Winter yelled. "It's Titan."

I spun around to find Titan on his back, squirming in pain with a stinger stuck in his eye.

CHAPTER EIGHTEEN

The amount of blood pouring from Titan's eye had to be dangerous. Between that and how deep the stinger had dug in, I was worried it might have hit his brain. The stinger was wedged in at an angle, though, so hopefully, it had missed his brain. If we lost him, that would hurt both his and Sadie's packs.

Blood wasn't my friend, but it didn't bother me as much in dragon form. The animal side did come in handy. If I'd been human, I would have vomited my lunch everywhere.

Titan's injured, I linked with Egan, not sure what the hell to do. *And so am I. I can't hold them off on my own.*

He responded, *I'll be right there.*

"Help!" Winter screamed as she fell to her knees next to her mate. "Somebody, please."

The alpha flailed around and groaned in pain like he was unsure what to do.

Pounding footsteps grew nearer, and the familiar scent of Kayda and Ladon blew in the air. They raced into view, Ollie running right behind them.

Ollie hadn't hidden. He'd gone to get help. I kind of felt

bad. My gut reaction had been to think poorly of him. Little did he know, I hadn't had the bracelet on me this past week to see how he would act. I needed to know if I had to use it for him to comply. I had it hidden under a floorboard in my and Egan's room since the falcon's sight was better than his sense of smell. And despite my little test, when things had gone south, I'd thought the worst of him.

The oldest dragon rushed to Titan, pushing past his king and queen. The little bit of gray hair he had stood straight up from how fast he'd been moving, and he said, "We have to get that stinger out of his eye before the poison spreads and kills him."

"Wait." Ladon tensed, reminding me of his son. "I thought the stingers weren't poisonous."

"To dragons. But to humans and several other supernatural creatures, they are." The older man placed a hand on Winter's arm. "I'll need you to move so I can get this out before it's too late."

"Of course," Winter said and stood to let the older man sit on the side of the injured eye.

She moved to the other side and stood behind Ladon and Kayda as she reassured her mate, "I'm right here. Long is going to help you."

Long's amber eyes surveyed the injury. "Titan, this is Long. I'm going to yank the stinger out of your eye. It'll hurt like hell, but if we don't, you won't survive."

Wings flapped nearby, and I tore my eyes away to find Egan hurrying toward us. Even in beast form, his forehead was lined with concern. Titan was a man he respected and cared about, so this was hard for him to see.

"Fine, just do it," Titan grunted, his breathing shallow. "The pain is getting worse."

"Ladon and Kayda, hold him down," Long instructed. "The less he fights me, the less risky this will be."

I felt so helpless in this form. All I could do was stand here and watch. *What do we do?*

We do nothing. Egan touched my wing as he examined my wound. *You're injured and need time to heal.*

I'm fine. As long as I didn't move my wing, the pain was manageable. *But we need to prevent something worse from happening to Titan.*

We'll stay here and make sure nothing attacks them while they work on Titan. Egan's dragon hand brushed my arm. *We should be safe since most of the manticores are dead, but we don't need to be careless, especially with your injury.*

I had no arguments there. *Okay.* I scanned the area for threats. The smell of flames and smoke was thick around us, but that was a good sign. That meant there were plenty of us left to fight and proved we'd gained the upper hand. Unfortunately, the manticore had acted out of desperation in trying to take out Titan before they all died in vain. But I didn't understand it all. What in the hell had the fae dragon king promised them to convince these creatures to come here and risk their lives? He had to be either very convincing or leveraging hatred in some way.

"We've got him," Kayda said with determination. "Go ahead, Long."

Winter paced behind them, her fingers pulling at the end of her ponytail. Her sea-blue eyes turned cobalt, and her body shook with emotion.

Maybe Sadie should be here with her. I hated seeing Winter like that. She reminded me of my mom outside of the surgery room when the doctors had been trying to save

Dad. That look of heartbreak and fear almost made me feel eight again.

No, she's needed in the fight out there. Egan looked skyward as a manticore raced away, retreating from the battle. *Her fae magic is doing the most damage, even more than the swords since she can shoot her magic from several yards away and hit the same targets all the others are having to get close to.*

I couldn't argue with his point. If she was the reason we were making such a big dent so quickly, removing her from the fight could give the manticores the upper hand, and who knew how many others could get hurt like Titan. *Does she at least know?*

I'm sure one of his pack members told her, Egan reassured me. *Several have taken a protective stance around the area.*

How don't I know that? I looked around for his people and noticed a few wolves had scattered. But it wasn't good that I hadn't been paying attention to this. I'd been more focused on my pain and emotions than the battle at hand. That was how people got hurt.

He took my hand, which was odd in beast form, and replied, *Because I flew over here when Winter was screaming for help. I saw his men come to assist, but the manticores attacked as they got close. It looked like it was a calculated move.*

Yeah, it did, which meant I needed to hand out the weapons. *We need to let the wolves focus on helping Titan while we take over their job. If they run out of weapons, we could lose the upper hand.*

You're right. He let go of my hand.

Titan cried out in pain as Egan and I walked past them

and grabbed a few swords lying several yards away from the iron pile.

Do not touch anything in the iron pile. Only the swords, Egan said as he gathered some of them. *They'll drain your power and slow down your healing.*

Good to know. *Got it.*

With our strange dragon hands, we couldn't carry too many swords, but we made it work. I wound up carrying at least twenty by holding them in my arms instead of in my hands. The sharp blades didn't cut into my scales.

Egan examined me, looking for any signs of discomfort. *Are you hurting?*

Even if I had been, it wouldn't have dissuaded me from what we had to do. *No more than when I'm standing, and the pain is receding.*

Good. Your dragon is working overtime. Egan's jaw relaxed marginally.

We ran toward the fighting, and I foolishly looked at Titan one last time before leaving. The stinger was out, but his eyeball had come with it. Veins hung limply from the end, and a large hollow hole remained where his eye had been.

Even with shifter healing, there was no way he could come back from that. We could only hope and pray that they figured out a way to prevent the poison from spreading.

"We need to scrape the inside to make sure we got all the poison out." Long leaned over Titan again.

As we walked through the trees that blocked Titan, the alpha screamed in agony.

A younger man who was swinging a knife at a manticore's mouth turned his head toward the alpha, missing his mark. Before he could regain control of the weapon, the manticore lunged and ate him whole.

That was at least two deaths I'd seen done in this same method. Blood didn't even dribble down the creature's mouth. He'd eaten him entirely.

"No!" Torak screamed and carelessly ran at the creature. He held the sword over his head, hatred reflected in his usually warm green eyes.

Draco landed with a roar and engulfed the creature in flames.

The manticore stumbled forward from the force of the fire and tried to escape the flames. Each step it took, the dragon countered, keeping the flow constant.

Something blurred, and Cassius appeared, knocking down the alpha heir moments before he was about to run into the fire.

Athan appeared beside me and held out his hand. "I need one before Torak does something else stupid."

I quickly moved so he could reach a sword, hoping I wasn't making a bad decision. I didn't want him to get hurt either, even if he had tried to make Mom into a snack. In the past few weeks, I'd realized how hard he was trying and how much he struggled. He still apologized daily over what had almost happened to her.

Athan grabbed the sword, knowing how to hold it, and spun toward the manticore. The dragon halted the flames, and the vampire slammed the sword into its open mouth.

The creature sputtered, and its chest stopped moving.

"Look, they're all flying away!" a guy yelled from several feet away.

My attention turned to the sky. At least ten manticores were flying in the same direction as the other one had.

I wasn't sure if I should be relieved or concerned. If they returned to Fae, they would give the others more information about us, despite our location no longer being secret.

Mom flashed back into my brain. I needed to check on her. She was the only one who could've provided the location. I'd talked to her yesterday, so something must have happened between yesterday morning and now.

"Are we sure they're all gone?" an older shifter asked, glancing around the trees. So many damn manticores littered the ground that clean-up would be gruesome, especially with how huge these creatures were.

"They're gone over here too," someone said from a section of the woods we couldn't see.

One by one, the groups confirmed what we had hoped for. They had left ... for now.

Sadie and her pack ran right by us, rushing to get to Titan. Titan released another blood-curdling scream, and my blood ran cold.

The silence that followed seemed eerier. I'd held on to the hope that his screaming meant he was still alive. But what did the quiet mean? There were no cries of remorse, so maybe they were done doing God knew what to him.

Katherine walked into view and looked at Cassius, the wolf shifters, and the dragons. She said, as her eyes locked on Draco, "There was a bear. I think he led them to us. We need to find him. Now."

I had never seen this side of Katherine, but surprisingly, it suited her. Some thought the loudmouths and those who spoke their opinions were strong. And they were. But people didn't realize the strength it took to remain quiet ... reserved. Sometimes, there was more power in silence. People didn't understand the power that a quiet person commanded when they spoke with authority. Everyone stopped and listened.

And that's exactly what happened. No one questioned her; everyone left to obey.

I linked with Egan. *Let's take to the sky.*

Egan stepped toward me. *Can you?*

I moved my wings, and the excruciating pain was gone. There was still an ache, but I could handle flying long enough to search for the bear. *I'm good. If it gets to be too much, I'll come back.*

He nodded. *We can cover more ground in the air while the shifters and vampires track on land.*

We took to the sky as several other dragons followed our lead. Over half stayed back, and I watched as they blew their flames on the manticores.

They're cleaning up the bodies. Egan flew next to me, but his focus was on scouring the ground. *The easiest way to deal with the bodies is to burn them. We don't need humans stumbling upon their bodies or bones.*

Even though this was private land, the occasional human would stumble through while out on a hike. According to Cassius, it rarely happened. It was one reason they kept supernatural behavior to the hours after dark and close to home.

Attacking manticores was probably at the top of the list, but none of us had control over that.

We hung close to the trees, keeping our eyes and ears open for the bear or anyone that didn't need to see us.

One day, I hoped I could enjoy flying with the thunder. But like now, the only other time I'd flown with the thunder had been while fleeing the cave and desperate to get here. I had yet to experience a flight for enjoyment or relaxation with everyone.

"Over here!" Paul shouted from below.

I turned to the left, flying lower to look for him.

Egan flew right beside me as Draco flanked me on my left. Those two were already in protective mode, but I couldn't complain. They hadn't hovered during the battle despite us being outnumbered.

I'd expected to find the grizzly bear but, instead, found a naked man hiding at the top of a tree.

The guy had rich, dark brown hair and a long beard that turned more chocolate at the edges. His skin was a dark olive, proof that he spent a lot of time outdoors. His eyes were milk chocolate, and that was where I stopped looking. I didn't need or want to see his dangly bits.

Draco swooped down to the tree and used his back talons to latch on to the man's arms. The guy reached up, trying to dig his fingers into Draco's scales and escape the dragon's grip.

But nothing happened.

It probably felt like a tickle to Draco.

The bear shifter must not have been around dragons before, but if that was the case, how the hell was he working with the fae dragons?

Unfortunately, when Draco flew up, I got an eyeful of the guy's family jewels. I closed my eyes and spun away. When I opened my eyes, Draco flew underneath me, coming in front. I saw the guy's entire naked ass before I could shut my eyes again. I wasn't sure which view was worse, but the backside was a whole lot hairier.

Egan flew next to me. *Well, that was easier than I expected.*

What was he thinking? The bear shifter had been in the perfect position for Draco to grab and fly off with.

He chuckled. *Probably thought he could fight the vampires off if they found him, and the wolf shifters couldn't climb up the tree. Bears are good climbers, so he probably just wanted to get off the ground.*

He could have at least brought some clothes to change into. I'd have nightmares over what I'd seen.

I'm just happy you wanted him to be clothed. Egan winked. *Maybe I can give you a better visual when we get home?*

I purred at the promise. *Maybe.*

We all hurried back to the mansion, and it wasn't long before we were landing.

Once the bear shifter was back on the ground, the back door that led to the kitchen opened, and Torak came marching out.

He shoved the bear shifter hard in the chest, and the man fell on his bare ass. The alpha heir growled, "I'm going to kill you."

CHAPTER NINETEEN

The raw rage in Torak's voice was justified. I wanted to hurt the asshole too, but we needed answers first.

The back door opened with Cassius, Ladon, and Katherine running outside.

"Don't hurt him yet," Cassius said as he touched Torak's shoulders.

"Oh my God." Katherine's eyes widened when she saw the naked bear shifter. She held up clothes and nodded to Ladon. "Thank God we brought extra clothes."

She and I were thinking similarly. I'd seen more than enough of that guy, and I didn't even know his name.

Ladon pursed his lips, making the lines etched in his face more prominent. "Everyone outside of Egan and Jade should go help the others burn the manticores' bodies. Your clothes will be here when you get back. Egan and Jade, take what is yours and shift back so we can talk."

They placed the clothes on the ground. Egan and I picked up ours, and we ran into the woods to shift into human form while the other dragons headed back to help with the dead bodies.

"Put these sweatpants on," Cassius told the bear shifter.

I heard shuffling from that area, and then a deep voice replied, "There. Who would've thought a group of supernaturals would be that uncomfortable around nudity?"

Katherine cleared her throat. "We're more conservative."

"Sounds like where I'm from." The bear shifter chuckled. "I'd think people outside of Shadow City would be more accepting. Or that's what I was told growing up."

What's Shadow City? Yet another place I hadn't heard of.

Egan put the light gray shirt on. *Never heard of it.*

"So you're from Shadow City." Cassius clicked his tongue. "Interesting."

"What's that place?" Ladon asked.

"A supernatural city that was established a long time ago," Cassius replied. "I actually know someone from there."

Shifting back to human was harder than before due to my injury, but once I was back on two legs, the pain receded again.

After I'd zipped my jeans, Egan and I rejoined the others.

Torak's clenched jaw twitched from the strain. His hands were fisted at his sides as he glared at the bear shifter, who was now covered from his waist down.

Donovan and the others were huge, but the bear shifter was bigger than them. He wasn't as large as the dragon men but was stout. His muscular chest was pronounced even under the mass of hair covering it.

I hurried over to Torak and placed a hand on his shoulder to pull his attention away from the bear. Considering the way he was acting, I feared the worst. "How's Titan?"

Please don't say dead.

"He's alive but lost his right eye." His words were thick with emotion as his chest heaved with each breath. "Ollie took a dragon to a witch he knew to see if she can help him."

"Trixie?" Egan asked, standing in front of the bear.

"Yes, that was the name." Landon nodded. "Son, how do you want to proceed?"

"You're asking me?" Egan glanced over his shoulder and lifted a brow. "Isn't that your call?"

Ladon fidgeted. "No, it's not."

I was surprised that he was asking Egan to decide. He'd done this a few times, encouraging Egan to lead. I'd thought it was because he wanted to help transition him into the mentality of a leader, but maybe there was more to it than that. *We need to focus on the bear shifter. We can talk to your dad later.*

Egan's glowing eyes flicked to mine. *You're right.* He patted Draco's scaled arm. "Draco, shift back to human form. We've got it from here."

Hesitating, Draco hissed at the bear shifter then grabbed his clothes from the ground and headed into the woods.

The bear had grown nervous with our group surrounding him.

"Here." Katherine handed me my cell phone. "I thought you might want this."

For the first time ever, I had the urge to kiss a girl. She'd gone out of her way to get my phone so I could check on my mother, and it spoke volumes about her. "Thank you."

I typed a message out on Messenger to Mom and

pressed send. I stared at the screen, wishing those three dots indicating she was responding would pop up.

My mate didn't take any time getting to the point. "Who are you working for?"

The bear shifter sneered. "Like I would tell—"

Torak punched him in the nose, and the bone cracked loudly.

"What the—" The bear shifter pinched the bridge of his nose as blood poured down his mouth and chin onto his chest.

"Answer the question or I'll punch your face again," Torak spat, his hand fisted and ready to strike.

"Look." The shirtless man raised his free hand. "I'm not here to cause problems."

I laughed. I couldn't help it. "Really? You're going to lead with that?"

Something like respect appeared in the guy's eyes. "You've got a point, but this was nothing personal."

"Nothing personal?" Egan growled. "You attacked us. How is that not personal?"

Draco stepped back into the clearing and stood protectively beside Egan, staring the bear shifter down.

My phone buzzed, and I swiped the screen. I was relieved when I saw Mom's reply.

Hey. I'm fine. Is something wrong?

If they hadn't found our location from her, then how? That unsettled me. *Mom is okay and Vera is dead. I just don't understand how it is possible.*

If I hadn't seen the muscle in Egan's neck contract, I would have thought he hadn't heard me. But he finally responded, *We'll figure out how.*

My fear was that there was a spy in the camp, but I didn't see how it was possible. Egan's thunder was at risk, and the vampires and the packs were close and loyal. The alphas would've sensed an uprising, or I hoped so.

"Look, a friend told me that a woman was looking for a bear shifter that wanted some quick cash. I'd just escaped from jail and was desperate. I took the job, thinking it wouldn't be awful." The bear shifter shrugged. "She asked me to track down the wolf pack and lead some creatures to it. That's it. Once the job was done, she'd give me cash."

He kept saying "she," so my first thought was Mindy. Was she still working with the fae dragon king since we'd kicked her ass out? "Light blonde hair, tall, with honey eyes?"

You're thinking it's Mindy too? Egan rubbed his fingers together.

"No, not at all." The bear shifter shook his head, and the blood flow slowed from his nose. "Middle-aged woman with long caramel hair, very short, and light blue eyes that appeared cold. She was all human, which shocked me."

That description sounded so familiar. "Was her name Sarah?" My voice cracked.

"Wait. Yeah." The bear shifter looked at me. "That sounds right. We met outside Indianapolis, and she said dragons were causing problems and hanging around the pack that took down Tyler. Like Tyler would mean anything to me, but she thought it was a big deal."

"Tyler?" Katherine blinked. "A human mentioned Tyler? I'm going to get Sadie and Donovan." She headed back into the mansion on a mission.

"How does a human know about Tyler?" The shock on Egan's face would have been comical at any other time. He was usually good at keeping his emotions close. *Are you sure it's your aunt?*

It sounds like it is based on the city and description. But none of this made sense. Mom was okay, and Sarah was pretty much always home. If she knew about the supernatural world and was involved in it, wouldn't I have known?

"She mentioned that Tyler contacted her once she figured out her niece was a dragon's mate. She acted like he was a big deal. She got a phone call then became a lot less chatty." The bear shifter pursed his lips. "She said some wrongs needed to be righted and needed my services. She gave me a flannel shirt and jeans that had the wolf shifters' scents and told me it should be about thirty minutes east of Darmark. I picked up the scent after a couple of days. Those wolves like to run a lot. Honestly, she's a little crazy, but I needed the money."

But if Tyler had died before I'd made it to Kortright, how had she known I was a dragon's mate. The coincidence was too much, though. And unfortunately, Mom was the only one who knew the town closest to us.

Swiping my phone, I messaged her again. **Did you tell Sarah where we are?**

Her reply was immediate. **Of course not. Did something happen?**

If I knew Sarah, she'd be monitoring Mom's conversations. I had to be careful. I didn't need to alert her to anything and put her in danger. **Nope, just miss you.** *We need to get Mom. If Sarah is involved, we can't leave Mom there.*

As soon as we're done here, we'll go, Egan promised.

Sadie and her pack joined us outside with Katherine.

"I hear Tyler is involved." Roxy's nose wrinkled. "I shouldn't be surprised that he's still causing trouble beyond the grave."

"Why don't you go inside with Titan?" Sadie said, patting Torak's arm. "He was asking for you a minute ago."

Torak glared at the bear shifter for a few long seconds before responding, "Fine, but if you guys need me, just yell." He stalked toward the mansion.

"It looks like we missed some of the fun." Donovan gestured to the bear shifter's nose. "Has he said anything?"

We informed him of everything we'd learned.

"What do we do with him now?" Axel asked, gesturing to the bear shifter.

"Take him to the basement." Cassius gestured to the side of the house where there were stairs. "He won't be able to get out on his own. It's vampire-proof for when we find people who were just changed. I'll call the guy I know in Shadow City."

"Sounds good to me." Draco grabbed the bear shifter's arm and dragged him to the stairs.

Donovan ran ahead.

Sadie tensed, her eyes distant. "Rook and Naida are on their way. I informed them about the attack."

Two figures flickered into view, and the bodies took shape to reveal Rook and Naida. They were dressed in white, and Rook had a crown on his head.

"When you said they were on their way, you weren't kidding." Roxy sighed. "I still can't get used to that."

Sadie chuckled. "That's why I warned you. The few times I didn't, you almost peed yourself."

"Just because I shrieked doesn't mean I dribbled." Roxy lifted her chin. "I have a steel bladder."

"Sure you do, babe." Axel wrapped an arm around her waist.

"Every time I join you all, there is always interesting

commentary going on." Naida rolled her eyes. "Sometimes a 'hey' and general pleasantries are completely underrated."

Sadie's brows furrowed. "What's with the crown?"

Rook pulled at the collar of his white robe. "Things were getting out of control, so Murray and I agreed that was the best thing."

"But you didn't want that?" Sadie sounded upset.

"Don't worry, it's for appearances only." Rook rubbed his temples. "I'm the face of the monarchy, but Murray is handling all the affairs like normal. Something had to change to keep the peace in the fae realm, but things are still a little unsettled."

Roxy crossed her arms. "Meaning manticores coming to Earth to attack us."

"Yes, that's exactly what I mean." Rook rolled his shoulders. He obviously didn't like the royal attire. "The fae dragon *king* used Fae's divide to his advantage. He leveraged the location of the true dragon royal family on Earth to make promises to some of the more unfavorable creatures of our realm for their assistance."

"How many of these creatures are we talking about?" Cassius asked. "And do we have any idea of what we need to do?"

Donovan and Draco came back around the house and rejoined the circle.

"He's getting these creatures to attack us while he stays safe back in his realm." Assholes like him were the worst. He wanted whatever power he thought was rightfully his but wasn't willing to fight. "We need to make him come here. But what could make him want to leave to fight us himself?"

"The problem is we have no clue since we've been here for so long." Egan rubbed a hand down his face. "The dragons in Fae are essentially immortal. They live for thousands of years."

"That's true. The one in charge is the original brother who angered the fae gods and caused the split." Rook paced in front of me. "But he's getting older, and he's desperate to gain power. He only has one heir, so that should play to our advantage."

"Angered the fae gods?" I felt like I was always asking questions.

"Yes, they mind their own business, but the younger dragon brother tried starting a war like he's doing now, only in the fae realm. The fae gods punished them by taking away their fated mates, slowing their reproduction. When the older brother saw the destruction his brother was causing, he decided to leave, and the fae gods lifted the curse since they'd proved they cared more about Fae than the dragons that were staying behind." Naida's eyes turned a lighter teal as she told her realm's history. "They can only reproduce by the power of the land. Thus, the fae dragon king only has one heir."

"Which means the heir is our leverage." Egan inhaled sharply. "But we can't go into Fae."

"We need an ally willing to get them for us." Draco looked at Egan then Ladon.

"Is there someone you know who can help us?" Sadie grimaced. "I hate to ask, but Titan has lost an eye because of these attacks, and several pack members were eaten. We're all at risk."

"You have the strongest ally in Fae." Rook stepped to his daughter and brushed his fingers along her arm. "Your father, who so happens to be king."

"Look, I'm all about protecting Sadie and everyone here, but can we risk that?" Naida chewed on her bottom lip.

Grinning, Rook lifted a hand. "What is the one rule every creature in Fae must follow or suffer the consequences? The one law that has saved Sadie from our own kind."

"No one can attack a member of the royal family," Sadie answered.

"Exactly. We'll send guards to capture the dragon princess and bring her here," Rook said and hugged Sadie.

"Maybe we should write a note, making it clear it was us." We needed to make sure the asshole came here. "Add something to make his blood boil."

"I like the way you think." Draco nodded with approval.

"Of course, my guards will be here to help you fight too," Rook said confidently. "They will learn that the fae king backs the true dragon king and queen."

"I hate to do this, but Liz may be in danger." Egan took my hand and stared at the others. "We've got to go get her before Sarah realizes the attack didn't work."

Draco marched over to us. "I'm going with you two."

"Cassius, do you mind if we take your van?" Sadie asked the older vampire. "Donovan and I need to go too. A few extra hands would be helpful since we don't know what we're walking into."

"The keys are on the holder. Take what you need."

"Be careful," Ladon said as he hugged Egan then me. "I'll go write the note. You all go on so you can get back as soon as possible."

My phone buzzed again, and I glanced down to see a message from Mom.

Call me when you can.

CHAPTER TWENTY

We were about an hour away from Indianapolis, and my leg wouldn't quit bouncing. My back was significantly better since I'd sat pretty still, so that was a huge benefit.

The sun was setting, and I felt almost suffocated inside the van. I glanced at my phone again, but nothing else had come through from Mom.

As Egan drove, he reached over the center console, placing his warm hand on my thigh. He linked with me. *Everything is going to be okay.*

You can't know that, I snapped and immediately regretted it. He didn't deserve that. He was trying to comfort me. But it unsettled me that I hadn't heard back from Mom, especially after what we'd learned. Under normal circumstances, she'd have replied within an hour, so for four hours to have gone by made my skin crawl.

I sighed. *I'm sorry. I'm being an ass. It's just my aunt has known about us for God knows how long, and she orchestrated an attack meant to kill us. What if she hurt Mom?* I'd tried calling Mom when we'd left, like she asked, but it had gone straight to voicemail. She'd messaged shortly after saying she'd call me right back, but that hadn't happened.

Draco snored quietly in the back of the van. The faster Egan drove, the deeper he fell asleep. I had to admit, I was slightly jealous. If I could have knocked my ass out, everyone would have appreciated it. My nerves were on edge, and everyone around me felt it.

When the huge dragon had shoved himself past the middle row and into the back of the van, I'd thought it was rather odd. But he'd muttered something about needing rest before another attack and promptly lain down. He'd fallen asleep before we'd even pulled out of the mansion's driveway. I'd never been around someone who could fall asleep that quickly before.

"He better be glad Roxy didn't join us." Sadie sat in the middle row, right behind Egan, and she glanced at me as she gestured to Draco. "Because he'd never hear the end about his snoring."

That was an odd thing to say. "But he's not snoring that loud."

Donovan leaned over from behind me so I could see him. "Have you met Roxy? That girl lives on exaggerating truths and sarcasm. She'd make the rest of the world believe that Draco sounded like a foghorn on a peaceful night."

"Or a jet taking off in the middle of a forest," Egan suggested.

Both analogies sounded like something she would say.

"True, but she keeps things interesting," Sadie said in defense of her best friend. "And she's as loyal and steadfast as they come."

"I'm not arguing that." Donovan lifted a hand in surrender. "You know I love her like a sister, but facts are facts."

"Point taken. I'm surprised she didn't demand to come

with us." Egan glanced in the rearview mirror. "She normally goes wherever Sadie is and pitches a fit when she doesn't get her way."

"I asked her to stay back with Torak." Sadie tapped her fingers on her leg. "Someone needed to relieve some of the tension, and we needed them there for when Ollie and that witch came back."

Roxy thought the world of Sadie, so her staying behind made sense. If she knew that staying with Titan would make things easier on her and the rest of the pack, she wouldn't have thought twice about it.

"Don't forget the bear shifter in the basement." Donovan shook his head. "And here I thought all of our enemies and fighting were behind us and we could live a semi-normal life."

Egan frowned. "I'm sorry. This is my fault. This is all happening because of the dragons. I hate that I dragged you into it."

"Hey, that's not what I was getting at, man." Donovan's shoulders dropped. "Of course we're going to fight alongside you. You're family, and it's the right thing to do."

That statement resonated with me. They thought of each other as family, and more importantly, I did too. Sadie and the others were a pack, but if they needed us, I'd drop everything to be there for them. That was what families did. I liked to think I'd been so slow to come to this realization because I didn't grow up in a very supportive one.

In high school, I'd read that family could be formed beyond blood, and I thought the sentiment had been stupid ... until now.

My phone buzzed in my hands with a message from Mom.

With shaky hands, I opened Messenger.

I need you. Help.

I blinked at the message, hoping the words would somehow morph into something a lot less dire. But there they sat, and with each second, the words grew larger and more desperate.

Egan leaned over and read the message. "We're only a few minutes away." He pressed the gas, speeding past vehicles.

"What's going on?" Sadie asked tensely.

"I'm not sure." I forced my lungs to expand. Passing out wouldn't help anyone. "Mom just texted me that she needs our help. You'd think she'd tell me what kind of help she needs." Those words could mean so many different scenarios, but they all led back to the same thing—Sarah.

I chewed on my bottom lip as I looked out my window. "Maybe I should shift and fly over there." I already knew what they would say, but I was desperate to get to Mom.

"Babe, we're getting there as fast as we can, but the sun isn't completely down, and this is a busy city." Regret flowed through our bond. "And that neighborhood isn't exactly remote. We can't risk revealing the supernatural world to humans. It would only put a bigger target on our backs. Besides, we need to be careful that we aren't walking into a trap."

Every word he said was true, but they still irritated me. The thought of something happening to Mom plagued me. I couldn't live with myself if she died when I could've gotten there faster to help her. But if I acted rashly, I would put Egan and the others in danger, and I wasn't willing to live with that burden either. I was damned if I did and damned if I didn't.

"Why don't you try calling her?" Sadie suggested. "If she answers, you could get an idea of what's going on there."

What did I have to lose? At the worst, she wouldn't answer, and my situation wouldn't change.

What the hell.

I pressed the call button, and the line rang. After the fourth ring, my finger hovered over the red button, ready to disconnect, but right before I was about to press it, the other end picked up.

"Hello?" Mom sounded scared. "Jade?"

"Is everything okay?" There was no time for pleasantries.

A soft sob filled the line. "I ... I can't find Sarah."

"What do you mean you can't find Sarah?" I tried to remain calm, but if Sarah had disappeared, it wouldn't be a bad thing. Maybe she'd run away with some supernaturals, leaving Mom behind. In a way, that would be a blessing. Mom could live without the supernatural influence and Sarah's controlling ways.

"She was acting strange all morning. Almost cagey." A door shut on the other end. "And then she got a phone call about an hour ago and started freaking out. She told me to pack some things. Then about ten minutes ago, someone knocked on our door. She yelled at me to go to my room and stay put. I heard her let them in, and they headed out the back, near the window of my room."

I wondered if the phone call had been about the attack near the mansion. Could someone already know we hadn't gotten hurt? Several manticores had flown away. They must have returned to Fae. "Do you hear them talking?"

"No, it's been silent for the past few minutes. I heard Sarah shriek, but that was it." The floor creaked under her weight. "I saw the guy run away. He had oddly colorful hair, but Sarah wasn't with him."

"Oddly colorful hair?" The only creatures that looked human and had colorful hair were fae.

"It was a vibrant yellow-green color like nothing I'd ever seen before." Mom inhaled shakily. "The color seemed to glow, and so did his eyes. They were the same color."

"Fae," Sadie whispered with disgust. "A fae is helping them. I'm going to tell Dad."

Tell Liz to stay where she is. Egan linked. *She doesn't need to stumble on something and get hurt. We're close by.*

For once, I welcomed his bossy side. I was so torn about what to say or do that my brain felt like it was spinning in place. "Stay put. We're less than ten minutes out."

She exhaled in relief. "You're that close?"

"We knew something was off this morning, but I'll explain more later." I needed her to remain calm. "Just hang tight."

"Okay. Call me when you pull into the neighborhood?"

"Will do." I hung up my phone right as Sadie's rang.

"Who's that?" Donovan asked.

Sadie answered the phone and glanced at her mate. "Torak, is everything okay?"

With my supernatural hearing, I could make out every word on the other end.

"No. Something happened at Liz's house." Torak sounded more like himself. "The pack alpha has been trying to call for the last thirty minutes, but Dad dropped his phone when the ... uh ... incident occurred. A dragon heard the phone ring and brought it here."

That must have been when the fae had shown up.

"What did they say?" Sadie asked.

Torak cleared his throat. "He killed two of the three wolves standing guard. The third one barely got away and linked his alpha to inform him of what had gone down.

There are more shifters at the house now for backup, but it looks like the fae is gone. They're going to approach the house."

"No, tell them to wait until we get there." The last thing we needed was more supernaturals showing up and Mom thinking she was under attack. "Tell them we're five minutes out and to wait."

"Okay. Call us when you're heading back. I'll call the alpha now." Torak hung up.

Egan got off the interstate, and five minutes later, we were pulling into the neighborhood. We coasted down the street, hoping not to alarm any neighbors more than they might already be.

I typed Mom a message letting her know we would be there in a minute. I didn't want to risk calling her.

"Draco." Sadie turned toward him. "We're here, and something has gone down."

"Yeah, I heard." Draco sat up and yawned. "You all were jabbering, so I listened while resting my eyes."

The less we had to tell him, the more efficient we'd be.

"It's the house on the right at the end of the street." I pointed at the two-story white house. There was a wooden porch just large enough to protect you from the rain if you were standing right at the door. There were two double-pane windows on both sides of the front door.

Egan pulled into the driveway, and I leaped out of the car.

A few men ran over from a few houses down. Their olive complexion and thick, musky smell informed me they were wolf shifters.

Egan caught up to me and looked at the men. "Did you notice anything alarming?"

"There's nothing around," the older one said as he

approached. His gaze flicked to a few neighbors down the road. "But you need to go check out the back." He avoided our gazes. "It's bad."

Yeah, I was done waiting. I raced to the front door and turned the doorknob, expecting it to be locked, but the door flung open.

"Mom!" I rushed into the foyer that led to the living room and to the staircase.

"Jade!" Mom cried, and her footsteps pounded from her room toward us. "I ... I think something is wrong. A few minutes ago, I saw three strange men in our backyard."

Ugh, Torak must not have caught the shifters in time, but at least they weren't in animal form. "No, they were the wolf shifters that have been keeping an eye on you two." I was being nice by including Sarah in that, but in a way, it was true. If Sarah got hurt, that would put Mom at risk. And unfortunately, that had happened.

Her mouth dropped, and her head tilted. "They were still keeping an eye on us?"

The urge to smack her upside the head almost overwhelmed me.

Almost.

Egan stepped up beside me, so huge his body brushed against my side. "Of course. They were going to watch you until the whole dragon thing had settled."

"I ..." Mom seemed flabbergasted. "I didn't realize."

"It's fine." She needed to focus. "What happened?"

"I told you everything on the phone." Mom gestured to the back door. "I can't see her out there, but she hasn't come back inside."

From what the guys had said, I figured Sarah had been injured in the backyard. There was no telling what we would find. "Okay, stay right here. We'll go check it out."

"I'm going with you." Mom crossed her arms, lifting her chin. "She's my sister, and I need to go look for her with you."

Out of all of the times for her to decide to be strong, it would be now, when I had no clue what we might find outside. I'd opened my mouth to tell her no when Egan linked with me.

Babe, let her be part of this. She wants to be, and she's an adult. She at least waited on us.

He was right. Next time, she might not be willing. "Fine, but stay behind us."

She nodded. "Okay."

Egan took the lead, heading where Mom had gestured. A sweet floral smell trailed in the same direction.

We walked through the small mint living room, where a single brown leather couch sat against the wall, and toward the flaky white door. Egan opened it, and the stench of rust overwhelmed me.

My stomach hadn't been prepared to smell blood again today. It roiled as I found Sarah. She lay close to the side of the house, next to the white plastic chairs. Blood pooled under her body, and her caramel hair was fanned around her head.

If it hadn't been for the faint heartbeat and the way her cruel eyes found me, I would have thought she was dead. One hand clutched her stomach, but she had enough energy to lift her other one, despite it shaking. She said, her voice deep and filled with disgust, "You."

CHAPTER TWENTY-ONE

If I'd ever questioned how my aunt felt about me, I no longer did. Her face twisted, and she sneered. Pure hatred filled her ice-cold eyes, turning them a shade darker to sky blue. "You've ruined everything."

Mom took a hurried step toward the door to follow me out, but Sadie walked out the back door and told her, "Wait here for a second. The guys are checking the area one more time for threats."

"But ..." Mom hesitated.

"Just a few minutes," Donovan reassured her, stepping up next to Sadie. "You are human, so we need to make sure we don't have to protect both you and your sister, especially while she's injured."

The smell of their lie hit me hard, but I appreciated what they were doing. I didn't want Mom to see Sarah like this.

After a long sigh, Mom said, "Okay, but once it's clear, I need to get out there."

Not needing to worry about Mom, I dropped to my knees next to Sarah. "Where are you hurt?"

She jerked away. "You're the reason this happened."

Somehow, that stung even more. She was bleeding out, yet she was still so revolted by me that she didn't want me to touch her.

Egan growled as he placed a hand on my shoulder and glared at her. "How is she to blame?"

The gate to the privacy fence opened on the other side of the house, and Draco stepped around the house, his eyes scanning the scene, stopping on Sarah for a few seconds before he glanced at Egan. Draco shook his head slightly.

The message was clear.

Sarah wouldn't survive.

"Because she was supposed to be my ticket to power." Her voice grew louder until she was almost yelling. She hadn't noticed the other man who had entered the yard since she was focused on me. "I sacrificed everything for you."

My hurt morphed into anger. She'd sacrificed for me? She had to be living in an alternate reality.

I refused to let that be the way her story ended even if only in her mind. I jerked to my feet, enraged. "By controlling my every move after Dad died? Or beating me when Mom wasn't looking?"

"Why do you think your dad died in the first place?" she shouted, blood mixing with her spit. "When your mom told me about the strange people you met on the beach and how the little boy acted around you, I knew exactly what they were and what you were to them."

The most alarming fact was how long she'd known about Egan and me. "How the hell could you've known that?"

"Because I've known about the supernatural world since I was a little girl."

Her words stunned me. Obviously, she knew about the supernatural world, but for that long? That couldn't be possible. Humans were forbidden to know.

She chuckled. "Your expression is almost comical. You're so clueless and gullible, just like your mother. Thankfully, you took after her instead of your dad." Her face hardened, the smile morphing into a scowl. "That's why he had to go."

She was throwing out so much information that my brain protested. My natural inclination was to go numb, but I couldn't afford to do that. This was our only chance to get whatever information we could out of my aunt, so I couldn't shut down.

My dragon surged forward, easing some of my angst to help me focus. I didn't know which piece of information to latch on to. Where did I even begin? I wasn't sure how much time she had left, so I needed answers to the most important questions first, but hell, I couldn't tell which one I should address first.

"No." Mom stumbled outside and stood beside me. Her body shook, and her face was lined with confusion. "You wouldn't hurt Jeff. You wouldn't do that to me."

"Mom, why don't you go back inside?" She didn't need to hear this. I'd rather she mourn the death of a sister than struggle with the fact she hadn't known Sarah at all. "Go wait in the van for us. We won't be long."

"But ..." Mom glanced at me and then Sarah.

"Yes, be a good little robot, and do what you're told," Sarah mocked. "Lord forbid you have to listen or deal with anything unpleasant."

"I ... I can't leave." She needed answers like me. "Not until she tells me she didn't hurt Jeff." She held out a shaky hand and begged, "Please, just tell me that."

Sarah's hands were slick from the blood pouring out of her wound. "I had to kill him."

Mom gasped and wrapped her arms around her body. "You caused the car wreck?"

"I planned it." Sarah shrugged then winced from the pain. "When you called me on the way to the airport after you left the beach, and told me about the strange occurrence, I had time to set things up for him to die the next morning on his way to work when he planned to turn in his notice."

Draco stepped closer but stayed several feet back. He was watching the scene, keeping his focus on Sarah like she was still a threat.

But how could she be with the state she was in? The only potent thing she still harbored was raw hate for herself and those around her.

"You killed her husband and my mate's father because of me?" Egan rasped. "Why was finding a dragon that important?"

"I stalked Tyler and pinpointed him to a city. I ran into him at a restaurant that a local pack owned, and he was impressed with my ambition even though I was human. And he promised me power." Her eyes lightened with a wistful glow. "Promised that I would rule his kingdom next to him. Of course, he'd have to turn me into a wolf once I proved my worth by locating a dragon."

She had lost her mind. And maybe I had, too. My body felt numb to touch and emotion. "How did you even find out about this world?"

"I stumbled upon it one night years ago." She looked at the darkening sky. "I watched a vampire drain the life out of someone. It was amazing to watch. They held no remorse and enjoyed the act so much. I wanted to feel something like that. To dominate others and control their destiny."

This woman was so much worse than I'd realized. There was no telling what kind of monstrous acts she had committed to get to this point. Bad enough for the fae dragon king to want her dead after failing.

"So, I began researching and stumbled upon all these websites in my twenties." She coughed several times. Sweat beaded on her paling skin.

She knew she was dying. That was why she was telling us all of this. She wanted someone to know her story, her fall from grace, even though she might not see it that way.

For so long, I'd wanted to know why she acted the way she did, but now I was scared for her to continue. Yet, if we left before I heard it all, I would regret it.

I needed to hear her reasoning for everything she'd done.

It was strange watching Mom stand over Sarah as she bled out. Mom's chest heaved, the only sign she was struggling as she waited to hear everything just like me.

"Oh, God," Sarah groaned and wiped her mouth with her arm. Blood streaked across her skin. "This hurts so damn bad."

If she thought she'd get sympathy, she was clearly mistaken.

Egan cleared his throat. "So you learned about Tyler, then? I'm assuming you stumbled upon articles about him?"

"Yes, his family was revered." Sarah grinned. "And most importantly, feared. But after our first run-in, he refused to meet with me again. That was until my dear sister called to tell me about these tall, beautiful people who sounded like they were from another world. Liz babbled on about your family's mannerisms, but the biggest clues that narrowed my suspicions were the glowing eyes and a child so strong he could easily pull a girl from the water. Add in the facts that he catered to her and talked about how amazing it was to fly. I put it all together."

"I forgot all about that." Mom blew out a breath as she looked at Egan. "But you did. Jeff stayed close while you two were playing in the sand where the waves had crashed over you. You were telling Jade all about visiting another group of your kind that you'd never met before and how flying was amazing. I always thought you meant family and that you'd been in an airplane. But I remember it made Jeff so uncomfortable he wanted to go." Mom shuddered. "Your parents tried to explain that there was a storm while you were on the plane, but it didn't really make sense."

Egan ran a hand through his hair, and his shoulders deflated. "Dad jerked me aside and told me about the human world and how you would be at risk for knowing anything about us. He explained there was no way to protect you and warned me to be more cautious. He hadn't expected that I'd click with a human, so they hadn't considered reminding me, but the damage was done."

Remorse slammed into me through our bond as Egan linked with me. *I caused all this. I'd recently shifted and was so thrilled with my first flight and meeting others of my race that I didn't even think about not sharing it with you that day. But I was careless, and you've suffered and lost so much because of it.*

You did not cause this. My anger spread through my body, making my blood boil. Sarah would not make us doubt ourselves or manipulate us any longer. I was so damn tired of it. My dragon brushed against my mind, lending me some of her strength. *This was all Sarah's fault. Her choices. Her decisions. You were a child and did nothing wrong.*

I clenched my hands as I stood to look down my nose at her. How dare she try to make anyone feel accountable for her actions. "You used that to get Tyler to take you seriously and promise you the world. But how does the fae dragon king come into this?" That was the piece I was missing.

Sarah took in a ragged breath, her skin turning white. "Tyler was working with him. That's how he captured the fae king heir that he was holding hostage. Tyler's daughter —" Sarah paused and held a shaky finger at Sadie. "—failed him by not securing the dragon. Then the dragon helped take him down. But I had something Tyler didn't and was able to leverage it upon his death." She smiled. "I had you— the very weapon to take down a dragon and force them to disclose the location of the royal family. Little did I know you were mated to the prince himself." Malice dripped from her words. "You. Like you deserve to be with someone like that. You're too weak and pathetic."

A low growl rattled Egan's chest, but I touched his arm and said, *I need to stand up to her. I have to do this for myself.*

Okay, but if she tries anything, I'll kill her. His eyes glowed liquid gold with promise.

He always had my back, and it gave me the strength to face my demon in the face. Straightening my shoulders, I lifted a brow and scoffed, "Yet I'm not the one who's on the ground, bleeding to death. In fact, my mate, my friends, and I kicked the manticores' asses, which is probably why you're here dying."

She laughed, her teeth tinged with blood. Crimson leaked from the corners of her mouth. "Maybe I underestimated you, but it doesn't matter now. There's no way you'll survive. They all know where you are, and they won't stop until you're dead. I'll die peacefully knowing that."

Mom screamed and kicked Sarah in the jaw. My aunt's head jerked back from the force then flopped to the side.

"You killed him and hurt my daughter repeatedly," Mom screeched and kicked Sarah in the side. My aunt curled into the fetal position and groaned with the intense pain.

We have to stop Liz before she does something she'll regret. Egan stepped in front of me and grabbed Mom by the waist. He pulled her away from Sarah, and Mom fought against him, trying to attack her dying sister.

"I trusted you!" Mom screamed as tears rolled down her cheeks, contrasting with her red face. "And you did everything possible to hurt me and my family." Mom lurched desperately against Egan's hold again to get back to her. "How could you!"

I almost wanted to tell Egan to let her go, but I couldn't let Mom live with the regret.

"Jade," Sadie said gently as she stepped behind me. She placed a hand on my arm, diverting my attention to her. "Egan needs help calming your mother down."

That snapped me out of my shock, and I shook my head as the gravity of the situation crashed over me like torrential waves. Thank God my mate had stepped in because, if he hadn't, Mom would've finished the job of killing Sarah. He was right; she wouldn't have been able to live with herself once her sense of betrayal had simmered down.

"She's not worth it." In reality, I wanted my aunt to die slowly and painfully. Killing her quickly was too merciful for everything she'd inflicted on the world. I wasn't sure what kind of person that made me, but I'd examine it on the ride back to the mansion.

Mom continued her attempt to break free to attack Sarah.

She must not have heard me. She was only focused on hurting her sister. "Mom," I said loudly and pivoted to block Sarah from her view. "You need to calm down. This is what she wants."

"What?" Mom blinked and inhaled sharply. "She wants this? Why?"

"Don't you see?" I cupped her cheeks while keeping my voice calm. "She thrives on anger and pain. She wants to hurt us. Don't let her win."

Mom's bottom lip quivered, and she took faint breaths through her mouth. "You're right." She ran her fingers through her dark hair. "She's always been like this. Why didn't I see it before? You tried to tell me."

"Because you wanted to see the good in your sister." There was nothing wrong with that. In a way, I wished I could be more like Mom. Maybe I could be after all this shit was behind me. I was so tired of thinking the worst of people. Egan and his friends and family had taught me that not everyone out there was bad. In fact, most of them were good. "You need to tell her goodbye and head to the car. Don't do something you'll regret."

Realization flashed in her eyes. "She's going to die."

I nodded, not strong enough to say the words out loud.

"Okay." Mom looked over her shoulder at Egan. "You can release me. I'm good now."

Egan arched an eyebrow. *Should I let her go?*

Yeah, I guess we should give her that. It warmed my heart that he was allowing me to make this decision. He trusted me. *But stay close in case this is a bad call.*

He released his hold on her, and Mom stepped around me to stare at her sister. "I grew up idolizing you and didn't listen to Jeff or Jade when they warned me about you. I loved you and stood up for you. But I'm done lying to myself. I only hope I can earn Jade's forgiveness and that you burn in Hell." Mom spun on her heel and marched into the house. Egan and I watched her leave.

"Do you think I'm going out like this?" Sarah yelled. "If I'm going to Hell, I'm taking Jade with me."

"Watch out!" Draco yelled.

CHAPTER TWENTY-TWO

I spun around as Sarah lunged at me with a small knife in her hand. The faint glow of the sun glinted off the tip, but that wasn't what concerned me. Sarah's face set with grim determination as she used the last of her strength to strike at me.

People claimed that near-death experiences slowed time down, but that wasn't my truth. Everything accelerated like a fast-forwarding movie. All the actions blurred and didn't make any sense.

She aimed right at my heart, and Egan had been focused on Mom like I'd been, so he couldn't react in time.

My dragon took control, and I willingly submitted. Instead of shifting, I caught her wrist inches from my chest, ignoring my back screaming from my injury, and kicked her in her stomach. She released her hold and crumpled. The knife plopped to the ground.

She landed hard on the grass as blood gushed from the wound I'd made worse.

Draco stopped a few feet from me with a deep scowl. His nostrils flared in anger, but I wasn't sure why.

Hands pulled me in the opposite direction. Egan held me tight and rubbed my back where the manticore tail had wounded me. *I thought she was going to hurt you, and neither Draco nor I could get to you in time.*

Hey, it's fine. I kissed his cheek and stepped from his arms. *You have to remember I do have some training and a dragon that can come to my aid.*

He sighed. *You're right, but that doesn't make seeing you in danger any easier.*

I couldn't disagree there, but I had a sorry aunt to contend with.

She rolled her head slowly toward me. Her skin was almost white, and her heartbeat was very faint. "You won't win."

"Maybe." Who really knew? We had a lot to overcome to even get the fae dragon king to come here. "But you won't be the one to kill me. You never became powerful, and you never dominated me. You were just a pawn. I believe that makes you the dense and stupid one."

"I—" She coughed, blood pouring out of her mouth and down her cheeks. "—was not."

I squatted next to her, but for once, I didn't feel anger. I felt pity. Her entire life, she'd hated herself and spewed it everywhere. "If Tyler had bitten you, you would've died." I was being cruel, but maybe she'd finally see things for the way they were. "Over ninety-nine percent of people don't survive a bite, and the one percent who do have severe disabilities. You were never going to be queen or powerful. You got played."

Her eyes widened as the realization settled over her. Something like regret reflected back at me. She blinked as her breathing slowed. "Tell Liz ..." Her heart sputtered, and she sucked in one last breath. "Sorry."

Glassiness set in her eyes, and her body stopped moving even with her blood still pooling underneath her. Sarah had died, and it infuriated me that she'd used her last bit of strength to talk about Mom. Obviously, a piece of her had cared about her sister, but her greed and hunger for power had won until her last breath.

A heaviness weighed on me that I didn't understand. I'd hoped to feel relief. "We need to call 911."

A wolf shifter stepped from the house and asked, "Do we really want to bring that kind of attention here?"

"This is a neighborhood. If we don't, it'll bring more attention." For some reason, my feet were glued in place. I couldn't look away from Sarah.

Donovan joined us on the back porch. "She's right. I was human long enough to know that if someone finds her dead out here with no call in, reporters will dig even deeper."

"Are you three okay handling it so we can get back to the others?" Egan asked. He took my hand, pulling me toward him and away from my aunt. "There's a lot going on back at the pack house."

"Yeah, go." The shifter pulled out his phone. "We can handle it. Torak mentioned that Titan lost an eye in a fae attack."

"We appreciate everything you did." Donovan patted the shifter on the arm. "If you ever need anything, you know how to get a hold of us."

"We'll take you up on that." The shifter glanced at me. "It's best she gets out of here. Sadie took the other lady out to the van."

Egan stepped toward the door, but I stopped him. I faced the shifter, my voice thick with emotion as I said, "Thank you for protecting my mother."

He averted his gaze. "I'm sorry we couldn't do more."

"You did more than enough." They didn't have to keep an eye on my family. "You lost two of your own. Thank you."

The guy smiled. "Just know when we call in the favor, it'll be to both of you, not just Titan."

Egan bowed his head. "And we'll gladly return the favor."

Donovan, Egan, and I entered the house with Draco on our tail. I could hear the shifter calling in the accident as we walked out the door.

The other two shifters were out front, keeping watch. They'd propped themselves on the side of the house, appearing casual to any passing humans. But with the help of my dragon, I noticed their jaws clenching and the way their eyes scanned the area for threats.

Mom paced in front of the van, wringing her hands together. Her hair fell limply over her shoulder as she swayed with each step.

Sadie turned toward us, her mouth pressed into a line. A stark contrast to her normal friendly demeanor. "Are you ready?"

The question sounded innocent, but the real question was whether Sarah had died yet. Everyone knew it, even Mom because she stopped in her tracks and stared at me.

"Yes, it's time to go." There was no time to sugarcoat things for her. Mom needed to stand on her own two feet. She had no one else to rely on, especially if she didn't want to stay in our supernatural world. I met her gaze. "Where should we take you?"

Her eyes were bloodshot from all the crying, and she inhaled another shaky breath. "Can I stay with you for a few days?"

"Of course you can." Sadie smiled. "You can stay with Mom and Titan like before since you probably don't want to stay with us at the mansion."

"Sounds good." Mom nodded and opened the passenger back door to get into the van.

Egan asked, "Do you want to grab some things before we go?"

I already knew her answer.

She paused. "Actually, I do." She ran back to the house.

Everything told me to follow her, but I couldn't move. I didn't want to go back inside again. That chapter of my life had been pure hell, and this incident with Sarah had solidified that I'd never step foot inside again.

"I'll go with her." Egan kissed my cheek and went after Mom.

Thank you. That man proved over and over he'd do anything for me. I wasn't sure how I'd gotten so damn lucky.

He looked over his shoulder at me, his eyes smoldering. *Of course. I love you.*

"Hey, are you okay?" Sadie winced. "Well, obviously not, but can I do anything for you?"

"You and Donovan being here is more than enough. And thank you for taking Mom out here. I'm so glad she didn't see her sister like that." Sarah's pale, bloody face was seared into my memory.

Draco popped his knuckles. "Jade, I'm so sorry."

"What?" I faced him, completely confused by his comment. "Why?"

"I didn't protect you back there." His words were strained. "If you hadn't reacted the way you did, you'd be dead, and it was all my fault."

"You tried to get to me." I'd always known that Draco took his guarding job seriously, but he was putting way too much pressure on himself. "Egan couldn't even get to me."

"Egan shouldn't have been in the position to try." Draco's hands fisted at his sides. "That's the whole point. I failed you both."

"No, you didn't." He didn't need to beat himself up. "You were standing guard. You expected the threat to come from either inside or around the house. We all thought that. No one expected a dying woman to use her last bit of energy to try to kill me." Actually, now that I'd said that out loud, that didn't surprise me. Sarah had been certifiably insane. "There is no way to predict every possible situation. And part of my and Egan's responsibility is to not be completely helpless either. You can't protect all four members of the royal family at one time."

He tilted his head and scratched the back of his neck. "I never really thought of it that way."

"Jade has a way of making us think about things differently." Sadie bumped her shoulder into mine. "Especially with Egan."

Faint sirens sounded. The ambulance was on its way.

How much longer? The ambulance will be here soon. I hated to rush Mom, but we were running out of time.

The front door opened, answering the question for me.

Mom held a book close to her chest, and Egan followed behind her.

"Sorry, I had to get my journal." She climbed into the back of the van and sat, clutching the book as if her life depended on it.

Draco moved to climb in after her, but I stopped him. The poor guy was almost too big to sit back there alone, never mind with Mom. "Sit up front. I'll take my turn in the back."

"But you don't—" He stopped. "You want to be there for her. Okay."

Not wasting any time since the ambulance was growing closer, I climbed in the back as everyone else settled in. Egan pulled out of the driveway, and we made our way out of the neighborhood. The ambulance passed us as we turned onto the main road.

The van remained silent. So much had happened that no one had a clue what to say.

After thirty minutes, Mom lowered the book to her lap. She turned it to the side where there was a clasp, but it was broken. "Dammit," she said loudly. "I should've known." She dropped the book on the floorboard.

Her random act of anger startled me. I wasn't sure what had triggered it. "What's wrong?"

Mom turned to me. "Did something happen to bring you here?"

I couldn't lie to her, but something had caused her to ask. "We were attacked earlier. I was worried they might have gotten to you."

Mom sighed with defeat. "All this time, I stood up for her and turned a blind eye to everything wrong she did. I let her come between your father and me. That was why he was moving us away. Then when he was gone, I let her come between us. And all she did was hurt and betray me and those I love the most, over and over again."

What happened? Egan asked with concern. *She randomly got upset.*

I have no clue. It's like her journal pissed her off. The final piece of the puzzle clicked into place. *She realized the lock is broken.*

Sarah must have done that. "Mom, when did you start keeping a journal?"

"Right after I got back." Mom laughed, but it was devoid of humor. "She told me I should talk to a therapist after I was kidnapped and refused to talk to her. The therapist suggested I write down my thoughts and feelings about my experiences in a journal. She broke into it, and that's how she found you."

"You put our location in your journal?" I tried to keep the surprise from my voice. Mom had been manipulated; it wasn't her fault. A licensed professional had told her to do it, but I wanted to shake her. She should've known better.

"I only referenced Darmark." She placed a hand on my thigh. "When you drove me home, I realized you were staying thirty minutes east of there. Your father and I visited the waterfall on the outskirts of the town on our honeymoon."

"That was why she hired the bear shifter." Sadie groaned. "Because she knew our general location, and bears have the best sense of smell."

"I'm so sorry." Mom's shoulders shook. "I didn't know. Did anyone get hurt because of me?"

"There's no reason for you to apologize." Egan focused on the rearview mirror as his hands tightened on the steering wheel, his knuckles white. "You didn't do a damn thing wrong."

"Dude, Egan just cussed," Donovan whispered to Sadie like we wouldn't hear. "I've never heard him cuss before."

He'd said it loud enough that even Mom could have heard.

Sadie chuckled. "I know."

This was only the second time I'd heard him cuss too, but I loved that about him. "Like Egan said, you aren't held responsible. You had no idea it would happen."

"But I should've." Mom sniffed and turned away from me. "That's the thing."

I'd moved to slide across the bench to her when Egan linked with me. *Give her a second. You're a lot like her, and she needs time to process it first.*

And that proved he understood me better than I did myself.

THE REST of the ride home had been in complete silence. It was around one in the morning when we rolled up to the mansion. All of the lights were on. Everyone was awake and probably on edge.

"I'll go in and tell the vampires Liz is here," Sadie said as she opened the back door and ran to the front of the house.

She was gone in a flash as the rest of us climbed out.

Mom held the journal in her hands as she shifted her weight from leg to leg. "Should I head over to the pack?"

"Sadie and I planned on taking you." Donovan yawned. "But she's heading this way with Winter, Titan, and Torak."

"He's okay?" I'd been worried about him, but I'd been afraid to ask in case something bad had happened and Sadie wasn't ready to share.

"Yeah, Trixie was able to help him." Donovan turned to the front door as it opened.

The four of them walked outside. Titan had a black patch over his right eye.

"But not like we hoped," Titan said, his mouth set in a firm expression. "But she made sure the poison was out of my system and healed my eye socket so it wouldn't take days to heal on its own."

"And it's better than you being dead." Winter took her mate's hand. "It could've been a lot worse."

"You're right." He lifted her hand to his mouth and kissed it. "We're heading back to the pack. There's a lot we need to take care of now that I can't be alpha."

"You can't be alpha?" My heart broke for him.

"No, not like this." Titan patted his son's shoulder. "It's time to hand over the reins. I've been thinking about it for a while now anyway. I'm getting old."

"And speaking of leading, Ladon and Kayda want to meet with you two." Torak lifted a brow. "They're waiting for you in the kitchen. We'll take care of your mom from here."

"Thank you," Egan said as he walked next to me. *I have a feeling I know what this is about.*

Me too. I turned to Mom and hugged her. "I'll come see you in the morning. Get some rest, and if you need me, I'll have my cell phone on."

She hugged me hard. "I love you."

"I love you too."

Mom walked off with Titan, Torak, and Winter, leaving the rest of us standing under the moonlight. When they stepped out of view, Egan focused on me. "Are you ready?"

"As ready as I'll ever be," I replied and stepped toward the house. I lifted my chin and squared my shoulders. I was done cowering and running. Our futures were about to change rapidly once more. I felt it in my bones. And this time, I wouldn't run away.

CHAPTER TWENTY-THREE

Egan and I walked hand in hand into the kitchen with Draco following right behind us. Sadie and Donovan peeled off, heading toward the living room where everyone else was.

If the entire group giving us privacy wasn't a neon sign warning that something was waiting for us up ahead, I wasn't sure what else could be.

We found Ladon and Kayda sitting at the rectangular kitchen table with their backs to the windows. They watched us sit in front of them. I was right across from Kayda while Egan took the open chair next to me in front of his father.

Ladon tapped his fingers on the table. "Was Liz in danger?"

I wanted to shut him down and get straight to the point of this conversation, but he seemed concerned. Snapping at him would have been rude and wrong, given the circumstances.

"Not really, but a fae attacked my aunt." I rolled my shoulders, trying to keep the strange, remorseful feelings at bay. "She died shortly after we got there." A lump formed in my throat, and I tried swallowing it down with no luck.

Kayda leaned forward, her hair falling into her face. "Is Liz okay? I know how much she loved her sister."

My eyes burned, which was insane. Why was I getting choked up over this? My aunt had been awful to me. She didn't deserve any remorse.

Not wanting to risk a breakdown, I linked with Egan. *I'm sorry. I can't.*

He squeezed my hand comfortingly. "Many things came to light, and unfortunately, they were a little shocking to Liz. But she'll come around. She's stronger than she realizes."

"Yes, she is." Kayda smiled sadly. "But losing a family member is hard, especially when you grew up around them. I am truly sorry for your family's loss."

"Thank you." My voice cracked, and I cleared my throat. I hoped no one had noticed, but the concern etched around Kayda's eyes informed me they had.

Draco joined us in the kitchen, standing by the doorway. "Do you need me to stay, or should I join the others in the living room?"

"Please stay." Ladon squared his shoulders as his jaw ticked. "You should hear this as well."

Nodding, Draco stood stiffly by the door. Katherine's laughter filtered into the kitchen, and Draco flicked his attention in her direction.

He must have felt the same attraction as she did.

I only hoped neither of them got hurt.

"Your mother and I have been wanting to talk to you about this for a very long time, but we needed to wait until you'd found your mate." Ladon gestured at us. "Had we known we would be under a threat like this when you found each other, we would've started training Egan at a much younger age, but there isn't much we can do about it now."

Egan ran his thumb along my wrist. "We can start now. Yes, war isn't an ideal time, but we'll do the best we can."

"You're right." Ladon nodded. "War isn't the best time, but this is when the transition begins."

"Transition?" I wanted to hear him say it to ensure we were all aligned.

"Yes." Ladon took his wife's hand and placed it on the table. "The transition of the crown from us to the two of you."

There it was. The words I'd been expecting. "Now?" The timing was horrible.

"I know it's abrupt," Kayda said, "but this has been in the plans for a long time. Your father and I feel that we're not the right people to lead."

"Genetics say differently." Egan leaned back.

"That's not true," Ladon said sternly. "Every dragon king passes the torch when they feel their reign should be over, and there are two reasons we want to do this now. First, I've never wanted to be king. It's never interested me. The day I learned I would be taking over, I realized no one knew who I was except for a small handful with access to that privileged information."

"It's true." Kayda patted her mate's arm. "I'd only been part of the thunder for a week when your grandfather dropped the news on your dad. I thought he'd cry right then and there."

"So you'd like to pass that burden on to me?" Egan arched his brow.

Ladon sighed. "Which brings me to the most important point. You were born a leader. Your peers looked up to you.

Look at the strong alliances you've made during your short stint in the human realm. You are sharp, strategic, and have such a good heart. And with Jade by your side, you've grown into a stronger leader than I've ever been, and she's a solid rock beside you. If we're going to make it through this next battle, you and Jade need to lead the charge. You're our best hope."

I had to give him that. Egan was an amazing person. His presence alone made people feel safe and at ease. He had a natural charisma that made others want to follow him.

"But Dad—" Egan started.

"This isn't a question." Ladon made a slicing motion with his hand. "Effective immediately, you and Jade are the dragon king and queen." His attention turned to Draco. "Alert the other thunders and make the announcement. There's no point in keeping it secret any longer since the fae dragon king knows who we are."

Egan opened his mouth to argue.

If he doesn't want to lead, maybe we should take over. The last thing we needed was for Egan and his dad to be at odds. It wasn't like his dad would disappear. *If we fight with each other, the fae dragon king will win.*

He blew out a breath. *It just happened so fast. I feel like I have whiplash, and we didn't even have time to focus on us before a whole kingdom got thrown at our feet.*

And there was the real reason. He wanted time to focus on us, and I had to admit that sounded pretty damn amazing. *I don't want it either, but if we're supposed to protect our people, don't they deserve for us to step up? Especially if your dad doesn't want to?*

Turning toward me, he cupped my cheek. "Jade and I are in agreement even though we aren't thrilled with the timing."

Sadie shouted, "Egan! Jade! You may want to come in here."

Her voice contained no fear, which was the only reason I wasn't losing my mind.

Our group ran into the room to find Sadie, Donovan, Axel, and Roxy on one couch and Cassius, Dawn, Julie, and Paul on the other. Katherine, Lillith, Luther, and Athan sat in front of the fireplace under the television with Ollie and Trixie standing off to the side.

The witch's charcoal eyes locked with mine, and a smile twisted on her face, looking menacing with the deep wrinkles of age. Her hair spilled from what had once been a bun on top of her hair, and silver wisps hung in her face. Her brown dress was lined with sweat as she rocked in place.

But Trixie couldn't be why Sadie had called for us. I was searching for what had made Sadie shout when Rook and Naida flickered into view with a strange woman standing between them.

She was pale like the other fae beside her, but with a faint reddish hue and thin scales instead of skin. Long, pale cyan hair cascaded to her ankles, the color matching her eyes. She stood as tall as Egan and wore a dark green robe with a tiara made of turquoise stone.

"What are you?" The word vomit had already begun. I wished I could take the words back, but they'd flown out before my brain could process what I'd said.

A hint of a smile peeked through, making her breathtaking. "And all I heard back in the fae realm was that humans lied and played games of the brain. But she asked a direct question with no disdain."

"Playing games of the brain?" This had to be a dream or a nightmare. I wasn't sure which way it would go.

Her forehead creased. "Manipulate to get what you want."

Rook chuckled. "She means mind games."

"That makes so much more sense." Roxy tapped her head. "I was really confused for a second."

"Please excuse these two." Naida glared at Roxy then me. "They sometimes don't know how to behave. This is Libelle, the fae dragon king's daughter."

"And you didn't chain her up?" Draco rushed past Egan and me to stand in front. "We need to restrain her now."

"Actually, we don't." Libelle crossed her arms, and smoke trickled from her nose. "I came here willingly."

"Why should we believe that?" Lillith stood as if the move would put them on the same level, despite the dragon princess having almost two feet on her.

"Fair question." The princess walked around the room, taking in every detail. "My father has been a dictator since before I was born. He starves those who anger him, treats everyone as if they are his slaves, and when bored, he enjoys beating his own people." She ran a hand over the wall. "Even his own family isn't off the table. He does whatever is necessary to instill fear and has broken the spirit of our entire thunder."

"When she says thunder," Rook added, "she means every fae dragon. They don't live apart like you."

Ladon stepped beside Egan. "We didn't until the fae dragon king began hunting us."

"I remember the day my father began reaching out for human contacts." Libelle walked next to Roxy and touched the leather couch with her finger. "It was after the harpies had laughed at him when he'd told them to leave the lands outside our volcano. They informed him that no one revered him and that many wanted the fake fae dragon king,

Otin, dead since he didn't possess the true dragon king power. After that, things got worse for all of us, me included."

"So you want us to kill your father?" Donovan said carefully. "Because that's what it'll take to end this."

"Of course I do." Libelle stared at him. "It doesn't bring me joy to say it, and I refuse to do it myself, but he's lived for over two thousand years and had a full life. He's shown cruelty to everyone, and my people are already speaking of rising against him before he gets more powerful. With all the turmoil, he's made some allegiances, making him more ruthless. The more power he gets, the crueler he becomes."

She didn't smell of a lie. Rook and Naida seemed comfortable around her, so maybe we could trust her.

"I understand it's hard to believe, but I want the best for my people." She placed a hand over her heart. "My people have tried rallying for him to let me step up and lead, but he killed the ringleader and told me if I tried to overthrow him, he'd kill my best friend. We're all at his mercy, and his terror must end."

"I understand that all too well." Sadie leaned over Roxy and placed a hand on her arm. "I've lived a life similar to yours, and sometimes doing the right thing isn't easy or fun."

"Same here." Maybe that was one reason Sadie and I had connected from the beginning. We'd both grown up with people who didn't love us and punished us for just breathing, and it had made us see something in each other, similar to how we could see something in Libelle now.

"My guards informed me that she was dropping information on Otin's plans for attacking the kingdom while the civil war was going on." Rook lifted a hand toward the princess. "She's been helping us, and it's why we regained control so quickly once I took the throne. I believe we can trust her."

Do you think she's telling the truth? Egan asked.

Taking my time before answering, I watched her a little more. *Yes, but that doesn't mean we trust her blindly. I say Draco and a few other dragons stay close and guard her. She seems genuine, and if she is, we want to make sure she trusts us in return.*

Nodding, Egan inhaled sharply. "Then we appreciate your help. Draco, please contact the thunders and tell them to make their way here. If Libelle is staying with us, I'm assuming her father won't be far behind."

"You're correct." Libelle took in the entire room. "My capture will make him look weak. He won't tolerate it. I suspect he'll attack before a day cycle."

"Day cycle?" Katherine asked and scooted closer to Draco.

Naida sighed. "Within twenty-four hours."

"I'll text them now." Draco pulled the phone from his pocket and typed a message.

Libelle watched, her head tilting so far I was afraid it would fall off. "This is such a strange, wonderful place."

"It is a lot different from back home," Rook said.

Naida stood stiffly and on edge like always. "Rook, you better go back and ready the guards. Sadie or I will alert you when it's time for the guards to come."

"And the rest of us need to get some sleep while we can." Egan tugged me toward the hallway. "Draco, why don't you, Ollie, Trixie, and Libelle sleep here? I'm sure we can get blow-up mattresses for you all."

"I'll grab some now," Dawn said and hurried from the room.

"Jade and I are going to get some sleep. She got injured

earlier and needs time to heal." Egan held his hand out toward me. "Call us or come get us if anything happens."

"Wait." Trixie took a few shaky steps toward me. "Let me heal her so she can rest better."

Just like last time, I felt extremely uncomfortable around the witch. "After what you did for Titan, I'd hate to put you out."

"Nonsense." Trixie circled me. "Where is the wound?"

"On her back," Egan said and touched my arm to calm me. *It wouldn't hurt to let her heal you.*

I don't trust her. I didn't know how to explain it, other than that.

He pointed to my back where I was hurt. *It's only because her magic is different than ours.*

I hoped that was the case because before I could move, Trixie's hands touched my back, and magic pooled inside me.

My flames flared, fighting back, and my head grew light. Something was wrong.

CHAPTER TWENTY-FOUR

My dragon roared as the flames increased. *Something feels off.*

Egan tensed. "She says something feels off."

"You know why." Trixie pushed more magic inside me. "Do you really think I'd do something stupid in a house full of supernaturals?"

"Maybe," Egan growled. "If you have a death sentence."

Flames licked my skin as my dragon fought against the foreign magic. I wouldn't be surprised if I spontaneously combusted. My mind screamed to move, but between the two warring magics, I was mercilessly stuck in place.

"I may be old," she tsked, "but I'd like to live as long as Mother Nature intends me to."

The magic receded, and I sucked in a breath. I'd been so focused on the warring parts inside me that I'd forgotten one of the most basic survival techniques. Maybe my gynecologist had been right all along. He always reminded me to breathe during my annual exams, and I'd thought it strange until now. Granted, this had been way more invasive than that.

After a few seconds, she removed her hand. "There. She's physically healed."

Her choice of wording was correct. Maybe I was healed on the outside, but I was completely drained inside. My dragon coursed through my body as if she was waiting for another magical attack.

I sagged against Egan, more exhausted than ever before.

"Do you have everything you need?" Egan asked as he lifted me and cradled me in his arms.

His touch soothed my dragon, but not enough. The fire still licked my skin, and in my weakened state, I could barely hold off the shift.

"Yes, get her to bed," Sadie said. "It shouldn't take long before we all can get a little bit of sleep."

"The thunders are moving." Draco sounded almost excited. "Everyone is eager to meet their new king and queen and remove the fae threat that's kept us in hiding for so long."

If all of the places were beautiful like where Egan's thunder had stayed, I wouldn't consider it a horrible sentence. But if I'd had no option but to stay there, I'd have felt trapped too.

"Good." Egan headed toward the stairs. "We'll need all the energy we can get to make it out of this alive."

"Word of advice," Roxy interjected. "Don't tell them that. It's a real morale killer."

"I hate to agree with Roxy." Lillith snorted. "But a little bit of 'go team' would be ideal in this situation. Don't be a dream crusher."

"I'll consider your suggestion," Egan said seriously, but I felt a trace of humor through our bond.

Out of the corner of my eye, I watched Katherine and Draco slip away, hand in hand. I tried not to worry since it was clear they were interested in each other, but I cared about them deeply and hoped no one got hurt.

Roxy cleared her throat loudly. "That makes me part of the royal decision-making. I should probably receive a formal title."

"Now's not the time." Julie chuckled. "Go take care of Jade, Egan."

The group bantered, and with each step, their voices grew farther and farther away.

Seconds later, Egan sat me on the edge of the bed and brushed my hair from my face. "I'll go warm the water for you."

A warm shower didn't sound appealing. *Can you make it cool? My dragon is still agitated.*

Of course. He gathered our things and headed into the bathroom. The sound of running water trickled into the room.

Gaining distance from the witch had helped, but some of her magic remained inside me, maybe finishing up the job, so my dragon wouldn't completely calm because of it.

I slowly undressed. Thankfully, my shoulder didn't scream or twinge with pain as I pulled off my shirt. I dropped my clothes on the floor and entered the bathroom.

"I was going—" Standing by the shower, Egan turned around, and his eyes glowed as he scanned my naked body. In a low, husky voice he linked with me. *Turn around.*

Obliging him, I slowly turned and pulled my hair over my shoulder so he could see my back.

He closed the distance between us, and his fingertips brushed along where my wound had been. "You're completely healed. There's not even a scar."

Even in my exhausted state, his touch ignited warmth inside me. The very kind that a shower wouldn't extinguish.

Only he could.

I spun around, and my breasts brushed his hands. The amount of need coursing through my body took me by surprise. I'd always wanted him, but this bordered on desperation.

My hand clutched his neck, yanking his mouth to mine. Not bothering with foreplay, my tongue slipped inside his mouth, showing him what I wanted.

Jade, it's been a hell of a day. Maybe you should take it easy. But his body responded despite his protests. His fingers pinched my nipples, and I moaned.

I stepped forward, wanting to dominate him. I needed him and wanted control. *I need to feel you. Make me feel alive.*

I'll do whatever you need me to. The tangy scent of his arousal and his consent charged me more than ever before.

Get naked, I commanded and stepped back, unbuttoning his pants and pushing them from his body.

He stepped out of them as his back hit the glass door of the shower.

Not wanting to step away from him again, I grabbed the top of his button-down shirt and ripped the buttons off, shredding the fabric from his body.

There was no way we were making it into the shower. I couldn't wait. I climbed him and wrapped my legs around his body. His hands moved to my ass, and his fingers kneaded my skin.

He slid down the glass wall until he sat propped against it. I eagerly straddled him. The tile cut into my skin, adding to my desire. Egan sucked on my nipple as I slipped him inside me.

There was no time for slow as I rode him. I gasped as his teeth nipped, and I groaned in pure ecstasy.

Using the glass as leverage, I spread my legs wider, wanting him as deep as he could go. He thrust in sync with me and leaned his head against the glass wall supporting him.

Lowering my head to his neck, I grazed my teeth against his skin. I wanted him to experience what him being rough with me felt like. I always thought he wanted to be gentle, but I refused to give him that tonight.

A low, deep growl rumbled from his chest. *Damn, that feels good.* His emotions poured into me—love, arousal, and pure pleasure.

Emotions only I could invoke, and I felt powerful.

I sucked on his neck, not giving a damn if I left a mark. He bucked against me in a frenzy, and the pleasure built between us.

Maybe he'd realized that gentleness was overrated sometimes.

He pinched my breasts, and I fell over the edge as he slammed into me. Responding, I dug my teeth deeper into his skin, leaving a slight metallic taste on the tip of my tongue.

He groaned as he climaxed, bringing me further over the edge. My body quivered as the largest orgasm ever rolled through me.

My body sagged against his as we came down from wherever the hell we'd been. Our breathing was ragged and somehow in rhythm. As the world crashed back over me, I glanced at the bite mark I'd left on his neck. *I am so sorry.*

Don't be. He kissed my lips gently. *That was amazing.*

I couldn't argue with that, but pure exhaustion hit. I wasn't even sure I had the energy for a shower. *I love you.*

I love you too. He kissed the tip of my nose and grabbed

my waist, lifting me off him gently. *You're exhausted. Let's clean up and get some sleep.*

We climbed into the shower, and Egan washed me. I'd never realized a man could be so loving. The pure joy radiating off him from taking care of me made me fall even more in love.

I hadn't even known that was possible.

Fate knew what she was doing. He was my perfect match. Even if we hadn't been mates, I would've fallen in love with him. It just would've taken a whole hell of a lot longer. And I was so glad it hadn't. I never wanted to experience another moment without him.

Minutes later, we cuddled in bed and fell fast asleep.

SOMETHING COLD and unsettling charged through me, waking me. Egan's breathing grew rapid as he released me and sat up in bed.

You feel it too? Maybe I hadn't lost my mind.

He looked at me. *Yes. I have a feeling the fae king may have arrived on Earth.*

Of course he had. I threw the comforter off and stood. "Then we have no time to waste."

We ran to our closet, each picking out old jeans and a shirt. We didn't have any armor, and we'd be shifting soon, so we didn't care what we wore.

Throwing our bedroom door open, Egan yelled, "It's go-time. The fae king has arrived."

Sadie's door opened. Just like us, she and Donovan were dressed and ready to go.

"Yeah, I felt their arrival too." Sadie shivered. "It was

faint but malicious. It was almost a sinister feeling as he arrived in our world."

"If we can feel him, why didn't we feel the harpies and manticores?" Some things still didn't make sense to me.

"They probably didn't transport close to us. Fae travel to Earth all the time, and we only pick up on their energy when it's close to us." Sadie headed toward the stairs.

That only raised more questions. "But I don't feel anything with Rook and Naida."

"That's because you knew Naida as human before you shifted into a dragon. Since they're my family, you recognize their energy, and that's why you don't register the dizziness that warns of fae. If someone you don't know transports over, you'll grow dizzy."

"She's right, although it's very faint," Egan said and followed Sadie as Roxy and Axel's door opened. "Maybe if it's the same race as us, we feel it more prominently."

"I don't know if I should be relieved or upset that I can't feel anything." Donovan waved his hand, indicating I should go next. "All I know is that it's time to kill some assholes. We warned Titan's ... I mean, Torak's pack."

Axel and Roxy joined us in the hallway as Axel shook his head and said, "Dude, that change will take some getting used to."

"Ah, just don't say it too much." Roxy rolled her eyes. "Or Torak will get an even bigger head."

I hurried after Egan as Donovan chuckled. "He's not bad at all. Several others have a bigger ego than him."

We entered the kitchen, and it was packed with all the dragons, vampires, Ollie, and the witch. Libelle, Cassius, Ladon, and Draco were at the door leading outside.

"Did everyone feel them come over?" I asked, surprised our group was already assembled.

"All the dragons did." Cassius inhaled. "They alerted everyone."

Good. Us being split across the house had come in handy.

Sadie scanned the group. "Where's Naida?"

"She transported to Fae to get the guards." Libelle pursed her lips. "My father striking this early isn't a good sign."

Egan took my hand, and we moved toward the front. He asked, "What do you mean?"

"He must know not every dragon is here yet and he's trying to capitalize on it." The princess's skin turned a shade darker, making her scales more prominent. "How far away are they?"

"I'm not sure." Draco frowned. "They're on their way but in dragon form. There's no way to communicate with them."

"You can't communicate with them?" She tilted her head as the corners of her eyes crinkled in concentration.

"No, only wolves can pack-link when they're in the same pack," Egan explained. "Dragons can't unless it's with their fated mate."

"I can't hear my father either." She moved her head from side to side like she was trying to catch a frequency. "I felt him and figured he'd reach out to me, wanting to know everything about you. I'd hoped to play that to our advantage."

"Maybe the fae realm allows that sort of connection." Ladon chewed on his bottom lip. "And Earth prohibits it. There are different rules between the two worlds."

"That makes sense." Libelle glanced out the window. "I'm already feeling weaker from being here."

"At least, we have that to our advantage." Ollie pursed his lips. "Is there a way to drain the fae dragons faster?"

"Make them use their magic." Libelle shrugged. "It's the only way."

Katherine drank from a blood bag. "Will the iron work?"

It was strange watching her drink like that. They always used cups, but we were in a hurry. Then I noticed that all the vampires were drinking.

Egan must have felt my confusion since he explained, *Vampires are strongest after they eat.*

Gotcha. We needed everyone at their peak. I'd carry the blood bags personally if that would make us win.

"Iron?" Solid scales formed around Libelle's nose as she squinted. "What is that?"

"A material that drains the fae." Sadie lifted a hand. "I discovered it when the fae were trying to kill me."

"Ah, yes, since you are a half-blood." The scales became less visible, and her face smoothed. "If that works on them, it's worth trying on the dragons. Our magics are similar."

"Good." Donovan sighed. "The pile they brought during the manticore attack is still in the clearing. We should head out and get it before it's too late."

A roar rocked the mansion, and I looked outside to see the strangest sight ever.

If I'd thought our dragons were huge, I'd been wrong.

So wrong.

These dragons were at least twice our size. They were varying colors of light pinks, yellows, purples, and blues. They were gorgeous, but their faces were contorted. Eyes narrowed, they bared their teeth with smoke trickling from their noses.

In other words: pure rage.

"Outside!" Draco yelled. "Before they set the mansion on fire."

They were out to demolish us.

Ten circled the house as blue flames poured from their mouths, hitting various points of the mansion.

Shit, we had to move.

Draco opened the door, and we poured outside, which was exactly what they wanted.

"Your Highnesses, stay close to me," Draco commanded as he stood in front of us. He looked at Katherine, and then his gaze flicked toward me, making it clear he wanted her with us too. "My family will be here soon, but until then, I have to keep you alive. Otherwise, the fae king will get what he wants."

Katherine stepped toward me, listening to his silent command ... or was it?

Did they mind link? I had to be seeing things. They were different species. But hell, so was I.

That should be impossible. Egan sounded confused. *Maybe she just understood his physical cues.*

The magnitude of the situation washed over us as more dragons flew our way. There were hundreds.

They were here to wage war and win.

I only hoped we could survive until the others got here.

CHAPTER TWENTY-FIVE

Blue fire erupted from all sides of the roof as the fae dragons concentrated their attacks. One of the manticores must have seen Ladon and the others run from the mansion during their escape back to Fae and informed Otin.

My dragon surged forward, wanting me to shift, but I pushed her away. We all wanted to shift, but it would put us at a severe disadvantage. "Don't shift. Stay human so we can use the trees as coverage."

The trees had budding leaves that would partially hide us as we ran to the supply of iron and waited for the other thunders to arrive.

"Listen to the queen's orders!" Draco shouted and motioned for us to run in front of him. "And follow her to the others."

"Libelle, keep close to Ladon and Kayda," Draco commanded. "I need to protect you as well."

Even though his words were sincere, he also wanted to keep an eye on her. Since this was her thunder attacking, we didn't need her to tell them our plans.

Wait. He wanted to move in front. *I thought he wanted us to stay behind?*

That was before more dragons came. We'll be safer in the woods. He can guard us better from behind. Egan chuckled even though humor didn't flow through our bond. *He'll want to get in front again soon enough. Don't worry.*

A cyan dragon flew down from the house, heading after those running into the woods. Not all of us would make it into the woods before it reached us. We had to do something, or people would die in the first few moments of battle. "We have to hold him off."

I stopped and spun around, staring the crazy-ass dragon in the eye. I searched for something, anything to protect our people.

"Dammit, Jade!" Draco spat. "Run."

Sadie rushed over to me and touched my arm. "I've got this, and Naida is on her way."

Did she expect me to leave her? She was one of the most important people in my life. "But I don't want you to get hurt either."

Egan held me in place, "I promise she has this handled," Egan rasped. "I wouldn't leave her behind if I wasn't sure."

Smoke trickled from the fae dragon's nose; he was close enough to spew flames. He roared, blowing Sadie's pink bob behind her and filling our noses with the stench of brimstone.

Naida and several other fae flickered into view, and Sadie lifted her hands. Pink magic spilled from her palms. The flames charged toward us, but when they hit the pink barrier, they blew back in the dragon's face.

The dragon roared again, and I braced myself for a smell that never came. Not even Sadie's hair blew from the breeze.

My mouth dropped. "What the hell?"

"It's like a force field." Egan moved toward the iron. "She's been practicing her magic with Rook, and she's gotten stronger. Just shy of pure-fae-blooded levels."

Draco stepped beside us and frowned. "We need to get to the other dragons before it's too late."

Donovan walked over to us. "I'll stay here with her and the fae. We'll catch up to you, but I'll let them drain the dragons as much as possible before we leave."

I felt stupid for not wanting to leave her since she was more than capable of handling herself. "I'm sorry, I didn't know."

"There's nothing for you to be ashamed of." Egan brushed his fingers against my cheek. "You didn't know, and you love her. Any one of us would've done the same thing."

He was right. I'd lost any concern I'd had about growing too close to any of them. They were my family, and I was willing to risk my life to protect them.

My life had changed so drastically, and I wouldn't alter it for anything. "Okay." I turned and ran back toward the woods.

Ladon, Kayda, Libelle, and Katherine had stopped to wait for us, probably due to Draco requesting it. He wanted us together, which wasn't a very strong plan.

We ran quickly with the other dragons toward where we'd fought the manticores.

Egan and I needed to be in agreement before we got to where the battle would truly begin. *The four of us sticking together isn't smart. All it'll take is one strike, and the whole royal line will be wiped out.*

You're right. He replied as a few of the fae dragons flew overhead. *Let's split up from my parents, but Draco will have a fit.*

It doesn't matter. I understood that Draco wanted to protect all four of us, but there was only one of him and hundreds of fae dragons. *This plan is the best way to ensure our people stay safe.*

"We're heading right," Egan informed Draco.

The warrior's head snapped in our direction. "No, stay the course. I can't protect you if you're over there."

"That's the point," I butted in. We didn't have time to waste by not fighting in the battle. "Focus on keeping Ladon and Kayda safe. Egan and I will protect each other."

"But ..."

"Let them go," Katherine said softly. "It's better that way, and you know it."

Blowing out a breath as a muscle in his neck pulsed, Draco nodded stiffly. "Fine, but if you are attacked, let the dragons closest to you help fight. Once my family arrives, I'll come looking for you two."

"Wait!" Libelle shouted. "Hold me captive so Dad will ignore me." Libelle's eyes glowed pink. "If he suspects I'm working with you, he'll kill me before I can help. Once we get to the clearing where my people can see me, I'll take a stand beside you."

"You want to be our prisoner?" Egan asked slowly. "That means we'll have to restrain you."

"In other words, we're both taking a leap of faith with one another." Libelle let the truth of her words settle over us.

Egan lifted his hands and wiggled his fingers. "I don't have any rope."

"This should work." Ladon pulled out the dagger Vera had tried to use on me back in the cave. The rising sun reflected off the dark silver edge, and the two golden jewels at the top of the slender handle glowed, making the black wings that sprouted from the neck appear to move.

Libelle stumbled back. "Where did you get that?"

"From the witch that attacked us in the cave." The memory of her attacking me with it still gave me nightmares that I refused to admit to anyone.

"I wasn't sure you could win." Libelle's gaze stayed on the dagger. "But you have the one weapon that can kill any fae. You could succeed."

We deserved a break after everything we'd been through. "What do you mean?"

"That's the fae realm dagger." Libelle lifted a hand like she was considering touching it. "I can't believe Dad gave it to that witch. He's even more power-hungry than I realized."

"Vera was crazy." Egan ground his teeth. "She was all about killing us."

"Everyone thinks he hid it somewhere, so scratch my plan." Libelle grinned. "I'll show him I'm on your side to completely piss him off. His anger will make him more ruthless—that's why I wanted us to hold off—but we have this. We need him crazy with rage so we can use this to our advantage."

"Then I'll need that so I can kill him." Draco took the dagger and sheath from Ladon and placed it through his belt loop.

"The plan doesn't change." I nodded to the right. "Egan and I will catch up with the dragons that ran off that way."

Draco sighed but grunted his agreement.

I hated to cause him more grief, but we all knew this was the best plan. Before he could argue, Egan and I ran to the right, straight toward Long and a few members of the thunder. Cassius and Dawn were right beside them with Ollie and the witch only a few feet behind.

It surprised me that the older witch could keep up, but hey. She might creep me out, but I didn't want something bad to happen to her. She'd only helped me ... so far.

Our group pushed as fast as we could, and after a few more steps, paws pounded the ground. I turned to find a vibrant red wolf and a darker brown one racing toward us. Roxy and Axel were keeping up and informing Donovan and Sadie about what was going on.

We were less than a mile away from the spot we were aiming for. It was between the pack house and mansion but, most importantly, where the iron was. Even though we dragons couldn't touch it, the vampires and wolves could, which would hopefully give us more of an advantage against the fae dragons.

Several fae dragons flew overhead, but unlike the others, they were flying lower, searching in between the leaves. They circled the sky like a flock of birds.

Mind linking would have been amazing, but unfortunately, that wasn't happening. I wanted to tell them to slow down, but I couldn't without giving our location away.

Egan and I crouched behind a tree, hoping that they wouldn't see us.

"Hide!" Long shouted as the dragons circled back.

The others scattered towards safety, but the dragon's eyes were latched on to the older dragon.

He was sacrificing himself for us.

We've got to help him. We couldn't hide and let the poor man die for us.

I jumped to my feet, and Egan was right in sync with me. He linked with me. *I want to help him, but he's saving us.*

Long's silver eyes widened, and he shook his head as I tried to reach him in time. I had no clue what we would do, but I had time to figure something out.

Jade! Egan yelled in my mind as he raced toward me.

When I was only twenty feet away, something slammed into my back, and I fell into the brush. Egan landed next to me, and I realized Roxy and Axel had tackled me.

I fought against their hold and glanced at the older man. Relieved that the wolves had taken us down, he mouthed the words "thank you" as a buttercream dragon swooped toward him.

Bucking against the wolf on top of me, I watched in horror as the dragon bit into the older man's back and stomach. The dragon's teeth thrashed through his skin, and the sickening sound of flesh ripping and bones breaking hit my ears. The dragon released its hold, and Long's body split in half.

I'd never seen a sight so disgusting or heartbreaking in my entire life. His slashed organs hung outside his body.

The urge to vomit overtook me, but I swallowed the bile back down. The buttercream dragon flew higher in the sky with blood dripping down its mouth.

After a few seconds, Roxy and Axel got off me. Tears rolled down my face.

Egan pulled me into his arms. "You can't do that again. Those dragons would have found us. Long saved us, and his sacrifice would've been in vain if Roxy and Axel hadn't stopped you."

"But he died." I wiped the wetness from under my eyes, knowing I had to pull myself together. We were at war. I didn't have time to break down.

"Because he was old and wanted to protect us." Egan kissed my forehead. "We'll fight too, but we can't be reckless. If we die, our people will fall under Otin's rule, and Libelle told us how it is there. His own daughter is turning away from him."

He was right. I'd been careless.

I don't like it either, but it was his call to make. Egan intertwined our fingers. *Now, let's make sure his death has purpose.*

His words invigorated me; he knew exactly what to say to drive his point home.

The other dragons reemerged as Ollie and the witch caught up to us. We all took off, and soon, we were approaching the clearing. I glanced to my left and found Draco and the others a hundred yards away.

"Let's shift!" Egan shouted. "It's time to fight."

All of the dragon shifters called their animals forward, and we all stepped into the clearing, ready to fight.

Fae dragons approached from every direction in the sky. Each flap of their wings sounded like a battle cry. The pack and the other dragons broke into the clearing on the other side, already shifted into their dragon forms. Half of the wolf shifters were still in their human form, racing to the iron along with our vampire friends.

Most surprisingly, Ollie flew out in his falcon form with the witch right behind.

Only Libelle was missing.

Where's the princess? She'd been so steadfast in joining our fight and helping us win.

I don't know. Egan rasped as our group formed a circle, our backs facing one another. *But it doesn't matter. At least, we know what the dagger is.*

The dagger.

I glanced at Draco, wondering where the dagger was now that he was in beast form.

Katherine stood beside him, wearing the dagger peeking out from her waistband. She wouldn't leave his side, so he'd have easy access to it.

The fae dragons flew into the clearing, their eyes locked on Egan and me. A limestone-colored dragon flew at me and opened its mouth. Blue flames shot out, and my own fire bubbled inside. I blew my red flames out and prayed I would survive.

CHAPTER TWENTY-SIX

Our flames collided, crackling loudly. When I didn't feel immediate pain, I opened my eyes to something amazing. The red and blue flames connected, neither one advancing, creating a vibrant purple that would have been breathtaking under normal circumstances. Various hues of purple sparked from the connection and hit the ground. The grass quickly went from brown to black.

My eyes remained locked on the beauty of the chaos until the fae dragon roared and pushed his flames harder toward me.

All of the other dragons followed his lead and attacked the others with a vengeance. I'd hoped to get some help, but that wouldn't happen.

I was on my own.

Shit, I had no clue how to fight a dragon. *Only your flames don't hurt me, right?* A lot had happened, but I vaguely remembered Egan telling me that. The fae dragon was determined to set me on fire, but I'd assumed a lot about this world and was usually wrong.

Any fire outside of mine will hurt. Fear and determination wafted from Egan and slammed into me. *Hold on. I'm coming.*

I found Egan in a battle of his own with a peach-shaded dragon. Instead of attacking my mate with flames, he leveraged his size. The mammoth dragon dug his talons into Egan's shoulders. Blood dripped from the puncture wounds, and Egan clawed at the enemy dragon's feet.

The crackling turned into sizzles, bringing my attention back to my own battle. The dragon had pushed his flames closer to me, and a few sparks hit my large, scaly hands. The sensation reminded me of the sparkler injury I'd gotten on the Fourth of July when I was six years old. I'd screamed in pain, and Dad had rushed over with water, telling me that was why we didn't play with fire.

I chuckled at the memory of his words. Little had he known his little girl would grow up to be a fire-breathing dragon.

As the blue flames receded, I fixated on the fae dragon again. Even in his dragon state, his forehead lined with confusion, and he turned his head side to side slightly as if looking for an attack.

He had to think I was crazy to laugh in the middle of a battle unless I had the upper hand.

Finally, my strange personality was coming in handy. I laughed harder, which sounded like a cross between choking and burping in beast form.

Maybe that was why he was confused. He wasn't sure whether I was about to attack or die.

Egan turned his head to me, distracted from his own fight. *Are you okay? You're laughing.*

Aw, at least, he knew not to ask if I was insane. His mom, Sadie, or I must have trained him well. Maybe it had been a group effort. *Yeah, just a random memory, but it's confusing the fae dragon, so I'm using it to my advantage.*

The peach dragon attacking Egan dug his talons back into my mate's shoulders.

Pay attention and fight. I'm fine. I focused back on the limestone dragon, needing to end this. If Egan became severely injured, we would be hurting. At least his current wounds would heal relatively quickly.

Taking my own advice, I locked eyes with the enemy dragon, who still seemed unsure.

Projecting my fire toward him more, I concentrated the rolling liquid inside. I wasn't sure what to do, but I was letting my beast side take over more than usual.

My dragon's hot magic coursed inside me, spreading through my body. My skin grew hotter than ever before.

A loud *kak* sounded overhead as Ollie's white feathers flew toward the limestone dragon. Compared to the dragon, the falcon looked like an ant, but Ollie didn't falter as he flew right at the beast.

Ollie had lost his mind.

He had joined the fight without me commanding him to. I regretted ever doubting the guy, but right now it didn't matter.

I had to survive.

The falcon flapped his wings and landed on the limestone dragon's nose. The blue flames extinguished.

The bird perched on the dragon's face, fluffing his feathers. Taunting.

This couldn't end well.

The dragon roared and swiped at the bird, but Ollie hopped over to the dragon's eye and pecked.

A screech echoed in the clearing as the dragon stumbled

backward. The limestone-hued dragon bared its claws, his intent clear.

No, I couldn't let Ollie die after he'd risked his life for me.

I flapped my wings, lifting off the ground. My flames erupted and hit the limestone dragon in the chest. I continued a steady stream as the dragon tried charging toward me.

He hesitated, not knowing which attack was more lethal.

Ollie jerked his head back and dropped an eyeball. Blood spilled down the dragon's snout. He ignored the blood like it was nothing out of the ordinary, hopped over to the other eye, and got to work.

And I'd thought seeing the girls without a throat and eyeballs on Kortright's campus had been bad, but seeing him in action was even worse. At least, my beast form eased some of the trauma.

This time, he was on our side, and injuring an enemy was the same regardless of whether it was through their chest or eyes.

The dragon cried for help, and the peach dragon fighting Egan paused.

Egan threw the peach dragon to the ground, jarring the earth. Within a second, Egan was on top of the enemy dragon, sinking his teeth into its neck. He jerked his head to the side like a wolf and ripped the dragon's throat out.

Peach scales hung from Egan's mouth, contrasting with his dark olive complexion. He looked furious and dangerous in his current form. He spat out the scales, and they landed next to the dying dragon.

I'd always heard that war was ugly, but I'd never understood the meaning until this very moment. This was more gruesome than all of the other attacks. Maybe because they were dragons like us and didn't know any better since they were fighting for the only king they'd ever known.

The limestone-colored dragon fell on its back, desperately searching for anything or anyone beside it. Ollie had managed to remove both eyeballs.

No longer under direct attack, I surveyed the area.

I saw Torak and his pack still in human form, wielding iron poles like they were their sole chance of surviving.

Maybe they were.

The few shifters that had been in wolf form were scattered throughout the clearing, dead, and Long had given up his life to protect us. I didn't see Roxy or Axel's bodies, but only the unshifted wolves, vampires, and dragons seemed to remain. I had to believe they were somewhere else fighting.

Still, my heart broke. We'd lost so many in a short amount of time, and the only fae dragons that were injured or dead were the two Egan, Ollie, and I had fought. This was a fucking massacre, and my heart felt ripped in two.

We were losing and fast. We needed help.

Mom, Winter, and Titan were absent, which gave me some comfort. Not everyone I loved was at risk.

A low rumble filled the air as a light red fae dragon flew overhead. She turned her head side to side, making sure everyone heard her call.

My dragon acknowledged the sound as one of battle.

It was Libelle.

But I wasn't sure if she was rallying her troops or pinpointing who to attack.

Stay close to me. Egan linked as he stepped beside me, our sides brushing.

Libelle darted toward Egan and me, and we both tensed. My heart pounded, ready for the fight, but I hoped it wouldn't come down to that. I chanted internally, *Please be on our side.*

Wings flapped loudly behind me. It had to be a larger dragon. *Stay focused on Libelle,* I commanded as I spun around and found a sand-colored fae dragon flying at me.

Now would have been a great time to have the dagger, but I couldn't reach Katherine before the enemy dragon caught me.

The enemy dragon flew at me with purpose. Its matching sand eyes revealed a cruelness I'd only ever found in Vera's. Each move was calculated like we were playing a game of chess.

Inhaling sharply, I steadied myself. Overreacting would get me hurt. My years of martial arts training had taught me not to overreact. That was when a fighter got careless and lost.

My biggest advantage was my fire. That should hold him off long enough for us to determine which side Libelle was on. If it was ours, Egan could step in and help.

The magic churned in my stomach as I prepared to expel the flames, but Libelle flew over my head and landed right in front of me.

She expanded her wings, blocking Egan and me from the dragon's onslaught.

The fighting around us paused as several enemy dragons turned toward their princess. Even though we couldn't speak, their confusion was clear by the shaking of their heads and their hesitation.

Libelle rumbled again and paced around Egan and me.

Is that equivalent to a dog marking its territory? I hoped his answer was yes.

Egan chuckled. *I'm not sure.*

The enemy sand dragon roared and threw his head back

in disgust. Libelle stood her ground protectively in front of us.

He stomped then charged. His mission was clear.

He would attack us, no matter what.

Libelle's blue flames covered the sand dragon, and his body dropped. He didn't even attempt to fight back. Instead, he tried getting away, but she countered each move.

She's killing one of her own. When she'd said she didn't want to kill her father, I'd assumed she'd meant all fae dragons.

Egan turned his attention to the other dragons watching the show. *He looked like a warrior dragon like Draco. She's showing that she's standing against her father, and we're under her protection.*

Thank God. *So, this is over?*

No. Egan was so tense a strong gust of wind couldn't have blown him over. *It means things are about to get nasty, and we have to wait for an attack to know who isn't on our side.*

His words made me feel raw.

We would be on the defensive since there was no way for us to know which fae dragons were on her side and which ones weren't. I'd thought her help would strengthen us, but I hadn't processed the risk. *There has to be some way to tell a friend from foe.*

Every opponent had a tell that signaled their next move. We just had to figure out what the fae dragons did when they were about to attack.

A scarlet enemy dragon roared as he flew toward the clearing. He was easily the biggest of them all and wore a white-gold crown on his head. The crown reflected off the scales, giving off a sinister vibe.

That had to be the fae dragon king—Otin. Based on

Libelle's description, the scarlet red with the gaudy crown fit the asshole perfectly. His skin reminded me of the blood bags the vampires drank from.

His evil eyes locked on Libelle, and he pointed at her, baring his long, pointy teeth. He made the same rumbling sound and threw his dragon hand toward her.

They'd made their stances known. We'd soon learn how many people were loyal to Libelle and not her father.

All of the fae dragons glanced at one another, unsure what to do until an ivory dragon lunged at Luther fifty yards away.

The suddenness of the movement gave the enemy dragon leverage. We couldn't reach him in time.

As blue flames were about to engulf the vampire, Luther swung his iron pole in front of him in the nick of time. The flames blasted into the iron, almost like a vacuum. The enemy dragon tried flying away, but it was like the iron was anchored to the core of its magic.

Luther's eyes widened as his hands shook from holding the pole. "Uh ... this works."

"That's the trick!" Torak shouted enthusiastically. "The staff has to be the center focus."

Sadie and Donovan flickered into view, her arms wrapped around her mate. She'd teleported him along for the ride. She glanced around the clearing, taking note of the dead, as the rest of the fae appeared. They were spread around, their eyes locked on Otin, ready for war.

Otin roared like a general declaring war, spurring the dragons into action.

"No!" Sadie cried as she lifted her hands at the enemy dragons about to attack. "Only attack the ones who try to hurt us. Libelle and the other fae dragons should remain safe."

"You heard her," Naida said, supporting Sadie's order. "Now protect the Earthlings and take down the evil tyrant who has been hurting our own kind."

One by one, the fae shot their magic at the attacking dragons.

Maybe we could win this without anyone else on our side getting harmed.

Three figures ran from the woods to join the battle. My heart dropped when I recognized them.

Mom, Titan, and Winter.

No, they were supposed to stay back where it was safe. Mom and Titan shouldn't be here in their state.

Wearing his eyepatch, Titan rushed over and grabbed three iron poles. He passed them out to Winter and Mom. The three of them stepped onto the battlefield.

I wanted to fly over there and strangle Mom.

I linked with Egan as I lifted into the air. *I've got to get close to Mom.* I couldn't let her get hurt. She'd gone through so much already.

Egan screamed, *Jade, we'll go together!* He caught up to me, flying beside me.

Despite the battle raging around, we dodged all of the fighting.

When I reached Mom, her eyes widened with fear. "Jade!"

Something hot and soul-splintering hit my back. My wings gave out, and I fell.

CHAPTER TWENTY-SEVEN

I'd never felt pain like this before. The sensation was indescribable, and I crumpled face-first into the ground.

Egan roared with rage, and pure hatred flowed from him and into me.

He was pissed and scared.

"I've got this!" Mom yelled, and her footsteps pounded toward me.

Not wanting Mom to come near me and become more of a target, I forced myself back onto my feet. Every time I attempted to move quickly, pain ripped through me, and my core felt scorched.

Mom tugged on my arm like she could help. "I haven't been there for you in ten years, and it's time I make up for it."

Under normal circumstances, her dedication to mend the bond between us would have elated me, but I was injured. If I didn't steady my feet, I could fall over and hurt her. Her tugging put me further off balance.

Forcing myself to balance, I glanced over my shoulder. Egan was attacking the lavender dragon that had injured me. The enemy dragon kept spewing blue fire at my mate, who was barely dodging it.

He was forcing the dragon to pay attention to him instead of attacking me and Mom, but I couldn't allow him to get hurt. Mom had to get to safety.

Pink magic shot at the enemy dragon. Sadie had to be close by. I found her and Donovan running straight at us with Trixie in tow.

"Go heal her while we help Egan," Sadie said, gesturing to me. "Any funny business, and Donovan will be right on you."

"If I was going to hurt you, I would've done it by now," Trixie grumbled, rushing to me. "Damn shifters. They always think the worst of us."

My gut screamed not to trust her, so maybe she had a point, but witches like Vera didn't help that stereotype.

Mom stepped in front of me, blocking the witch. "Is this safe?"

"Of course it is," Trixie pushed by Mom. The witch touched me, and her foreign magic pulsed inside. Everything in me wanted to attack. My dragon cringed like a caged animal. I inhaled sharply as Donovan stood close by, splitting his attention between his mate and me.

"Here." Winter ran toward him with iron. "This works with their flames if you hold it in front of your body like a conductor."

"Thank God." Donovan took the metal from her. "At least, there's something our kind and the vampires can use."

Sadie blasted the lavender dragon in the chest, and she flew backward into a tree. The tree wobbled from the dragon's weight before tipping toward the clearing. The enemy dragon lay unconscious under the tree.

"Watch out!" Winter cried as Egan flew past us toward the enemy dragon.

The tree roots cracked, removing the tension that held the tree up. It started to fall, and Egan reached the tree moments later. He groaned as he pushed the dead weight in the opposite direction. For a scary moment, the two of them came to a standstill, then the tree straightened before toppling away from us, preventing so many injuries on our side.

Trixie removed her hands from my back. "All done. That went a lot faster in your beast form. I've never healed someone during their shift before."

Her magic receded from inside me, and I stood, feeling almost brand new. All of the commotion prevented me from focusing on the witch and the suffocating feeling her magic caused.

I'd say this was how she should always do her healing, but this was a unique situation. Besides that, I hoped I'd never need healing again.

Egan landed beside me and examined my back. *Are you tired like last night?*

No. But I'm pretty sure it was the entire day, not just her magic, that had exhausted me. That was not a day I ever wanted to relive. *But the pain is gone.* Several fae dragons were fighting their own kind. Libelle's followers were coming through.

I'd been worried they would fear her father too much to take a stand.

"Help!" a shifter yelled several yards away. Three dragons were attacking, and he couldn't use his pole. All of the fae warriors around him were engaged in battle, so Sadie rushed to them.

Mom screamed, and I spun around to face her. She

charged the unconscious dragon, her face the same scarlet color as Otin. She raised the iron over her head and yelled, "You hurt my daughter! I'm going to kill you."

Dammit, I had to get to her before something happened. I pushed my healed wings while Egan followed right behind.

I understood why she was angry, but throwing herself into a supernatural fight or killing something wasn't the healthiest outlet.

Later, she and I would have a serious talk about acceptable risks.

Now I understood how Egan had felt when I'd been mostly human, determined to fight beside him. He hadn't seen me as weak; rather, he knew the strength the supernaturals held. I'd been too arrogant and self-righteous to see the real concern he had for me.

Titan dropped his iron and caught Mom as she ran by him. She swung her weapon down, unaware of who'd grabbed her.

The former alpha caught the iron before it could strike his head. "Liz, it's me. You need to calm down. This is war. You can't lose your head."

I didn't know Titan well, but that right there solidified my undying loyalty to him.

She tried jerking from his grip, but he kept his hold steady, and she sagged in defeat. "You're right."

The thunders. Egan linked as he looked at me. *They're here.*

Four hundred dragons were heading this way, all in varying shades of greens, browns, and blues, contrasting drastically with the fae dragons. It was easy to see which ones were tied to Earth.

A roar of warning emanated from a fae dragon close by.

The larger dragons glanced skyward in trepidation, drawing the attention of the shifters and vampires too.

Bright yellow blurred as an enemy dragon attacked. Its blue flames erupted over Athan.

Athan yelped in surprise, and then the sound quickly changed to heartbreaking agony.

The other enemy dragons charged, their fighting more desperate and determined.

We would soon outnumber them.

"No!" Katherine yelled, watching as her brother rolled on the ground to extinguish the flames.

But the dragon kept pouring them on, burning his flesh, which smelled like burnt cotton candy. I had to help him before it was too late.

A few feet off the ground, something hit me solidly in the side, and claws pierced my arm. I stumbled and caught my balance as Egan appeared beside me in a flash. He sank his teeth into the offending dragon's wing. The enemy dragon spun toward my mate and lunged for his neck.

Not happening.

I blew flames at the enemy's back, relishing that he'd know how it felt. My flames engulfed him, and Egan slashed the fae dragon's neck with his claws. Blood poured out as the dragon gurgled in pain.

I found Athan motionless and doused in fire. Enemies picked off every shifter that tried to get to him.

Katherine's face morphed into pure rage as scaled, black wings ripped the shirt from her body. Her pale skin turned scaly, and her body grew, splitting her pants from her body. The dagger fell beside her.

My eyes had to be playing tricks on me, but every time I blinked, nothing changed.

A black, smaller dragon-like creature stood where my sweet vampire friend had been.

I'd say she and Draco were definitely fated mates.

Roaring, she picked up the dagger and took flight. She flashed across the field, and stopping behind the attacking dragon, she stabbed him in the back.

The dragon's scales thinned as it roared in pain, and its scales disintegrated into sand.

As the blue flames lessened, what once had been Athan came into view. Only a pile of ash remained.

"Athan." Julie's voice cracked as a sob left her chest. "No."

My heart hurt for them, but if we disengaged, we wouldn't make it out of this alive. To end this, we had to go after Otin.

But first, we had to find him.

Of course, he wouldn't fight in his own war. He'd hang back and reap all the rewards, though. *That means he's hiding in the woods where he can watch without putting himself at risk.*

Paying attention to the tree line, I found a patch of scarlet behind Titan, Winter, and Mom. *I see Otin close to the tree that almost fell over.*

There were more enemy dragons concentrated in that area than the rest. They were protecting their king.

Our thunder reached us and engaged in battle.

Only a small portion had been trained for battle since they'd planned to remain in hiding. But dragons were natural fighters, so they weren't completely defenseless. Going forward, Egan and I would change that. We needed our people to be strong.

There would always be someone looking to tear us down, and it was our responsibility to protect our people and, most importantly, ensure they could protect themselves.

Two navy blue dragons flanked Egan and me, their stature similar to Draco's.

I'm pretty sure that's Draco's family, Egan confirmed.

Good, we needed warriors. *Let's go.*

Please stay close to me, Egan asked. *These people want to kill us. We're what's standing between their king and the throne.*

I promise not to be careless.

We took off with the warriors staying close to us. Libelle fought another dragon. It tried to get away, not fighting back at all.

I had to be missing something. *Why aren't they trying to take Libelle out?*

The best way to solidify your reign is to have an heir. Egan sounded disgusted. *Even though they don't want to kill her, her father will punish her.*

By killing her best friend. No wonder Sarah and the king had gotten along. They were the same type of people, using whatever they could to force others to their knees. That was probably why Libelle had been hesitant, so we couldn't lose. She had just as much, if not more, at stake.

Every fae was engaged in battle, and it took several wolf shifters to hold their own against a single dragon, even with the iron. Our dragons had gone straight to battle, but the enemy dragons had training.

It made sense that Libelle had questioned our abilities. Otin obviously never paused their training.

We flew across the field, avoiding any fighting since our people had the lead.

As we flew closer to the tree line past Mom, five fae dragons flew from the woods, swarming us.

This had to be the king's personal guards.

The warrior dragons went straight on the offensive. Each fae dragon charged our warrior dragons, but that left three to focus on Egan and me.

Crap, this was what the fae king wanted. He'd held several dragons back, hoping to split us off from the others and attack. We'd walked into his trap.

What do we do? I linked with Egan. *We're outnumbered.*

Stay close to me, and we fight dirty. Egan's voice held an edge I'd never heard before. *Do whatever it takes to make it out alive.*

Fight dirty.

I could do that.

If I could figure out how with these creatures.

The three enemy dragons circled us. Two locked eyes on Egan, and the eggshell-colored dragon extended its talons, making its way toward me.

Squaring my shoulders, I prepared for the impact and pain. If I could reach his neck or injure his wing, that would put us on more even ground. I was already a slightly smaller dragon than the others because I'd been human.

But when it flew over my head, avoiding me, my blood ran cold.

He wouldn't have let me go unless something horrible would happen.

I spun around right as the enemy dragon swooped down and picked Mom up by his talons.

"No!" Mom swung the iron like a bat, desperately trying to hit the dragon. "You aren't hurting me or my daughter again."

Terror took hold of my gut as the memory of the harpy holding her exactly like this blasted through my mind. The harpy had dropped her from two hundred yards high, letting Mom spiral to her death.

I almost hadn't caught her that day, but I had, just like I would today.

I spread my wings, ready for a game of cat and mouse. Unease pulsed through me when the dragon stayed put.

Mom pounded the dragon's feet with the iron. The dragon seemed to droop as his eyes focused on me.

He had to be growing weak and couldn't get away.

But that would only make him more dangerous. I wanted to yell at Mom to stop. If he took off with her, I wouldn't have a chance at saving her unless I left Otin alone. But if he didn't move, he'd get desperate and be willing to do anything.

He dug his talons deeper into her shoulders, and Mom sucked in a painful breath. She stopped moving her arms and faced me, tears filling her eyes. "Jade, I'm sorry. I love—"

The dragon spread Mom's shoulders apart, cutting off her words. Bones cracked, and blood oozed down her arms. Her body went slack, and the dragon released her.

Hot rage consumed me, and my vision hazed as a roar racked my body.

They'd killed my mother.

Pain consumed me, mixing with the loss of Dad. Now I had no parents left. No one to see my children or stand beside me during birth, telling me I'd be okay. My heart shattered, and I couldn't breathe.

Tears threatened my dragon eyes, but I blinked them away. They would not get the pleasure of seeing me fall apart.

That was what they wanted.

And there was one thing I was good at—retribution.

I'd mourn her when this was done, but I had to focus on serving justice to these assholes.

I relinquished all of my control to my dragon for the first time in my life. Letting her flames consume my blood, I felt on the edge of combustion. I encouraged the feeling, allowing it to grow.

I trusted her a whole hell of a lot more than I did the king.

It was time to bring that bastard to his knees.

CHAPTER TWENTY-EIGHT

When I opened my eyes, the world seemed sharper ... clearer. Even the bond between Egan and me had amplified. Strength pulsed through me as I roared with rage and pain.

Egan's own pain mixed with mine, making the void and anger that much stronger.

Spinning toward the mango-colored enemy, Egan grabbed its neck and jerked it hard to the side. His bones cracked, and he dropped dead.

Without missing a beat, Egan spun to the other fae dragon and expelled orange flames instead of the normal red. The enemy responded with his blue, but Egan's easily cut through it, covering his opponent. The heat from his new fire pulsed hotter than before.

Something had happened. He was stronger too, like me. But how? *Do you feel different too?*

You let your dragon completely free with our thunder here. Egan watched the two warrior dragons fighting the fae. *The true royal power got transferred to us. This is what Otin is after. It makes us stronger.*

Good. We needed it.

Satisfied with how the warriors were fighting, he linked again. *You handle the dragon that killed your mother, and I'll go after the king.*

Sounds like a plan. Both of them had stolen too much from us to make it out alive.

Please be careful, and let me know if you need me. He flew off into the woods, searching for the fae king.

I hunkered down to charge at my target. *I will be. You be careful too.* I scraped the ground with my claws and clutched fistfuls of dirt. I wouldn't allow this bastard to die with dignity. It'd be gritty and nasty.

The kind of death he deserved.

Forcing myself not to look at Mom, I stared at the enemy and ran. I could see each breath he took and hear his heart even from farther away than normal. I welcomed the insight into their emotions.

He inhaled, planning to spew flames, so I jumped.

His eyes followed me, and smoke seeped from his nose. His focus flickered to the ground, telling me he planned on hitting me as soon as I touched down.

Nope. Not today.

I flapped my wings at the last second, and his flames missed my feet by inches. He threw his head back, chasing me with his fire as I flew higher. He was determined to end me with magic.

But I was faster than him. Before his flames could catch up, I hovered over his head and threw dirt in his eyes.

His fire cut off as he rubbed his eyes. A rumble, followed by a choking sound, escaped him as he pawed at his eyes. He shook his head back and forth like that would make the dirt fall out.

I flew behind him and extended my talons, slashing his wings in one slick movement.

His cry for help hurt my ears, but I wanted to debilitate him one agonizing inch at a time.

I waited for the joy of victory to come, but it didn't. Watching him be helpless didn't comfort me because the pain he felt wouldn't come close to losing Mom, and it wouldn't bring her back.

The truth slammed into me. I didn't want to do this ... become this. Taking pleasure in someone's death was wrong, even if they were cruel. If Otin had taught me anything, it was that revenge was pointless and would only get me hurt.

Ready to end the eggshell dragon's suffering, I slashed his throat with my claws. The crying cut off as blood poured down his throat, onto his chest, and dripped onto the grass. I'd made sure the cut was deep so there would be no coming back from it.

He stumbled, dropping his hands from his eyes to the more serious injury. He wrapped his dragon hands over his neck, but they slipped.

"Jade!" Winter yelled. "Egan needs you."

Those words chilled me. My head jerked toward my mate.

Egan and Otin were engaged in hand-to-hand combat. They charged each other, throwing punches and trying to bite each other.

Blood oozed from bite marks on Egan's neck and thick scratches down his arms and wings.

Dammit, we might have king and queen power, but that dragon was thousands of years old and from Fae. They weren't an even match, which meant we needed leverage.

Libelle's earlier words repeated in my brain. The easiest way to kill a fae was with the dagger.

I needed to find Katherine.

Finding a vampire dragon shouldn't be hard.

I turned around, and as expected, I found her within seconds.

She and Draco fought their own dragon side by side. Katherine wielded the dagger and used her extremely long and pointy teeth to thrash some throats along the way.

Throwing my head back, I roared and stomped on the ground to get her attention. I couldn't leave Egan.

But she was too focused on her pain and anger. Her normally brown eyes were deep red, almost like she'd finished drinking blood, but the pure anger of her movements conveyed her rage. Where I wanted to slowly hurt the dragon that had killed Mom, Katherine wanted to hurt every enemy she came into contact with.

Either reaction wasn't healthy.

Our loved ones weren't coming back.

Lillith stood a few feet away from Katherine with an iron pole in her hand and smacked a fae dragon engaged in battle with Sadie over the head. As she turned to look for the next fae to help, her eyes locked on mine.

I could count on her help.

Pointing at Egan, I only hoped the vampire would understand my message. Not being able to speak in this form was a huge pain in the ass.

She looked at my mate, and realization dawned on her face. "Katherine, Egan and Jade need you."

But it was like Katherine couldn't hear. She stabbed the next fae dragon instead of acknowledging her friend.

"Oh, hell no," Lillith hissed as she flashed over and

smacked Katherine on her arm. "Your friends need your help." Lillith wouldn't be ignored.

Katherine spun around, her long teeth dripping blood. She went to strike her best friend but abruptly stopped like what she'd said had sunk in.

"Bitch, you better be glad your ass didn't bite me," Lillith warned. "Now, go help Jade."

She nodded and turned to Draco.

The warrior dragon glanced at me, and they flew over the clearing toward me.

They had to be mind linking. There was no question they were fated mates.

Knowing they were on their way, I flew past Draco's family still engaged with the fae dragon warriors. It looked like they were gaining the upper hand.

As I rushed to my mate, Otin bit into Egan's shoulder and shoved him into a tree. Egan's head bounced against the trunk, and he tried to claw at Otin's face, but the king fought his hands off and sank his teeth deeper into Egan's scales.

Lowering my head, I steamrolled Otin in the head, making his jaw pop. Growling, he released his hold on my mate and turned his blood-red eyes on me.

Jade, I've got this, Egan said and slowly climbed to his feet.

Nope, he was worse off than me. Trixie had healed me, and I barely had any injuries.

Otin bared his claws and swiped at my chest. All of my martial arts training kicked into gear. I'd grown up with hand-to-hand combat.

I ducked his attack and rammed my head into the asshole's stomach, throwing his large frame over my shoulder. I intended for him to fall on his back, but he clutched my wings, stopping his movement, and pulled at them until the scales couldn't give any longer.

The asshole was going to rip the wings off my back.

No! Egan shouted as he flew over my head and sank his talons into Otin's shoulders. He flapped his wings, lifting him and Otin into the air and off me.

When they'd elevated several feet into the air, Otin flapped his wings, and Egan lost his balance. Otin swung his feet toward Egan's face and cut deep into his cheeks.

My mate fought back, but Otin flipped him over. He landed on his back with a thud.

I moved to reach him, but the Otin bared his claws and swung at Egan's throat.

No! I was hurrying to him when something black darted past me, but I didn't care.

I had to save my mate.

No matter how hard I pushed myself, I wouldn't get there in time. *Egan!*

As the claws were only inches from killing my mate, the dragon king sagged forward, landing on top of Egan and revealing the dagger plunged into his back.

My legs gave out when I saw Katherine standing over them.

Otin cried as his scales turned to dust.

I dropped next to my mate. Tears dripped down my cheeks and splashed across his dark olive scales. *You asshole.* I sobbed and snorted at the same time. I was pissed at him for putting himself at risk but so damn relieved he was alive. *I thought I was going to lose you.*

Never, Egan groaned and brushed his hand against my arm. *Even death couldn't steal me away.*

The sounds of the fight quieted, and Libelle's roar echoed through the trees.

I crumpled near my mate.

Thank God. The fight was over.

Three Months Later

"I STILL CAN'T BELIEVE you decided to live here and not near us!" Roxy pouted as she stood in front of Egan's and my brand-new, two-story brick house.

She'd been giving us shit about that since we'd agreed to buy a spacious section of land from Cassius and build a neighborhood for our thunder. "You live too close to the city. We can't fly, even under the cover of night, like we can here." This was the hundredth time I'd explained that to her.

In moments like these, with Egan by my side and our best friends surrounding us, I felt a sense of peace. The loss of Mom and Dad still hurt, but they'd given me so much. Dad had tried to save his wife and daughter and give them the best life possible, and Mom had found the strength to stand on her own.

Kayda told me what finally made peace with her parents she'd lost too soon was to find the best in them and hold that close to her heart. That doing that would allow me to carry them throughout life. Even though Kayda would never replace my mom, she and I had grown closer over the past few months while building the homes in our new neighborhood. Egan's family was now my own.

"I'm just pissed that Katherine is living here too." Lillith crossed her arms and arched a brow at her best friend. "Just because you're half dragon doesn't mean you can't still live with us."

"No," Katherine giggled. "But being mated to the lead warrior protecting his king and queen made that decision for me." She looped her arm through Draco's and stared lovingly into his eyes.

At first, we'd been confused about how those two could be fated mates, but Cassius had come up with a theory. A vampire who never killed anyone retained their soul. Because Katherine had kept her humanity, she could forge the bond with Draco. Since their souls had connected, Draco had taken on a few vampire tendencies too. Just like I'd become a dragon, both he and Katherine had merged into hybrids. Katherine had been thrilled that she could get rid of her all-liquid diet now that she could taste food again.

"Leave them alone," Sadie said, wagging a finger at Roxy and Lillith. "Besides, we're all heading back to Kortright in the fall, so it's not like we'll never see them."

"Let's not forget that your nest lives ten minutes away." Donovan shook his head. "I think you're good."

"For many reasons, we will not be living in the dorms." Draco surveyed the group. "We will rent a large house and stay together. Trying to protect you two in a dorm building would be a strategic nightmare."

"Don't forget to add that we'll be sleeping with our mates." Axel pinched Roxy's ass. "And might have some pissed-off roommates if they don't agree to let us bunk together."

When Draco had realized we all wanted to go back to college, he'd gotten excited. He'd always wanted to get an education, so convincing him to come along hadn't been the difficult task I'd imagined. Egan's parents agreed to look after the thunder while we integrated more with humans. It wouldn't be a hard job now that Libelle had proven to be a very supportive ally, and the other fae races respected her position since Egan and I had given her our blessing to rule over the dragons that had decided to remain in Fae.

Also, things had settled down for Rook and Murray. For once, everything appeared to be calm in the fae realm and on Earth.

Our entire group would get to have a somewhat normal college experience, despite being responsible for a thunder with over four hundred members.

Katherine pursed her lips. "I'm still shocked they let us come back for another semester."

"Money has a way of making people agreeable." Sadie frowned. "Though I hate it was Tyler's money."

"Hey, you grew up with that bastard." Roxy huffed. "And he swore you were his daughter. You deserve it. And you've put it to good use by helping restore the packs Tyler and his minions tore apart and bribing our way back into college over and over again."

"Let's not make the latter a habit." Donovan wrapped an arm around his mate's waist. "Next semester, we promise there won't be a creepy bird pecking people's eyes out or a rabid vampire gorging on Hidden Ridge locals."

"Now that's something I can agree to." Lillith lifted an imaginary glass in a toast. "Even if I'm the only single one surrounded by couples." She shuddered.

"Don't worry, girl." Roxy winked. "I got you covered. I already ordered you a body pillow you can cuddle."

The vampire scowled as we laughed.

This was love. This was family. And we'd all make it through together.

Hey, I want to show you something. Egan linked with me. *Follow me?*

Always. I'd go anywhere with him.

"Where are you going?" Lillith hollered. "I need all the backup I can get."

"Just give us a second," Egan said as we entered our brand-new home. He shut the door behind him.

I stepped into the living room. Rose petals covered the rosewood floor. In the center of the pale-yellow room, four candles surrounded a seashell on the coffee table.

"What's all this for?" Today was special since we were officially moving in together. Alone. No one else in the house but us. Something we'd never had. But I hadn't expected him to go all out.

"I wanted to do something to signify what this day means to me." Egan cleared his throat and walked over to the table. His khaki pants almost matched the candlelight, and he pulled at the collar of his green dress shirt. "You see, this shirt is jade, which is my favorite word in the world." His face turned a shade of pink as he pointed at the candlelight. "And the flames remind me of our bond now that our souls are connected."

"Okay." I couldn't keep the smile off my face. This might have been incredibly cheesy to some, but the effort he'd put into this and his sincerity left me breathless.

"The rose petals represent my love for you." He picked up the shell, cradling it in his hands. "And this seashell reminds me of the first time I laid eyes on you."

"I love you." I waved my hand around the room. "You didn't have to do all this to prove anything to me."

He raised an eyebrow. "Will you let me finish?"

"Of course." I placed my hands on his.

He laughed nervously. "We kind of did things backward. We didn't really date. We more or less danced around each other then went all in. The time we spent getting close involved constant threats. And now we've already completed the mate bond and will live together."

This was taking a drastic turn. "Are you saying you don't want this?"

"What?" His mouth dropped. "No. That's not it at all."

He removed something from the center of the shell and bent to one knee.

Oh, my God.

"Jade Storm, I want you in all ways. As a fated mate and as a wife. Will you marry me?" He held out a white-gold band with small diamonds that surrounded a three-carat diamond in the center.

Yes. I linked since I couldn't speak, my throat thick with emotion. *Of course.*

A huge smile filled his face as he slipped the ring onto my shaking finger. I hadn't realized how badly I wanted this, but like always, he knew me better than I did.

His lips landed on mine, and my heart felt full. Exactly the way it should.

The End

ABOUT THE AUTHOR

Jen L. Grey is a *USA Today* Bestselling Author who writes Paranormal Romance, Urban Fantasy, and Fantasy genres.

Jen lives in Tennessee with her husband, two daughters, and two miniature Australian Shepherd. Before she began writing, she was an avid reader and enjoyed being involved in the indie community. Her love for books eventually led her to writing. For more information, please visit her website and sign up for her newsletter.

Check out my future projects and book signing events at my website.
www.jenlgrey.com

ALSO BY JEN L. GREY

Shadow City: The Silver Wolf

Broken Mate

Rising Darkness

Silver Moon

The Hidden King Trilogy

Dragon Mate

Dragon Heir

Dragon Queen

The Wolf Born Trilogy

Hidden Mate

Blood Secrets

Awakened Magic

The Marked Wolf Trilogy

Moon Kissed

Chosen Wolf

Broken Curse

Wolf Moon Academy Trilogy

Shadow Mate

Blood Legacy

Rising Fate

The Royal Heir Trilogy

Wolves' Queen

Wolf Unleashed

Wolf's Claim

Bloodshed Academy Trilogy

Year One

Year Two

Year Three

The Half-Breed Prison Duology (Same World As Bloodshed Academy)

Hunted

Cursed

The Artifact Reaper Series

Reaper: The Beginning

Reaper of Earth

Reaper of Wings

Reaper of Flames

Reaper of Water

Stones of Amaria (Shared World)

Kingdom of Storms

Kingdom of Shadows

Kingdom of Ruins

Kingdom of Fire

The Pearson Prophecy

Dawning Ascent

Enlightened Ascent

Reigning Ascent

Stand Alones

Death's Angel

Rising Alpha